About the Author

Alan Frost is an experienced IT professional, being a Fellow of the British Computer Society and a Chartered Engineer. He has spent his life moving technology forwards from punch cards to AI, but always knowing that the key constituent in any system is the liveware, the users.

Blind to the Consequences

Alan Frost

Blind to the Consequences

Olympia Publishers
London

www.olympiapublishers.com
OLYMPIA PAPERBACK EDITION

A CIP catalogue record for this title is
available from the British Library.

ISBN: 978-1-80074-200-0

This is a work of fiction.
Names, characters, places and incidents originate from the writer's imagination.
Any resemblance to actual persons, living or dead, is purely coincidental.

First Published in 2022

Olympia Publishers
Tallis House
2 Tallis Street
London
EC4Y 0AB

Printed in Great Britain

Dedication

To Victor Frost, the very best of brothers

1

Introduction

Most introductions are fairly tedious affairs. This one is no different. The reader just wants to get on and read the book. But the author wants to revel in its magnificence. The introduction is a chance for him or her to convince the reader that they should devote a valuable portion of their precious time on Earth to reading it.

Well, that's not the case here. I wouldn't bother reading it. The quality of the writing is acceptable, but it's not TS Elliot. This story is quite mundane, and there is no point dashing to the last page of the book as it ends with a damp squib. To be honest, I couldn't think of a good ending, but the rest is hardly what you would call good either.

I should know as I'm both the Narrator and a participant in the story. A significant part of this tale is true. In fact, the most unlikely part. The rest is just embellishment added to make the story more entertaining and, hopefully, to sell more books.

This might seem dishonest or even improper, but I have little time for that type of sentimentality. I want the reader's hard-earned money in my wallet. So a little bit of embellishment to make a true story more entertaining makes logical sense.

As the Narrator, I will assist the reader in highlighting the truths and the lies as they appear. Whether you believe it or not is up to you. When I wrote this, I wondered whether your acceptance of the truth made a difference or not. Frankly, it doesn't, and I don't care either way.

So let's get on with the story. I would turn the page, and we can begin. By the way, I haven't allowed facts to get in the way of a good story or in this case indifferent story, so don't tell me that mobiles weren't available then. I don't care.

2

Background

This is a true story, with embellishments. As the events unfold, it will seem more like fiction. Most of the readers will file it away in their memory as an imaginary tale, but they would be wrong. To protect the participants, we need to disguise the names and location. It's a shame, but I don't want any lawsuits, especially from my ex-wife.

So who are the participants? Well, there is me and my ex-wife; a mother and father with their two children; an elderly Irishman, and The Friend. The story demands that you know more about us, which I will cover in the next chapter.

So when did this story take place? It was 1972. As an author, this is an opportunity for me to add some stuff from Wikipedia. It helps to pad out the novel, and it might help set the scene, especially for our younger readers.

Firstly, we had the same queen then as we do now. She looked a bit younger, but the art of smiling was still to be mastered by her then. That wasn't easy when you had a PM like Edward Heath. Rather than produce a lot of narrative, I thought I would list the events and characteristics under three categories: Good, bad, and indifferent.

Good

- Miniskirts
- David Bowie and the release of The Rise and Fall of Ziggy Stardust and the Spiders from Mars
- Creation of ABBA
- Rose Heilbron became the first female judge to sit in the Old Bailey
- CND demonstration
- *I'm Sorry I Haven't a Clue* was broadcast for the first time

on Radio 4
- First gay pride march in London
- *Jesus Christ Superstar* premieres in London
- School-leaving age raised to 16
- *Mastermind* broadcast for the first time
- Thousands of Ugandan Asians arrived in the UK
- The lifting of restrictions on broadcasting hours permits an extension of daytime television
- Access credit cards were introduced
- Green Party formed
- Inflation falls to 6.4%
- British car production peaks at 1.9 million units
- *Watership Down* published
- Liam Gallagher was born
- Jude Law was born
- Pink Floyd's *Dark Side of the Moon* tour was premiered at the Brighton Dome
- Wings and ELO made their live debuts.

Bad

- *Last Tango in Paris*
- Spurs beat Wolves in the UEFA Cup Final. The referee was probably blind
- Leeds United beat the marvellous Arsenal in the FA Cup Final
- Coalminers' strike
- Bloody Sunday in Northern Ireland
- Mounted police charged protestors in London
- Heath declares a state of emergency
- IRA bomb kills six people in Aldershot
- Derby County won the Football League First Division title
- Bloody Friday, more deaths in Belfast
- Dockers went on strike
- Idi Amin expels 50,000 Asians from Uganda
- GB only wins 18 medals in the Olympics (4 golds)
- Second Cod War

- The government introduces price and pay freezes to counter inflation.

Indifferent
- Linda Lovelace's *Deepthroat* was released
- Ford launched the Granada
- The merger of the Church of England and the Methodist Church failed to go ahead
- The Queen met her uncle, the Duke of Windsor, in Paris before he died
- Ceylon became Sri Lanka, what's in a name?
- The M6 was completed
- Thomas Cook was privatised
- Geri Halliwell was born
- The pound was floated
- Bank rates abolished
- The first episode of *Emmerdale Farm* was broadcast.

It was, however, an excellent time for albums:
- *Electric Warrior* by T. Rex
- *Harvest* by Neil Young
- *Fog on the Tyne* by Lindisfarne
- *Machine Head* by Deep Purple
- *Exile on Main Street* by The Rolling Stones
- *Never a Dull Moment* by Rod Stewart.

There was no real point in doing this. I enjoyed it as I have a great liking for lists. You as a reader will just skim over it, but subconsciously you will note the bits that are of particular interest to you. Some of you, I suspect, will not have my love for Arsenal or my choice of albums, but as the writer, I decide, until the editor has a crack at it.

So we have listed the participants and set the time period. Now we need to know where. All of the events happened in Haywards Heath in Sussex.

It would be wrong to call Haywards Heath a boring, tedious commuter town with no real historic or cultural value, but that's what I'm going to call it.

I'm not sure if you can just include chunks of Wikipedia in your novel, but if you can, it hardly improves the image of the town. Here is the text:

'Haywards Heath is a town and civil parish in the Mid Sussex District of West Sussex, within the historic county of Sussex, England. It lies 36 miles (58 km) south of London, 14 miles (23 km) north of Brighton, 13 miles (21 km) south of Gatwick Airport and 31 miles (50 km) east northeast of the county town of Chichester. Nearby towns include Burgess Hill to the southwest, Horsham to the northwest, Crawley north-northwest, and East Grinstead north-northeast. Being a commuter town with only a relatively small number of jobs available in the immediate vicinity, mostly in the agricultural or service sector, many of the residents commute daily via road or rail to London, Brighton, Crawley, or Gatwick for work.'

The Sussex County Lunatic Asylum—now called St Francis Hospital—is one of the historical highlights, as was Bannister's Cattle Market. It used to be the twelfth largest in the UK. It's now the site of a Sainsbury's supermarket.

The list of local attractions is mind-blowing:

- Victoria Park
- Clair Hall Community Centre
- Haywards Heath Leisure Centre
- Borde Hill Gardens
- Beech Hurst Gardens
- Haywards Heath Recreation Ground
- Haywards Heath Library
- Haywards Heath Cadet Centre.

I can summarise by saying that it was an interesting year but a boring place to live. As summaries go, that was rather simplistic, but it has set the scene.

3

The House

As already mentioned, Haywards Heath is a commuter town. The quickest way in or out is the railway line. It was always a pity that the station was not in the town centre and that the car parking was rubbish.

I used to commute to East Croydon. I waited at the same spot on the station and got in the same carriage at the same time every day. It was a rare day when a seat was available. It was even rarer to find the train on time.

The second escape route was the A23/M23, but the traffic queues into Croydon were a nightmare. The chances of getting to the office on time were slim.

All of the above is true but not really relevant to the story. It's always hard to judge how much scene-setting is needed. Anyway, the house where the events took place was not that far from the station. A modest semi-detached property that had been extended over several years by the owner who was a builder by trade.

It included a small flat which was rented to an Irishman, but he shared some of the facilities in the main residence. I had never been upstairs but knew downstairs quite well. It had a very modern kitchen, for the time, a sitting room, and a lounge. The lounge opened out into the hall where the stairs were also located, along with a toilet. The events I'm going to discuss occurred mainly in the hall. The truth will be revealed.

The lounge was a bit like a Habitat showroom. They had spent some money, but it was really a mismatch of conflicting designs. There were too many patterns, too much furniture, and too many wall decorations. Obviously, this was my opinion, and no one has ever accused me of having good taste.

They had a Technics Hi-Fi system, which I suspect was rarely used. It was more for show. Their music collection was tediously and embarrassingly middle-of-the-road: Matt Monroe, Cliff, Shirley, Black and White Minstrels, John Denver, Val Doonican, and lots of compilations. It was hardly progressive.

They had sofas where the seats were so large that you couldn't sit down properly. You had to loaf about, especially when it came to the corner unit. They had a drinks trolley full of exotic concoctions such as pear schnapps, cherry brandy, and eggnog.

The large colour TV was one of their prize possessions. By today's standards, it was relatively small, but it had two doors that could be closed to hide the screen. What a marvellous innovation! The wood veneer cabinet was a thing of beauty.

To sum it up, the house was large and modern looking but cluttered. They aspired to be sophisticated but fell short. It was doubtful if they knew what sophisticated was.

4

Me

I'm Adam Strange (it's a false name; I told you I would let you know about the lies). This is where I describe myself, not as I am today, but as I was nearly fifty years ago. The main objective here is to help the reader create an image of me in their mind's eye. So what sort of image do I want you to create?

It's probably best to make a list:

- Five-foot six inches tall
- Broad shoulders and chest
- Size 10 shoes
- Short legs
- Slightly overweight, but starting the journey towards obesity
- Dark hair and lots of it
- Robust features with a Roman nose
- Friendly smile.

I've been accused of being handsome, but the jury may still be out. I could always pick up the birds, but it might have been down to my deep, sexy voice.

I got three A-levels at Haywards Heath Grammar School and joined American Express, where I mastered punch-card technology. I ended up as the IT Manager, with over 150 staff reporting to me. I then joined Babcock and Wilcox when I was tasked with setting up an ICL-based data centre. Eventually, I became a Fellow of the British Computer Society, a Fellow of the Institute of Analysts and Programmers and a Chartered Engineer.

This proves that I have a logical, rational mind. I'm not religious. I don't believe in God, heaven and hell, astrology, witchcraft, homoeopathy, the Loch Ness Monster, or any other weird superstitious mumbo jumbo. I don't believe in good or bad luck, but I do wonder about the presence of UFOs. There does seem to be a lot of objective evidence to support their existence.

The above is genuinely relevant when we look at the events later in the book. Here I'm trying to prove that I'm a reliable witness. A witness to events that I can't explain. Events that have no rational explanation.

At that time, I had no medical problems. I've never had any mental health issues. I've never spent any time with a psychologist or psychiatrist. I've never taken any recreational drugs, and I hardly drink. I've got no history of illusions.

You couldn't ask for a better witness, could you?

5

My Ex-wife

At the time, she was still my wife. Her name is Dolores (this is another lie). We met at American Express. It was love at the thirtieth sight.

I feel another descriptive list coming on :

- Five-foot two inches short
- Reasonably attractive but rapidly putting weight on
- Shoulder-length blonde hair
- Thin lips
- Twenty-nine years of age but dressed older, much older.

Dolores had been married before and had a daughter who was staying at her grandmother's, on the night in question. Both were friends of the family living in the house.

Dolores left school at the earliest opportunity and had no formal educational qualifications. She was casually interested in the supernatural.

Our relationship was even showing signs of strain in those days. We hadn't been married long, and the lack of a sex-life was becoming a significant problem. We only had sex once before we got married. There was no sex on our wedding night and little during the honeymoon. This was partly because she suffered diarrhoea, an over-indulgence of alcohol, sunstroke, and sunburn. It may, of course, have been an act to avoid a good todgering.

However, the lack of sex continued until a steady state of abstinence was achieved.

So the question is, does Dolores make a good witness?

She has suffered from several medical conditions but none related to mental illness. She has never taken recreational drugs, and despite the honeymoon, she is not a drinker.

In court, she would be regarded as a sound witness.

6

The Man of the House

Doug and his wife owned the property outright. He was a qualified builder and purchased dilapidated properties and did them up before the idea became fashionable. To be fair to him, he did a good job, and by his mid-thirties, he was mortgage-free. Not a bad achievement in the 1970s.

This achievement only exacerbated his natural arrogance. He was a large, athletic man who enjoyed embarrassing lesser mortals. His intellectual ability was more limited, but he knew he was right. He found it challenging tolerating those who disagreed with his right-wing views. He was strongly anti-immigrant, anti-gay, anti-scrounger, anti-unmarried mothers, and anti-trade unionism. He would spit venom if his audience was weak.

No one could call him a wife beater, but mental cruelty was a day-to-day occurrence. His wife was naturally inferior; in fact, *all* women were inferior. For him, it was the natural order of things. Women, as he often said, lacked the intellect to have robust views on things and lacked the ability to elucidate a logical argument. Apparently, their place was in the home.

I heard but never had any objective proof that he was somewhat challenged in the trouser department. My ex-wife was keen for me to verify the fact by having a good ogle in the gents' loo. My task was to follow him in and select the public urinal next to him. I would then assess the length and girth of his genitalia. I explained to her that it wasn't the done thing. My refusal was another nail in the coffin of our marriage. To be honest, I did have a quick sneaky look disguised by a cough. He *was* challenged. I refused to let the wife know, but it did my confidence a lot of good. My twelve-incher would certainly trump his minnow, and that is not a lie.

Well, perhaps it's ten inches, but on a good day when it's really hard, it looks like twelve inches. Anyway, this section is not about my magnificent cock. It's about the rather diminutive Doug. Tiny Doug as I now call him. He was a small, racist, sexist, tiresome, arrogant twat. Not that I would say it to his face as he was a big bloke, but not where it counts.

Anyway, he was married to June and had two children. It couldn't have been easy for them.

7

The Woman of the House

June had been incredibly attractive with long blonde hair and blue eyes. She was the classic prom girl. Everyone wanted to get in her knickers, and she let them in. This included a large proportion of the boys at school, most of her husband's employees, any male worker who came to the house, and the local vicar. It wasn't that she was deliberately promiscuous; she just didn't know how to say no.

Well, sometimes she said no, but she didn't mean it. At school, she was the local bike, but she didn't care. She took precautions and thought what the hell. It was better than doing lessons. Fortunately, in those days, there was no social media and no smartphones, so her reputation never got that tarnished.

When she started work, she discovered that life was a lot easier if she dropped her knickers. She got nice presents, additional time off, holidays—sorry, *business trips*, salary increases, etc. She wasn't always that popular with the other female employees, but she didn't care. She was going places.

Then she met Doug. Big, strong, tall Doug who treated her like a lady. He made no attempt to get in her knickers, which she found frustrating but at the same time endearing. He wanted her for herself. She wasn't just a sex object. Marriage was proposed and became necessary when she got pregnant. She had a quick fumble with Doug in the car but wondered if penetration had actually been achieved. She didn't mind that much as penetration had been accomplished twice that day already, but not by Doug. The vicar and the vicar's son had both blessed her.

Anyway, the past is the past. She was still an attractive woman with curves in all the right places, a full bosom, and a nice arse. Two children had done some damage. Her legs had varicose veins, and there was slightly more sagging than was ideal. Even more damage had been inflicted upstairs with overdyed hair, decimated eyebrows, and sun-ravaged wrinkles.

She was one of those women who was attractive but not beautiful. She was not pretty, but she was fuckable. She oozed sexuality. A bit of bosom here and there, tight pants, a loose towel, a twinkle in the eyes, pouting, some serious pouting, the occasional accidental touch, and lots of suggestive chat.

It was debatable whether she wanted children or not. She was a good mother. She was always there when her children needed her. She went to all the school events, provided the almost obligatory children's taxi service, cooked reasonably balanced meals, and even helped with their homework. But did she *like* kids? The answer was 'No'. They were time-consuming, irritating, infuriating, annoying little shits on which you wasted a large proportion of your life for little return.

And as for Doug, he was one big arsehole with a tiny little pecker. She didn't hate her life, but she sought solace from the church. They were a godsend. It wasn't religion but the help and assistance provided by the vicar and his son. Together they had been administrating their good works for twenty-odd years, sometimes at the same time. Amen.

8

The Children of the House

As the Narrator, I've given you a fairly good insight into the adult players. They were a fairly typical couple struggling to get through life. They had the same trials and tribulations as everyone else. They had their secrets and aspirations, their foibles, and idiosyncrasies, and they wanted their children to have a better life than they'd had.

Well, that wasn't likely as their son was a little shit, and the daughter was a nervy, panicky, anxious nightmare. Let's eliminate the son as he takes no part in this story, although we might use him later to embellish the tale. Let's assume that it is not the case.

This child shall remain nameless as I never knew his name and still don't. I could invent a name, but there doesn't seem much point. He is a mini-Doug. It's hard to believe that an eight-year-old could be so strongly anti-immigrant, anti-gay, anti-scrounger, anti-unmarried mothers, and anti-school. This little fascist was prime material for the Hitler Youth. He even enjoyed squashing insects, sometimes with his tongue.

Let's move onto one of the key players: Isabella or Isi for short.

Let's list her key characteristics:
- Twelve years old, approaching thirteen
- Puberty had reared its head, and a sports bra had been acquired
- Skinny to the point of almost being anorexic
- Obsessed with her looks. There were signs of prettiness, but only time would tell
- Brown hair, brown eyes: she didn't take after her mum
- She didn't take after her father, but perhaps she did. If only they knew who the father was.
- Brighter, certainly brighter than Doug

- She hated her parents but not as much as she hated her brother (Probably best to call him Bob as it will save calling him 'brother' all of the time, and it does make my job as the author easier).
- She likes school but not her classmates
- She was not one of the in-gang, out-gang, or any gang. She was probably in a gang of her own. Occasionally she teamed up with an autistic lad. She wondered if she was on the spectrum, then she wondered if everyone was. Clearly, her brother was.
- She knew that schizophrenia ran in the family.
- Her political leanings were towards the left. She wasn't too sure if they were her beliefs or whether she had just wanted to irritate her father
- She was a virgin and intended to stay that way
- Her emotional age was probably two or three years younger than it should be. She knew that and didn't care
- She was quite interested in the concept of suicide, but she was not suicidal.

That might be enough on Isi. In many ways, this is her story.

So far, practically everything is true. There are still two players to go. You must be bored by now. If you want to shut the book in disgust, that is fine with me. As they say, it's no skin off my nose. Actually, there is a lot of skin on my nose. Well, it's a big nose after all, but not as big as my cock. But where were we?

9

The Old Irishman

As mentioned in the second paragraph in chapter two, they had a lodger. I didn't know that they had a lodger, and there is no reason that I needed to know, but later, he became a crucial part of the story. All I really knew was that he was Irish, he was old, and he wasn't a drinker. I was going to say that it was odd as all Irish people are heavy drinkers. That's the main reason they were put on this earth, to drink.

Clearly, that's unfair as there are sober, tea-drinkers in the emerald isle like everywhere else in the world. But all I can say is that I attended a wake in Mullingar. I was wasted for three days. There were bodies in the street, bodies in the church, bodies in the pub, and bodies in the park. One of those bodies was me.

There had been a serious outbreak of drunken alcoholic consumption that would challenge most medical institutions. I can't remember the service, the funeral, or any other social interaction. I know that I lost the ability to stand up, but gained the ability to pee down the inside of my trousers unaided.

So we know that he was Irish. I also knew that he was an accountant, one of the living dead. That probably meant that he lacked any sign of a personality, but he could count.

We also know that he was old. It turned out that he was fifty-two. That's young in my book, but since he was an accountant and certified, it probably added quite a few years to his age. It can't have been easy to be hated and despised. Who wants young children pointing at you and saying, 'There goes an accountant'? And to be fair, they are not all emotionally damaged, and for those that are, several effective treatments are now available on the NHS, including cognitive speech therapy.

The critical points here are that he was Irish and almost a teetotaller.

There is only one more player to go, but let's get on with the story, and the player details will become apparent.

10

So what were the Family Connections?

You have been wondering how the wife and I were connected to this household of misfits. Well, we are not connected in any family way; we were not relations. We were, in fact, the poor help. We were babysitters.

Let's be honest, our finances were not in the best of order. Working for a finance company, I got a very reasonable mortgage, but it was hard. The mortgage was £60 per month, and my salary was £70. My ex-wife brought in £30 per month, and consequently, we could just about survive. Things were gradually getting better as my wages increased, although inflation was a real worry.

At the time, I didn't know that there was a shitstorm just around the corner. Dolores had a very irritating habit of lecturing others on the need for household budgeting. She would explain in great detail that you needed two columns—one for the ins and one for the outs. It was vitally important that the ins were bigger than the outs. This was clearly very prudent and shrewd advice. If only she had followed her own fucking advice.

I had few debts before I got married. It wasn't that I was a goody-goody. It was because I had a good household accounting system. I made sure that the ins were bigger than the outs.

The problem with Dolores was that she had secret ins. The ins usually came by post and were ritually burnt. Apparently, this made them go away. If they weren't burnt, they were tucked away safely at the back of the drawers until you reached the point where the drawer couldn't close.

Eventually, the ins caused a massive bust-up. There was a husband-wife verbal confrontation. The husband demanded to see the ins. Initially, there were no ins, then there were some, then there were more, and in the end, the ins equated to their joint annual salary. Then more ins appeared. Sometimes the ins were escorted by aggressive money collectors in dirty macs. It was handy that their aggression could be calmed by giving them your TV. Well, it only worked once.

Our unhappy marriage just got steadily unhappier. The minimal level of sexual activity descended to a new low. It wouldn't be fair to go into the sordid details, but after two years of marriage, I still hadn't seen her fanny. I sometimes wondered if she had one, but the chances of that were pretty low.

So what was all this about? Simply put, we needed money. Dolores wasn't keen to go on the street, so we cleaned offices in the evening, delivered newspapers, and provided babysitting services. Doug and June were one of our best customers.

They paid well, provided snacks, and had a colour TV. I looked forward to the snacks because they were edible. My mother was probably the worst cook in the world. I could spend ages telling you about her culinary nightmares. I won't bore you, but I must tell you about her stew. You had to wolf it down; otherwise, a layer of thick fat would settle on the surface. Once you reached that stage, it was almost impossible to break through to the gruel below. Warmed-up vomit looked more appealing and probably tasted better.

Anyway, I was saying that my mother was probably the worst cook in the world. That was until I met my ex-wife. Her cooking skills were, let's say, rudimentary. In fact, they were downright dangerous. Food poisoning was a daily risk; diarrhoea became a hobby. But let's get back to the story.

We were their regular babysitters. Dolores had known June for some time, so we were seen as a safe pair of hands. We got to know the children quite well. Not that we liked them, they were horrible kids.

Doug saw us as scum and often left little tasks for us to complete, everything from washing up to hoovering. He wanted his money's worth. He also used it as an opportunity to lord his superiority over us. He really needed a hard kick in the balls, but I can't really condone violence.

Anyway, we had been booked to babysit. It would be a day like no other.

11

The Event, Minus One Hour

I can't think of any reasons for delaying the main event any longer. Now the real story begins.

We walked to their house in the pouring rain. There wasn't much of an alternative. We didn't have a car, and there was no point in paying for a taxi. We didn't have enough money. There were too many ins.

Dolores was not looking her best, not that her best was that appealing. Marriage was a good excuse for gluttony. The weight was piling on. I was half-convinced that she was doing it to stop me from fancying her. If that was the case, it was working.

On the other hand, June answered the door in her underwear. She said something like 'don't mind me', but I was too busy ogling her tits. The nipples were hard, dark, and protruding. She spotted me looking and made no attempt to cover them up. Her panties were brief and semi-transparent. Her curly bits were showing.

Dolores tugged at me in an attempt to stop my ogling. She said, 'Why are you staring at her, as I'm enough woman for you?' I could have been rude, but I was keen to hide my erection. I knew precisely what fantasy I was going to masturbate to that night.

Doug walked down the stairs putting his tie on. He shouted at June to get dressed. He made the point that 'our guests don't want to see you running around with your boobs hanging out'. He was wrong there.

June got some drinks and snacks ready for us and left them in the kitchen. She then explained that Isabella had been suffering from nightmares and that it would be a good idea for us to leave the lounge door open in case she needed comforting. I was more interested in comforting her dangling delights. She still wasn't dressed. Some would say that she was making the tease last as long as possible.

I don't want you thinking that I'm some sex-crazed pervert. I object to the word pervert. I just had my fair share of testosterone. I appreciated the female form, and I definitely wasn't getting my fair share.

June did eventually get dressed. They did eventually leave. They promised to be back at a specific time. That had never been achieved in the past. There was often a slippage of two or three hours but never an apology, but it cost them more so we were quids in.

We settled down to watch *Columbo* on tele. I couldn't stand the show, but Dolores was older than me and almost the same size. She was in charge of all things TV-related. That was one of her rules.

12

The Event

We were both sitting on the sofa watching *Columbo*. The lounge door was open in case Isabella had a nightmare.

As we were sitting there, an elf ran across the doorway and stopped and looked at us.

Yes, I did say an ELF!

It was about two feet tall with a perfectly proportioned body. It was a bit like a miniature Robin Hood, dressed in green with a hood. The face was well worn, bearded, and had large brown eyes. There was a tiny pair of spectacles resting on a prominent nose. He wore black boots and a black belt.

He or it was surprised that we had seen him or it. For the purposes of this story, let's assume that it is masculine. The beard is a good clue, but it's not conclusive. My mother sported a fairly impressive growth, below her nostrils. In fact, her legs were so hairy that I thought she was a werewolf for many years. Apologies for getting a bit personal, but could she fart?!

The elf, if that was what it was, was actually shocked that we saw him. In reality, we only saw him for a few seconds, but that image was locked on our collective consciousnesses forever. I can see him now in my mind's eye. He didn't strike me as being unkind or evil, rather naughtier, and mischievous. I got the feeling that he liked playing games. I was wrong, he turned out to be an evil little bastard, but we will cover that later.

The elf mumbled something and disappeared. We turned around and continued watching *Columbo*.

Now that is the frightening part of the story. We saw it, and we did not say a word until we got home a few hours later. Let's be honest if you saw a two-foot-tall elf in your house you would shout, 'What the fuck is that?'

You would be shouting. You would be animated. You wouldn't just sit there and watch *Columbo* without saying a word, would you?

So why did we not react? Did it put a spell on us? Were we hypnotised? Did we just imagine the whole thing? Too many questions.

Did our minds filter the image out? Or are there things that happen just beyond our vision? Things that we occasionally see from the very corners of our eyes.

Or were we programmed to simply carry on? I've told this story many times, and I've been asked if I was frightened. The answer was no, but I had goosebumps. My fear reaction had been stimulated. Was this creature a danger to humanity?

I have no answers. I know that I would pass a lie detector test. I saw an elf. Dolores saw an elf.

13

A Few Hours after the Encounter

Eventually, the owners of the house returned extremely late in a somewhat drunken state. I didn't like to ask how they got back, but their car was in the drive. The drink-driving laws were hardly enforced in those days but, nevertheless.

It was annoying that they had used all of their money on alcohol and that they would have to pay us the babysitting cash later. Last time that happened, it took weeks to get the money. June was soon out of her dress. Doug complained that no one wanted to see her in that state. He was wrong again.

In her inebriated state, she was finding it difficult to stand and even to keep her puppies under control. Dolores decided that it was time to go in case I saw something that would arouse my manhood. We had a long walk home in some good old Sussex drizzle. A lift was offered, but it looked far too risky. We joked that we liked walking in the rain at three a.m. And I had work the next day.

We got home drenched. Our clothes were sticking to us. After a warm bath, we got into bed, and I asked Dolores if she had seen anything. She wondered why I was asking. I said that I saw something and wondered if she had. She wanted to know what I had seen, but I was too embarrassed to tell her. A stalemate with an accompanying silence had been achieved.

Dolores then said that we had to get up early in the morning and that if I didn't tell her, she would scream. I considered the options and quietly mumbled, 'It was an elf.'

She said, 'Fucking no way, you saw the elf?!'

I was embarrassed before I told her and was even more embarrassed afterwards. Then she told me that she had seen it twice. Once while we were watching TV and later, she saw it creeping into Isabella's room. She then told it to go, and it rushed by her and disappeared.

This is where I have a dilemma. I'm a logical, rational human being who doesn't believe in the supernatural. But two people witnessed the appearance of an elf. I was still in denial. Apparently, I had done well, and we cuddled. I mistakenly took that as a come-on. She said, 'I saw the way you looked at that half-naked strumpet. You can go and fuck yourself.' That struck me as a rejection, and the cuddle ceased. She turned over and said, 'If you are really desperate, you know where it is, you can help yourself.' To be honest, I was still a bit vague about the exact location. I had only been married for two years, and it takes a while to orientate the female body.

It was almost time to get up before I got to sleep.

14

What Happened Next?

That could almost be the end of the story, but I've only written 6,000 words. I need another 74,000 words to get it published.

So far, everything has been true or almost true. I did try to lie about my cock size, but I corrected it later, so we are doing quite well.

June and her sister May fixed a date for tea at our house. They were actually coming round to give us the babysitting money. I should point out that June wasn't born in June, and May wasn't born in May, irrelevant but interesting. It was a bit annoying that Dolores spent more money on the tea than we were going to receive for babysitting.

This is almost back to her problem with the ins and outs. She also bought June's children some presents. Madness! It was no way to run a business.

Then we discovered some juicy stuff. Isabella's nightmares were getting steadily worse. There had been complaints about her behaviour at school. She had sworn at one of the teachers and bitten a classmate. Her eating disorder was also getting worse. She would only eat if the table were laid out for her friend.

Her friend insisted on a cup, saucer, plate, knife, fork, spoon, and a napkin. They had to be laid out in a specific way with the cruet set nearby. Only brown sauce was acceptable, never tomato sauce.

June explained that this had gone on for a few years, and if the rules were not followed, then there was mayhem or worse. She said that Isi would come down the stairs, tap on the radiator by the lounge door, and her friend would appear to Isi. He would consume the imaginary meal, and life would be reasonably amicable. She couldn't, however, work out who was consuming the brown sauce as they were getting through a bottle a week.

June felt that she could cope with it if things stayed the same, but things were deteriorating. What were these 'things'?

'Things' included alcoholic drinks for her friend, Mars bars, cigarettes, dirty magazines, razor blades, and stamps. Isi would leave the house late in the afternoon and not return until very late at night. She often disappeared at weekends.

June had attempted several treatments, but Isi's friend wasn't interested. In the end, they dragged Isi off to seek medical assistance. They had no doubt; it was a clear case of schizophrenia. It runs in the family, you know.

June wasn't sure. She didn't want to admit it, but she had seen a short, shadowy figure lurking by the stairs. It left behind a distinct smell of brown sauce.

Nevertheless, Isi took the recommended medical treatment for schizophrenia, and she ceased to exist as a person. She became an empty, personality-less shell. The spark had gone, but June continued to see a short shadowy figure. June had to do something as she wanted her daughter back.

Dolores casually mentioned that she had also seen a figure in their house. June looked into Dolores's eyes and said, 'What did you see?' Dolores realised that it was a loaded question.

Dolores said that both of us had seen an elf, 'That's my husband and me,' she added.

June just started screaming and waving her arms about. May tried to calm her down, but June was hysterical. She was almost a danger to herself. May slowly walked her out of the house and out of Dolores's life forever. They never met again nor even spoke a word. At least it saved money on Christmas cards.

Dolores was quite upset by this encounter. She couldn't understand why June was so upset. Now dear reader, Dolores will never know, but we will.

I almost forgot to say that this part of the story was true.

15

What Happened after That?

The unnamed old Irish lodger started coming home as pissed as a newt. These old metaphors are a bit tedious, but they make a point. He had never been a serious drinker. He had the occasional Guinness but little else.

So why the big change? June had decided that Doug was going to have to talk to him. Doug would have to lay it on the line. No more drinking, no more boisterous activities, no more singing 'Danny Boy' at the top of his voice. June lectured Doug on the urgent necessity as the Irishman was frightening the children.

Doug puffed up his chest and knocked on the lodger's door. He was invited in. Inside the accountant's room, there was a considerable collection of whiskey bottles. There were a few Bushmill bottles, but most were Tullamore. The man had good taste.

Doug, being Doug, was hardly subtle. He came straight to the point and asked what the hell he was playing at.

The unnamed old Irish whiskey drinker had tears running down his face. Tears of distress, tears of anguish, tears of a man who thought he was going mad. Perhaps he was. He carefully considered his reply and then decided to remain silent.

Doug, being Doug, upped his voice and demanded a response. The unnamed Irish insolvency practitioner wanted to respond, but he knew that his response would not be what Doug wanted to hear. Doug was the sort of man who wanted to hear what Doug wanted to hear.

Doug swore at him and told our Celtic friend that he had to leave. His case was already packed. He stood up and left, leaving the outstanding rent on the table. It was exactly the right figure, but then he was an accountant.

So why did he go?

He went because he was fed up with paying for the room and having to share it. The Leprechaun should get his own room and pay for his own drinks. At least he wouldn't have to listen to that awful rendering of 'Danny Boy' any more.

This section is possibly true, but there is no objective supporting evidence.

16

So, Which Players are Left?

The players haven't changed that much.

The story continues with the four family members playing key roles. Even the son gets more involved. The Irishman might make a return, but Dolores ceases to take an active part. There will be the occasional cameo from May and one or two other bit players.

I continue as the Narrator and will provide regular updates on my sex life or rather the lack of it. I have reached the stage where I need to consider other options.

But now is the time to introduce the main man, or whatever it is.

17

The Main Man or Whatever it is

Narrator, 'I'm the Narrator.'

It, 'No, you are not, you are the babysitter.'

Narrator, 'So you remember me?'

It, 'I remember everything.'

Narrator, 'What is your name?'

It, 'I don't remember.'

Narrator, 'Are you going to be an awkward little bugger?'

It, 'Probably.'

Narrator, 'Is it worth carrying on?'

It, 'That's got to be your decision.'

Narrator, 'I can only do my job if you cooperate.'

It, 'What's your job?'

Narrator, 'I'm writing this book about inexplicables. And you are one of them.'

It 'Is there any money in it?'

Narrator, 'Possibly.'

It, 'I need my Tullamore.'

Narrator, 'OK, I will give you a crate of Tullamore in exchange for this interview.'

It, 'Fair enough.'

Narrator, 'So, what is your name?'

It, 'I've had many names over the years. I take the name that is given to me.'

Narrator, 'What shall I call you during this interview?'

It, 'Danny.'

Narrator, 'OK, so what are you?'

Danny, 'I have no name for what I am. I appeared, I live, I never die,

I am what others call me.'

Narrator, 'How about Leprechaun?'

Danny, 'I'm sometimes called that. And pixie, elf, goblin, fairy, imp, gnome and many others.'

Narrator, 'Which do you prefer?'

Danny, 'Its humans that want to label things. I am all of those and none of them.'

Narrator, 'That's a bit enigmatic.'

Danny, 'Is that a crime?'

Narrator, 'No but terrorising a household probably is.'

Danny, 'And you think abusing your wife, fucking the vicar, crushing small insects, and biting classmates isn't?'

The interview will continue, but June is up to something.

18

June was up to Something

June wanted her daughter back. She had been lost to the ministrations of the medical profession. She decided to try a different profession. It was time to visit her clergyman friend. It meant that she would have to drop her drawers, but that wasn't a bad thing as she needed a good todgering. Doug's feeble attempt last night had only just got her interested. Now she needed finishing off.

She walked a couple of miles to the vicarage. It was a nice walk down a country lane with wild primroses and milkweed. The later had already been infested with the Monarch butterfly caterpillars. They were busily chomping away, which made her smile as the vicar would be chomping away at her soon. He liked to chew her tits. Sometimes he was a bit too enthusiastic, but any attention was good. She wasn't wearing any underwear under her short summer dress. She could feel the summer breeze circulating around her moist pussy.

June knocked on the vicarage door, and Polly, the vicar's wife, answered. Polly said, 'What is it today, a religious encounter or a good fuck?'

June, 'A bit of both really. I need some help regarding Isi, and I thought John could help, but I doubt if he will assist until he had his wicked way.'

Polly, 'John and his libido. As you know, I've always been grateful for your assistance. Too much cock makes my fanny sore, and as you know, he can go on for hours.'

June, 'Is Nigel around?'

Polly, 'No, he is still at university, so you will only be getting one cock today.'

June, 'That's a relief. Being fucked by both of them at the same time

41

is a bit too much.'

Polly, 'Like father like son. Anyway, I wouldn't know, but John's brother-in-law gave me a good seeing to once. He's a big lad.'

While they were talking, Polly put the kettle on.

At that moment, the vicar walked in. He wanted a nice cup of tea, but he wanted June more. He walked up to her, kissed her on the mouth, pushed her over the table, lifted her dress, smiled when he realised that she was knickerless, and entered her. The fucking was quite intense.

Polly, 'John, I've asked you before not to fuck the parishioners on the kitchen table.'

John was listening, and Polly sat down to watch the action. She handed June a cup of tea, which she was going to need because it looked like a long fucking session.

Polly watched John's cock repeatedly enter June's sweet little cunt. John liked to almost withdraw and then force his way back in with some gusto. It certainly made it difficult for June to drink her tea. Her approaching orgasm also made tea drinking a bit challenging.

John pumped away mercilessly. Her first orgasm only encouraged him to up his game. He was in full sledgehammer mode. Polly had always admired her husband's stamina. His technique might be wanting, but you knew that you were being fucked. The orgasmic look on June's face was making Polly feel a bit randy.

Then there was a knock on the door. Polly answered it but kept the door semi-closed to hide the action. It was one of the churchwardens. She wanted to know if the vicar was free. Polly told the warden that he was administrating at the moment but should be free in an hour.

Polly sat down again. It looked like John was going to finish soon as his cock had reached its full size, and he was slowing down. It was time to prepare for the scream. It didn't come. Instead, June was pushed to one side, Polly was grabbed and thrown over the table, and his cock slid up the inside of her knickers straight into her willing cunt. There was no subtlety. His cock just exploded in her fanny. Spunk went everywhere.

Polly, 'What made you do that?'

John, 'I didn't want one of my parishioners walking home with spunk running down her legs.'

Polly, 'That was very thoughtful of you.'

John, 'Hello June, how are you?'

June, 'Very well, thank you.'

John, 'How can I help you?'

June, 'Well, I believe that an elf has possessed my daughter.'

John. 'There is a lot of that about nowadays.'

June, 'Can you help?'

John, 'I can't do exorcisms myself, but I could assess the situation and then get the help of an expert.'

They agreed on a date and time. Then the churchwarden returned. Polly let her in this time. She walked up to the table and lifted her heavy church gown, exposing a plump arse. The Vicar already had his cock out. You had to admire the man.

19

A Doug Update

As the Narrator, I thought it only fair that all the participants should get a chance to express themselves.

Doug was still revelling in his latest love-making experience. He said to himself that he might not have the largest todger in the world, but he knew how to use it.

He was a bit surprised that June had fallen asleep halfway through, but her explanation made sense. She found the experience so erotic, so unbelievably sexual, that her mind couldn't cope, and for her own protection, it closed down. It wasn't the first time it had happened, although her snoring was a bit off-putting.

Anyway, he was genuinely concerned about Isi and decided to buy her some chocolates.

20

The Exorcism doesn't Go Well

The vicar turned up on the agreed date and time. He was a bit early so that he could exercise his love stick. June took him into the downstairs toilet and let him roger her until he came. She was far too nervous to enjoy the experience.

They both went upstairs to Isi's room. Isi was sitting on the bed in her normal gormless state surrounded by chocolates. Clearly, the chocolate plan wasn't working.

John wanted to be on his own with Isi. June wasn't too sure if that was a good idea as John couldn't be trusted with any female body. In the end, he persuaded her that it was the best way forward. When June left, Danny appeared, sitting on the bed next to Isi.

John was shocked. Shocked to the point where he was speechless and paralysed.

Danny, 'You may have noticed that you are paralysed, but you can talk.' John couldn't believe that this piece of filth in front of him could communicate. He wondered if it was the devil or just an everyday demon.

John, 'Keep away from me you vile pile of shit, you demon from the pit, you godforsaken excuse for a man, you beast from the depths of hell.'

Danny, 'Are you sure that I'm the beast?'

John, 'How can you say that, you monstrosity?'

Danny, 'I've never seduced an underage girl; I've never raped half my congregation; I've never fucked my mother; I've never committed thousands of indecent assaults.'

John, 'That's not true.'

Danny, 'Did you not force yourself onto June at Sunday school? Did you not tell her that it was the best way for the holy spirit to enter her body? Did you not rape her after the nativity play when she was in her angel costume?'

John, 'She was a willing participant.'

Danny, 'She was thirteen.'

John, 'She was a very mature thirteen.'

Danny, 'You are a philandering, paedophilic child molester whose time has come. It is time for you to be judged.' And judgement there was.

June heard the screams, but Isi's bedroom door was locked. June couldn't get in. She phoned Doug for help.

21

The Room will need Redecorating

Doug arrived. He was convinced that it would be a waste of time as June tended to overreact.

The door was firmly shut. Doug gave a fair old kick, and the door came off its hinges. Inside was horror. Something that Doug and June would never forget.

Their little girl was sitting there with a necklace around her neck. Hanging off the necklace was a penis and two testicles. The body of the vicar was on the floor with a large cactus sticking through his flies. On the wall written in blood was the message,

'Luke 17:2 It were better for him that a millstone were hanged about his neck, and he cast into the sea, than that he should offend one of these little ones.'

The police were called, and Isi was escorted off to a nice, safe padded cell.

June wondered about two things. Firstly, her daughter had never shown any religious inclinations before. How could she quote Luke?

Secondly, what caused the indentation on the bed next to Isi?

The police wondered how the genitalia was removed from the vicar's body. There was no blood on Isi's hands or teeth. In fact, there was none of the vicar's DNA on her body except around the neck.

Doug wondered what colour to paint the room. Now that his daughter had left home, he could have that study he'd always wanted.

Polly put the kettle on and wondered what to do with the insurance money.

The churchwarden cried and wondered who else would want to fuck a balding, seriously obese woman in her eighties. Then she remembered Nigel, the vicar's son.

22

Consequences

Danny wasn't sure what to do. He liked living in the house, but Isi had gone. He wasn't sure where. She just left without saying goodbye or even leaving a note. Humans were funny that way.

He had never been a decisive creature. Indecision, he thought, was a neglected art form. Quick decisions often led to disasters. There were countless examples in the Second World War. On the other hand, indecision often led to disasters. So, was the decision to be indecisive a decision?

Well, he had to make a decision soon. His whole metabolism was based on draining psychic energy off humankind. Young prepubescent girls were the best. Without that energy, he would disappear. He wasn't too sure how he knew that as he had never disappeared before.

Part of him wondered if energy draining was as bad as underage sex. At least most people survive the latter.

23

Police Confusion

The police weren't sure what to do regarding Isi. The facts were as follows:

- Isi was the only person in the room with the vicar
- The door and windows in the room were locked
- There was none of the vicar's DNA on Isi except around the neck
- There was none of Isi's DNA on the vicar
- Isi didn't do the writing as it was written using the vicar's penis and she would have had blood and DNA on her hands if she did it
- Where did the cactus come from?
- There was none of Isi's DNA on the cactus
- How were his penis and testicles removed?
- There was no knife in the room
- Who made the necklace?
- Who put it around Isi's neck?
- Where did the leather strap for the necklace come from?
- The vicar still had his trousers on, so how did the cutting take place?
- What made the indentations on the bed next to Isi?
- Isi had not mentioned the killing at all
- Does she have a memory of it?
- Who locked the door?
- There was no key in the lock, and no key was found
- There was less blood than there should have been
- What did the vicar die of? Shock? The autopsy was indecisive

Inspector Jones, who was no Sherlock Holmes, decided not to prosecute Isi and agreed to let her go.

June was thrilled that her daughter was coming home. June was surprised to see how well Isi looked. She was almost back to her normal morbid self.

Danny once again was grateful to his indecision. The food was back on the table. He needed a really good suck.

Doug had lost his study. He regretted redecorating the room now.

24

The Move

The house in Haywards Heath had too many disturbing memories. They decided to move to Burgess Hill or 'Bugs Hole' as the locals called it. If you thought Haywards Heath was a dull, boring commuter town, then Burgess Hill was an oasis of tiresome banality. It was the perfect place for a vicar-murdering, energy-sapping supernatural toss-pot.

Danny was quite excited about the move. It was going to be a fresh start, although he only needed a couple of months to finish Isi off. She wasn't going to be a great loss to the world, but he liked to line up the next victim before he put the knife in.

Isi didn't care whether they moved or not. She hated school. She had no friends. She couldn't see much point in living. She seemed to remember that she had felt happier in the police cell.

June was quite excited about getting a new kitchen. It had to be spacious with an island. However, the most important thing was that the new house had to seriously outdo her sister's house. It wasn't that she was that competitive, but May needed to know her place. She could be a bit of a snob, and she had to be taught a lesson.

June was starting to miss her representative of God on Earth. Who was going to look after her carnal needs?

The nameless son, who was actually called Ivor, hated the idea of moving. He also hated school, but he would miss his friends at the local branch of the Hitler Youth. How could he devote his life to the extermination of several ethnic groups if he lived in Bug's Hole? Alternatively, he might take up ballroom dancing to pick up the birds.

Doug just wanted a study. He didn't need a study. His reading and writing skills were minimalistic, but it would help create the right image. He was hoping that it would be a secure place to watch porn in private.

He liked the Japanese sex game shows.

A house was found, a deal was done, and a moving date was agreed. They all decided that it was going to be nice to say goodbye to whatever lurked in their old house. It was going to be goodbye to the little shit. June remembered what Dolores called it: an elf. How ridiculous, but it reminded her of the old joke: it was not good for your elf. It was stupid, but it made her laugh.

The Haywards Heath police informed the Burgess Hill police that a possible murderer was on the move.

You might consider this rather boring, but you won't have to wait long for an outbreak of serious action.

25

The Pets had to Die

Whenever Danny moved house, he had to eliminate all of the local pets. He liked to cause a bit of a stir. So while the family was moving in, he started his campaign of canine and feline extermination. He started with the cats as they were the most significant threat.

He used his Pied Piper skills to round up the local cats. He then gave them the most delicious food ever. It was probably magickal, and the cats could not get enough of it. Even when their stomachs exploded, they carried on eating. Only death stopped their feeding frenzy.

What do you do with twenty-six dead cats? The obvious thing is to sell them to the local Chinese restaurant, but Danny had style. He put them in a bag and delivered them to the local RSPCA charity shop.

Dogs were trickier as they often had humans attached to them. Sometimes you had to eliminate the humans as well. His first scan identified eleven dogs in the immediate area. It was challenging, but he got the job done:

Dog's Name	Status	Method Used	Owner
Richie	Dead	Electrification	Dead
Bob	Dead	Decapitation	Alive
Mr Boneyhead	Dead	Car accident	Brain dead
Jenny	Dead	Stabbing	Dead
Higgins	Dead	Poisoning	Hard to tell
Mouser	Dead	Microwave-oven accident	Alive
Darling	Dead	Novichok nerve agent	Dead
Beer mat	Dead	Drowning	Dead
Adrian	Dead	Broken neck	Nearly dead

| Alex | Dead | Crushed by tree | Alive |
| Trigger | Dead | Crushed by two trees | Almost alive |

Danny also eliminated eight budgies, two tortoises, four rats, two gerbils, a clutch of chickens, one salamander, and a horse. He failed to kill a pillow and a washing machine, but anyone can make a mistake. You couldn't be too careful.

The Burgess Hill Police Department contacted the Haywards Heath Police Department to ask about pet deaths. They explained that they'd had a similar experience about four years ago.

Funny how history repeats itself. Anyway, Danny was quite pleased with his performance. He was going to have an exceptionally massive suck tonight.

26

The Suck that went Wrong

Danny wasn't happy with the new house layout. He preferred to sleep in a radiator near to the outside door in case a rapid exit was needed. His exhaustion from the killing spree and his annoyance with the new house arrangements were just too much for him.

Besides, he hadn't realised how low Isi was feeling. Then it happened, he sucked her to death. He had a dead Isi on his hands. There was the added problem of the bedroom door being locked.

Isi rarely came down for a meal, so June had got into the habit of taking a tray of food up to her. That was seldom eaten, but she had done her duty. June knocked on the door, then thumped the door and eventually screamed, but there was no answer.

Doug came to the rescue. There was another kick, and the door gave way. There was their beloved daughter lying peacefully on the bed with a smile on her face. The fact that she was dead was less of a shock than the smile. Goodbye Isi.

The Burgess Hill police were called, and suicide was pronounced, but there were still too many unknowns:

- How did Isi kill herself?
- The post mortem could not identify the cause of death
- There were no drugs involved
- Was this related to the pet massacre in some way?
- Why was there a smile on Isi's face?

The world may never know the answers to these questions, but we know.

27

What went Wrong?

Doug and June's enjoyment of their new house was short-lived. The death of your only daughter does tend to piss you off a bit.

Doug was annoyed that they had moved. If Isi had died at their previous house, then he would have got his study, and it would have saved a lot of hassle.

June was pleased with the kitchen, especially as it made May's look somewhat dated. She still had no one to fuck. Doug, usually the place of last resort would have to do. Anyway, she had noticed that since he had his study, his libido had disappeared.

Ivor found that ballroom dancing was a poor second to the planning of horrific crimes against humanity. He was, however, fascinated about the local pet killings to the point where he mapped them out. Everything seemed to suggest that their house was the centre of this activity. He suspected his dad as he had never liked cats.

Danny was seriously pissed off. He was annoyed about his lack of professionalism. Isi died before her time. He should have got at least another six weeks out of her. Who was he going to suck now?

He had sucked June all through her childhood until she got married. Then she tasted rotten. It was a good job that Isi came along. He had never been a man sucker. Some of his kind were, but not him. They taste wrong, and they smell wrong.

Mind you, he had noticed recently that June was smelling better. It looked like she was the only option.

28

The Neighbour

June noticed that her neighbour worked from home, and she decided to introduce herself.

She actually introduced most of herself. She pretended that she had been locked out and needed his help to get her through an upstairs window. The neighbour, Jim, didn't know where to look as her skimpy nightie was somewhat revealing. He lived a relatively quiet life with his wife and two children.

The thought of an affair or sex out of marriage had never crossed his mind. He never even fantasied about other women.

Fortunately, Jim had a ladder that would reach the open window. June started the climb, followed by her neighbour. He had every intention of diverting his eyes, but he was transfixed by June's beautiful arse and the outline of her cunt. As she moved, her fanny beckoned him. Her crack was intoxicating. He could almost smell her sex.

When she got to the top of the ladder, she stopped, and Jim bumped into her. She could feel his erection through his trousers. She unzipped him, and his impressive penis bounced free. It wasn't free for long as June directed it towards her most intimate of places.

It was the first fuck on a ladder that either of them had experienced. It was undoubtedly risky. They managed to maintain their coitus as they twisted and climbed through the window. Then Jim came. You couldn't blame him, but June did. She needed and demanded satisfaction.

As Jim fell onto the bathroom floor, she landed on top of him. His penis was hopelessly limp as Jim had just experienced the greatest ejaculation of his life. Never again would Jim experience anything like it as she accidentally suffocated him with her vagina. She would have tried to revive him, but it was sometime before she realised, he was dead as she had been pleasuring herself with his nose.

The police were called.

29

It was Rape

After the forensic team had finished their work, Jim's body was removed. June explained that she was in her bathroom. After a shower, she opened the window as it was very steamy. She was putting moisturiser on her legs when she heard a noise outside.

A man was climbing up a ladder towards her window. She shouted at him to go away, but she realised that she was in trouble when she spotted an erect penis sticking out of his trousers. She tried to fight him off but to no avail. He took her and ejaculated deep in her vagina.

She continued to resist his attentions, and somehow, he was knocked unconscious. She was shocked to find out later that he was dead.

The Burgess Hill Police had no choice but to accept her story as there were no other witnesses. They did, however, have some queries:

- How did Jim know that June was in the bathroom?
- The post mortem showed death was caused by asphyxiation. How did that happen?
- Why are there no signs of struggle on either body?

The Burgess Hill Police phoned the Hayward's Heath Police to let them know that there had been another death.

The police also discovered Ivor's pet death chart on his bedroom wall, and in doing so, he became a prime suspect.

30

It was a Hanging

Danny loved his adopted family. The death of Jim generated a massive amount of negative energy. He sucked in every bit he could. He was expecting more.

Jim's wife, Carol, couldn't believe that her loving husband was a rapist. He had never previously shown any raping tendencies, although there was that time when he pushed her on to the bed and fucked her from behind.

Carol's Mum had always warned her about men. All they wanted to do was to get their dangly bits into a lady's private apartment. For years Carol had no idea what her Mum was talking apart. Now Jim had sampled another apartment. She was torn between disbelief and anger. But the facts were there to be seen.

It was their ladder, and he was found on the bathroom floor with his wedding tackle on full display. Our new neighbour had his sperm in her vagina. The police confirmed that was the case. Sperm doesn't pop into a woman's fanny without a handler.

She realised that she only had one course of action. She wrote a couple of letters to her children, phoned her Mum to say goodbye, and hung herself. Danny was bursting with energy. He may have helped her along a bit.

The children were young, too young to be good targets. Both were probably under three. Probably best to go for a short-term burst of energy. Danny proved once again that young children couldn't fly as he dropped them out of the window. The energy burst was thrilling. Young children have so much pent-up energy.

The police wanted to know how the children fell out of the window. They will probably never know, but *we* do, don't we, dear reader?

The Burgess Hill police phoned the Hayward's Heath police to let them know that the whole family had been eliminated. They decided to get together and review the recent deaths. Their list included:

- Reverend John
- Isi
- Jim, Carol, and their two children
- Five pet owners
- Twenty-six cats
- Eleven dogs
- Eight budgies
- Two tortoises
- Four rats
- Two gerbils
- Twenty-seven chickens
- One salamander
- One horse

Inspector Harrison asked if there was any pattern. There was no response.

31

Did you enjoy the Rape?

Doug was morbidly interested in June's rape. He repeatedly asked if she had enjoyed it. She told him that he was sick. He wanted to know what Jim's cock felt like. She told him to move on.

June wasn't feeling that happy with the world. Her lover had been killed in their house under mysterious circumstances. Her daughter also had a mysterious death. She realised that she was responsible for her neighbour's death, and felt guilty about the wife's suicide and even the death of the young ones. What a waste.

Danny realised that June's needs, which he may have prompted, could be a sure path to further energy sources. The options were endless. The sucking could be glorious.

Ivor was worried about the police. All he had done was to plot the pet deaths on a map. He got the feeling that the police were following him. That was because the police *were* following him, not because of the pet situation but because he belonged to several illegal organisations.

32

Another Interview

Narrator, 'Hello Danny.'

Danny, 'Hello, Mr Narrator.'

Narrator, 'I'm after some explanations.'

Danny, 'I thought that you might be.'

Narrator, 'Why did you kill the vicar?'

Danny, 'You must remember that I need psychic energy to live. I drain energy from human emotions, ideally negative emotions. You know fear, guilt, anger, pride, revenge. I've got to live.'

Narrator, 'Why the vicar?'

Danny, 'He was a paedophile and a liar. His victims were demanding revenge.'

Narrator, 'Did you enjoy castrating him?'

Danny, 'Not really, I'm not a sexual creature, but the punishment fitted the crime.'

Narrator, 'What about Isi. Why did you kill her?'

Danny, 'It's what I do.'

Narrator, 'Then you are no better than the vicar.'

Danny, 'You are wrong, very wrong. Our dear reverend pretended to be good and committed evil. I'm honest: I am evil, and I commit evil.'

Narrator, 'What about the neighbour's children?'

Danny, 'I killed them. It was best for them and good for me.'

Narrator, 'Why good for them?'

Danny, 'The future for two orphans has never been good in the history of humankind. Death was a better option.'

Narrator, 'Who are you to make those sorts of judgements?'

Danny, 'You can be a very irritating interviewer.'

Narrator, 'That may be the case, but what right do you have to be the judge and executioner?'

Danny, 'I don't need any right. It is what I am.'

Narrator, 'Did you kill all those animals?'

Danny, 'Yes.'

Narrator, 'And their owners?'

Danny, 'Yes.'

Narrator, 'And you don't regret it?'

Danny, 'No.'

Narrator, 'What do you plan to do next?'

Danny, 'A bit more killing and then a new family.'

Narrator, 'Who do you plan to kill?'

Danny, 'The rest of Isi's family, none of them deserve to live.'

Narrator, 'As you know, I'm writing a book about this. A decent book needs a good plot and an intriguing ending. All I'm getting are a series of spontaneous acts. Where are we going?'

Danny, 'I see what you are saying. You want me to change the way I do things to suit your novel?'

Narrator, 'That's right.'

Danny, 'Do you then accept the consequences of my actions?'

Narrator, 'That depends.'

33

More Consequences

So, dear reader, am I now complicit regarding the little bugger's actions. I'm really the Narrator, a passive observer of the facts. I'm just conscious that this story is going nowhere. There is no plot and no sign of one developing. I would like to think that a plot is being plotted, but it's not the way his majesty works. Well, you can't even call it work.

I'm also concerned that the story so far seems to contain numerous mentions of male genitalia. This was not intended; it just happened that way. In one of my more curious moments, I asked Danny how his kind procreate. The conversation went as follows:

Narrator, 'So, Danny, you are not interested in sex.'

Danny, 'Not really, it all seems rather mucky to me. It's a strange way to transfer bodily fluids.'

Narrator, 'How do your kind to do it?'

Danny, 'We don't, and I really wouldn't want to. The thought of it makes me feel ill.'

Narrator, 'I don't understand how you get baby elves?'

Danny, 'You don't, we arrive fully formed.'

Narrator, 'Fully formed?'

Danny, 'Are you deaf?'

Narrator, 'What do you mean by arriving?'

Danny, 'Are you stupid as well as deaf?'

Narrator, 'Let's assume that I'm stupid.'

Danny, 'That's fairly easy.'

Narrator, 'I would be grateful if you could explain your origins and how your race perpetuates itself.'

Danny, 'OK, in the world there are 39 of us, no more and no less. So about 1,000 rotations of the sun ago, I appeared as I am now.'

Narrator, 'You are that old?'

Danny, 'That's what I said.'

Narrator, 'For you to appear, does that mean one of your kind died?'

Danny, 'We don't die, we extinguish.'

Narrator, 'Extinguish?'

Danny, 'Why do you repeat everything?'

Narrator, 'Just to make sure that I've got it right.'

Danny, 'Yes, we extinguish ourselves, or we are extinguished.'

Narrator, 'You obviously are not thinking about extinguishment?'

Danny, 'Of course not, I'm having too much fun.'

Narrator, 'Would you consider it?'

Danny, 'Possibly if I got bored.'

Narrator, 'So boredom is a problem?'

Danny, 'When you live a few thousand years you have seen everything and done everything, then you get bored and stop chasing energy sources. If you let it carry on, you simply extinguish.'

Narrator, 'So there would only be 38 in the world.'

Danny, 'Don't be silly, a new elf appears fully formed.'

Narrator, 'And where does this new elf come from?'

Danny looked at the Narrator in a totally bewildered way, almost shocked.

Danny, 'Why do you want to know?'

Narrator, 'I was just being curious. Who is your creator?'

Danny, 'You don't know?'

Narrator, 'I've no idea. Until recently, I didn't know that elves existed.'

Danny, 'One day, I will tell you.'

Narrator, 'I will look forward to that. Do you have female elves?'

Danny, 'I've never checked.'

Narrator, 'Can't you tell without checking?'

Danny, 'I meant that I've never checked myself.'

Narrator, 'But you have got a beard.'

Danny, 'All elves have beards.'

Narrator, 'Not in *Lord of the Rings* they don't.'

Danny, 'Not that Tolkien claptrap.'

Narrator, 'So you are saying that you have never to see what gender you are?'

Danny, 'That's correct.'

Narrator, 'Why don't you do it now?'

Danny, 'I'm not sure how.'

Narrator, 'Take your trousers down and have a look.'

Danny, 'I've never taken my clothes off. I'm not even sure if they come off.'

Narrator, 'What about washing yourself?'

Danny, 'Never done that?'

Narrator, 'What about your clothes?'

Danny, 'Never washed them.'

Narrator, 'Are you saying that you have never washed yourself or your clothes in a thousand years?'

Danny, 'Yes, that is what I'm saying.'

Narrator, 'What about excretion?'

Danny, 'You mean shitting and pissing?'

Narrator, 'Yes.'

Danny, 'I don't do that either?'

Narrator, 'But I've seen you eat.'

Danny, 'I love eating! Steaks, burgers, fish and chips, pavlovas, cola cubes, apples, stingrays, tiger loaves, strawberries, shepherd's pie, cream, cat food, banana fritters, marshmallows, gravel, custard pies—'

Narrator, 'Stop! So you take it in, and it stays in?'

Danny, 'I guess so, there is the odd fart but no dung.'

Narrator, 'Let's get down to the basics. Do you have a cock or a fanny?'

Danny, 'I don't know.'

Narrator, 'Why don't you check now?'

Danny, 'What's the point? Anyway, Doug is dead.'

34

Doug is Dead

So Doug is dead. Danny said that it was on the cards, but how did it happen?

Doug woke up early in a good mood for a change. Most mornings, he suffered the bumpy grumpys. Normally his body ached, his mouth felt like shit, his eyes ran, and it took a while for his brain to engage. Some days it never engaged, and when it did, it struggled to get into third gear.

Today it was different. Today he felt alive. The sun was shining, the birds were singing, and the world felt at peace with itself. Then it happened.

Doug was supposed to be in Wivelsfield Green, but the appointment was cancelled at the last moment. That was fortunate as a colossal meteorite crashed through the atmosphere and removed the village from the face of the Earth. Unfortunately, a splinter shot off in the direction of Burgess Hill.

It shot through the Martlett's Shopping Centre, annihilated the WH Smith shop, bounced off the local cinema building, and removed Doug's head. He wasn't using his head at the time as he was having head from an accommodating lady who normally worked in the cinema. She never expected Doug to lose his head.

June was devastated. She got her newspaper from that WH Smith shop, and she had booked tickets to see a singalong version of *Mamma Mia!* at the cinema.

She was also concerned that the insurance company might treat the accident as an 'act of God'.

The Burgess Hill Police contacted the Hayward's Heath Police to let them know that Doug had been killed by a cosmic rock. They all agreed that he had met an unfortunate end.

Danny explained that the cancellation almost made him miss the target. If he had failed then the powers that be would not have been happy.

As the Narrator, I'm still trying to find out who these 'powers' were. Danny seemed to be in awe of them. I must admit I'm starting to wonder who or what is controlling the world we live in.

I need to have another go at Danny as there is still no sign of a story.

35

Doug's Death Investigated

I decided to do some on-the-spot investigation into Doug's death. I like to add some authenticity to my work.

Firstly, I visited Wivelsfield Green. Actually, I didn't. There is no Wivelsfield Green. There is one large smouldering crater and the remains of a meteorite in the middle of it. I'm not an astronomer or even a meteorologist, but it didn't seem right to me. The crater was far too big for the size of the meteorite.

I asked one of the locals what he thought.

He said, 'The crater is far too big for the size of the meteorite.'

That coincided with my thinking. There was an expert nearby. I could see that she was an expert as she was wearing a white lab coat.

I introduced myself and said, 'Young lady, I wonder if you could help me. I think that the crater is far too large for the size of the meteorite.'

She said, 'That is not unusual.' I later discovered that she was a cosmetics consultant at Boots.

I visited the remains of The Martlett's Shopping Centre. It looked like a giant rocket had ripped through the shops. It didn't matter that much as the centre was scheduled for demolition anyway. As far as I was concerned, they shouldn't have stopped at the Martlett's, the whole of Burgess Hill could go. That was an unkind thought, but if there had been a vote, then Bug's Hole would cease to exist.

When they said that WH Smith was demolished, they were right. June would have to find another newsagent. Then it was off to the cinema.

The side wall of the cinema had what looked like a massive scratch mark down its side. It was in the shape of an arrow with scorch marks at both ends. I knocked on the cinema door. An attractive young lady called Emma answered. I explained that I was investigating Doug's death, and she invited me in. It turned out that she was the actual girl providing the blow job. I asked Emma how she found herself in that situation.

She explained that she worked in the box office at the cinema for the minimum wage. After travelling expenses and paying her Mum some rent, she had very little cash left. So to supplement her meagre wage, she offered lightweight sexual services but never full intercourse. She was proud of the fact that she was still a virgin, although that might not be the case for much longer as the deflowering was up for auction on e-bay. So far, the bidding was at £860.

She argued that if she was going to lose her virginity one day, she might as well get paid for it. I wondered what had happened to romance. Doug had often purchased her used knickers and had even paid for some upskirting.

The trouble with offering lightweight sexual services is that you have to keep your clientele on the hook. There was too much competition. There was Big Bertha from the Brewery and Old Madge. The fierce local competition was pushing the prices down. Big Bertha was offering two for one. It was a cut-throat business out there.

Anyway, Emma decided to offer blow jobs. She had been practising her blowing all weekend. It came as a total shock to discover that sucking was required. She had been exercising the wrong muscles entirely.

Doug was her first blow-job customer. They went around to the back of the cinema, fought their way through an outbreak of stinging nettles, and found a reasonably comfortable spot where she could ply her trade.

Neither of them knew what to do, so Emma pulled his trousers down. She then slowly tugged at his Y-fronts. She felt a mixture of nervousness and excitement as she had never seen a live penis before. She was an attractive girl, and it was surprising that she never had a boyfriend. She put it down to her Quaker upbringing, her overzealous mother, Sunday school, and the fact that she had Tourette syndrome. Her symptoms were as follows:

General Condition	Emma's Condition
Blinking	Yes
Eye-rolling	Yes
Grimacing	Occasionally
Shoulder Shrugging	Yes
Jumping	No
Twirling	No
Grunting	Yes
Throat Clearing	Occasionally
Whistling	Occasionally
Coughing	No
Tongue Clicking	No
Animal Sounds	Yes
Saying random phrases	No
Swearing	Yes

Doug used to find her blinking, eye-rolling and grunting quite erotic. Swearing in his house was quite normal, so it was never an issue.

Emma found the exposure of his penis rather disappointing. In fact, it was shockingly disappointing. There was a tiny little protrusion in a forest of wiry black hair. She wasn't sure whether it was erect or not. This was not what she had expected after listening to the girl's stories at school. Were they all just fantasy?

She gingerly touched the little runt with her finger. It twitched. She touched it again, and it twitched some more. While this was going on, her grunting and shoulder shrugging reached new levels. She was struggling to keep control. She just hoped that the whistling didn't start.

Too late, the whistling started. That did surprise, Doug. Emma tried to grab hold of the little dangly prick. Unfortunately, she had to use her fingernails to pin it down. Doug shrieked in pain. Emma was surprised by that, which caused her throat clearing and grimacing to start. But she wasn't a quitter.

Emma got on her knees and used her teeth to hold the miniature cock in place. She wasn't sure how she was going to blow or suck with his todger firmly held between her gnashers. Doug hadn't expected to find his cock locked in place by Emma's choppers. It wasn't all bad, but it was slightly worrying. One quick bite and the little he had would be gone.

Doug was even more surprised when a meteorite removed his head. You don't expect that, standing behind Burgess Hill Cinema. There wasn't a lot he could do about it.

Emma was also surprised. She didn't expect to be kneeling amongst a bunch of stinging nettles with a tiny flaccid penis dangling from her mouth. It was just one of those days.

She was in two minds what to do with it. In the end, she handed it to the police, who eventually returned it to June. She never had much use for it and gave it to the dog to play with. She thought, 'Give the dog a bone'.

As Narrator, I thought that it would be kind of me to check on June. Well, to be honest, I was thinking that I might get a chance to exercise my trouser snake. Then I thought I couldn't really tell her about Danny, particularly as she was on the hit list. I wondered if I should warn her. But then you wouldn't want your Narrator caught in any crossfire, would you?

36

Doug's Death Aftermath

There are always consequences. Sometimes they are of major significance and world-changing. Usually, they are relatively insignificant and only of local interest. Sometimes they seem of little importance and evolve into something extraordinary.

In this case, there was no real aftermath. No real consequences. Few people attended Doug's funeral. June and Ivor felt obliged to go, but they left quickly after the service and had a McDonald's. The only other people there of interest were the police and Emma. Emma felt obliged to go as they had shared one last intimate moment together. She felt that they had bonded.

June guessed who she was and had thought about having a go at her, but what was the point?

The police being there may be the cause of future consequences.

37

Danny

As we know, Danny wasn't his real name. It wasn't his real name because they didn't have names. There are 39 of his type in the world. He knew exactly where each one was. They shared memories and experiences. He wondered if it was because they were all identical. He had heard of the word 'clone' and wondered if he was one.

He had grown fond of the Narrator and wondered if he should kill him. There was a lot of wondering. It was not something he or they were used to. Where do they come from? What happens to them when they disappear? Why don't they urinate or defecate?

Why do they suck energy from humans? In some ways, it didn't seem fair. They live pathetically, short lives, and we are nearly eternal. He had spent most of his life shortening their lives even further. But then life isn't fair.

He had never experienced regrets, as most humans deserved to be punished, but then what about those two children he threw out of the window. Did they deserve to die? Not really, but their terminal energy tasted really good. Was that enough justification for his actions? But who would he be justifying his actions to?

He had intended to kill the whole family, but should he rethink? He projected Ivor's life forwards and decided that there was no hope. He was going to turn into a nastier version of Doug. He was going to be an alcoholic, drug-taking, philandering, wife-beating, child-molesting bag of shit. On the negative side, he was going to provoke ethnic conflict and enjoy the persecution of the weak. Danny wasn't a judge, but he would enjoy sucking him dry.

June was really a walking vagina. He decided to give her a good suck and move on. Perhaps he was getting soft.

38

Ivor Problem

Ivor hated his father; he hated his whole family, and he hated humanity in general. He was mostly hate. But somewhat ironically, he missed his father. There was now a significant gap in his life.

He realised that he was now head of the family, even though there wasn't much left of it. He realised that he would have to take on all of the duties of his father, all of them.

He walked into the bathroom while his mother was having a shower. She never locked the door nowadays after their recent problems. Ivor looked her up and down and decided that she was still a good-looking woman. The breasts were firm, the buttocks were passable, and her fanny looked good enough to eat. He was going to enjoy taking on the paternal role.

June, 'What are you doing here? Get out.'

Ivor, 'I've decided that I'm head of the family now and that I'm taking over from my father, including fucking your arse off.'

June, 'No you are not, be a good boy and get out.'

Ivor unzipped his flies.

Ivor, 'You need to be taught a lesson, you whore.'

June, 'Don't you call me a whore.'

Ivor, 'But you are. I know all about your previous indiscretions. I know that the vicar and his son used to give you one. I used to go to school with the son. Don't you realise just how embarrassing that was?'

June, 'I'm sorry, but get out.'

She could see that he didn't intend to leave.

Ivor was playing with his now hardening tool and said, 'Not until I've had my way.'

June, 'This is your last chance, fucking get out.'

Ivor had no intention of leaving and leapt at her. June grabbed the soap container and squirted it at his eyes. He was immediately blinded, bashed his head on the side of the bath, and sank into the water. June hurtled out of the tub, screaming and wrapped a towel around herself.

She tried to revive her son, but it was too late. Danny had succeeded again.

At the funeral, there was no one to go to McDonald's with her.

June went home, sat by the kitchen table, and cried. In a few short weeks, she had lost Doug, Isabella, Ivor, and John. It was too much to bear. Danny was having a really good suck.

He was a bit surprised when June took the carving knife and slit her own throat. The sucking was brilliant but unexpected. He wondered what he was going to do next.

The Burgess Hill police updated the Haywards Heath police on the latest death. There was a discussion about having a case review. There were some suspicions that the Russians were involved.

39

A Third Interview

Narrator, 'Hello Danny.'

Danny, 'Hello, Mr Narrator.'

Narrator, 'Thank you for allowing the third interview.'

Danny, 'I quite enjoy them, they are thought-provoking.'

Narrator, 'What made you kill the whole family?'

Danny, 'Well, for once I didn't kill the whole family. As you know, I killed Doug and John. Isabella was an accident. Ivor had to go as he was going to be a real bastard, believe me, but I didn't kill June.'

Narrator, 'Who killed her?'

Danny, 'It was suicide.'

Narrator, 'The police said that whoever did it, cut her throat from behind.'

Danny, 'Well, she was making a real mess of it, so I helped her out.'

Narrator, 'Did she intend to go through with it?'

Danny, 'Of course.'

Narrator, 'Are you sure?'

Danny, 'She was a bit hesitant, and she didn't like the blood going everywhere.'

Narrator, 'You killed her, didn't you?'

Danny, 'Slightly.'

Narrator, 'You can't slightly kill someone.'

Danny, 'Let's move on.'

Narrator, 'Do I know too much?'

Danny, 'Probably.'

Narrator, 'Does that mean you are going to kill me?'

Danny, 'It's on the cards.'

Narrator, 'Apart from killing me, what are your plans?'

Danny, 'There has to be a connection between my kills, so I was thinking of Emma.'

Narrator, 'Who is Emma?'

Danny, 'She is the whore who was giving Doug a blow job when the meteorite hit him.'

Narrator, 'Does she deserve your attention?'

Danny, 'What's deserve got to do with it? It's either her or your family.'

Narrator, 'I think you need to see Emma. Can I ask some more questions about your world?'

Danny, 'Go on.'

Narrator, 'You mentioned that you just arrived. Where did you find yourself?'

Danny, 'I haven't told you, but all 39 of us are telepathically connected. So when I arrived, I was born into a network of friends. We always arrive at Ynys-witrin.'

Narrator, 'Just a minute I will google it. It's the Isle of Glass— Glastonbury.'

Danny, 'If you say so.'

Narrator, 'Do you all arrive there?'

Danny, 'What do you mean by all?'

Narrator, 'I mean all of your kind.'

Danny, 'The answer is yes, but many others arrive by the Island of Avalon.'

Narrator, 'Like who?'

Danny, 'Fairy kings and queens, goblins, pixies, and others.'

Narrator, 'You are joking.'

Danny, 'What makes you think that?'

Narrator, 'It's just so unlikely.'

Danny, 'You say that, and here you are interviewing an elf.'

Narrator, 'What others?'

Danny, 'When I was young there used to be a lot of creatures: dragons, centaurs, basilisks, ogres, satyrs, unicorns and many others.'

Narrator, 'Where have they all gone?'

Danny, 'No idea; I've no idea where I came from.'

Narrator, 'And you are sure about all this?'

Danny, 'Of course.'

Narrator, 'Do you have any proof?'
Danny, 'O ye of little faith. Do you want to meet a fairy?'
Narrator, 'I think so; is it safe?'
Danny, 'It will be for me.'

40

Emma drops her Knickers

Danny decided that Emma was a nice girl. Tourette's syndrome was an unfortunate mental condition that had no cure. She was just unlucky. Her low-level money-making sexual activities were part of a young girl's entry into womanhood. She had taken that route as compensation for failing to create meaningful human relationships.

Her brother and sister had a great relationship with each other and their parents. The siblings were twins and seemed to exclude Emma from their world. Her parents forgot that Emma existed. There was some great potential here for an experienced elf. There should be plenty of suckings.

Yes, Emma was a nice girl. Danny decided that he would have to change that.

Emma walked down the aisle of the cinema towards a dirty old tramp who often used the cheap pensioner's ticket to keep warm and have a good kip. Emma removed her skirt and knickers and sat next to him. He was surprised to have company and even more surprised to find that she was half-naked.

Emma placed his hand on her fanny. Joe, the tramp, had not seen or touched a live fanny in twenty years. He looked her in the eyes through the half-light of the cinema, and he swore that she nodded. Joe started caressing her clitoris. Emma quietly swooned and gyrated her body around his finger.

She pulled his cock out of numerous layers of clothing. It smelt of dried piss and Old Holborn, but that was not going to stop her. She lifted herself onto his lap and lost her virginity. Her screaming attracted attention, and Joe had to cover her mouth using his snotty motheaten gloves. She was a woman. He was an old tramp covered in the blood of a maiden.

Danny found the whole adventure very satisfying. The sucking was good.

41

Emma drops her Knickers again

Danny decided that Emma was still a nice girl, but that would have to change. This is not a story about sex and debauchery; it's more a story about the human condition. As humans are so short-lived, they have to focus on reproduction. They have got to knock out a few children before they give up the ghost.

Danny was not interested in sex. The sexual act was of no interest to him whatsoever except that lust was such a powerful source of energy. Prepubescent girls with their hormones and egg-laying capability were just manna to his cause.

Emma walked down the cinema aisle again, took off her skirt and knickers, and walked up to a row of four young lads. She squeezed past the legs of the first lad bent over and presented her open vagina. He grabbed a handful of popcorn, put it in his mouth, unzipped his trousers, and put his pecker in her pocket. He filled up her pocket and picked up some more popcorn.

He moved her on. The second lad was chomping on a hot dog but decided that this was hotter and doggier and deserved his attention. His own hot dog was soon doing the dirty deep down in Emma's tunnel of love. He sprayed her with his mustard sauce and moved her on.

The third lad had seen what was happening and was eagerly waiting for the loss of his virginity. Sloppy thirds were a lot better than the sniggers and sneers behind your back. Getting your pecker polished wasn't everything, but as he got near the polishing area ready for a poke, the pecker picked the moment to explode. The pesky pecker's poke missed the poking pit by a mile. All was not lost as no one but Emma would know.

She moved on disgruntled and dissatisfied. It got worse as the last lad declined the delights of her thighs. Her vagina, willing, and eager was rejected, refused, and rebuffed. She felt snubbed, shamed, and humiliated, but that was no excuse for sticking her hair clip up his nostril.

Management decided that the attack on the boy's nostril would not have been a sacking offence except that he was clearly gay, and consequently, she had to go. And so the budding career of a ticket seller and usherette was over. It had been a great way of earning extra money while at college.

42

Further Education

Emma's parents have been called to the school before. If your child has Tourette's Syndrome, it was to be expected, but they hadn't expected to have to visit the college.

Dr Downright, 'Mr and Mrs Brown, I've asked you here today as Emma's behaviour has got worse.'

Mr Brown, 'I'm sorry to hear that. The swearing can be difficult to cope with.'

Dr Downright, 'It's not the swearing.'

Mrs Brown, 'Then it must be the whistling.'

Dr Downright, 'No, it's not the whistling.'

Mr Brown, 'Grunting?'

Dr Downright, 'No, it's not the grunting.'

Mrs Brown, 'Then it's got to be the animal noises.'

Dr Downright, 'No, now listen, it's the nudity and sexual predation.'

Mr Brown, 'Nudity?'

Dr Downright, 'Yes, she seems to think that it is perfectly OK to walk around with only a bra on.'

Mrs Brown, 'She's always needed a fair amount of support. She takes after Aunty Joan. She had large breasts with big brown nipples.'

Dr Downright, 'I'm not interested in Aunty Joan.'

Mrs Brown. 'A lot of men were. She was never short of male callers. Now my nipples are smaller and pink in colour, aren't they Tom?'

Mr Brown. 'That's right. I'm not really sure where she got her brown nipples from. They don't run in my family.'

Dr Downright was getting annoyed. Downright annoyed and said, 'We are not here to talk about the colour of your daughter's nipples. We need to agree on a course of action.'

Mr Brown, 'So once again those with mental problems are going to be punished for their condition.'

Dr Downright, 'It's not just the nudity. She has turned into a sexual predator.'

Mr Brown, 'What do you mean by that?'

Mrs Brown, 'My daughter is a virgin.'

Dr Downright, 'If she is, then we have very different definitions of virginity.'

Mr Brown, 'How dare you?'

Dr Downright, 'Apologies, but your daughter has offered herself to countless students and staff, and I'm sorry to say that there have been quite a few takers. She is an attractive girl, and there is a lot of testosterone about.'

Mr Brown, 'How many are we talking about?'

Dr Downright, 'I would say about 130.'

Mr Brown, 'That's nonsense.'

Dr Downright, 'More if you count repeat performances.'

Mrs Brown, 'That's not my daughter.'

Dr Downright, 'You should see the queues by the cycle sheds. Shall we go and investigate?'

They all tramped down to the cycle sheds where there was a queue of a dozen boys plus a gang of onlookers. There was Emma taking three boys at once. Mrs Brown fainted. How could her daughter take one up the arse? Some of the boys shouted at them to join the queue.

Mr Brown put his jacket on Emma, and they all walked her away. The boys were not happy. It meant back to playing cards.

43

You need a fire to keep warm

Keith had never been close to his sister. Emma had always been a source of embarrassment, and now it had got worse. Most of his mates had slept with her. Some had even had anal sex with her. They were continually discussing her charms and describing what they had done and what they were planning to do.

He was still a virgin, which made it worse. And the fact that Emma walked around the house naked made it even worse. His Mum said that Emma was just transitioning to womanhood.

Anyway, he had decided to get his revenge. Danny liked revenge; it always led to good suckings. Keith had always enjoyed playing with matches; he liked seeing things burn. Under Danny's guidance, this turned into arsonistic tendencies, and there was no better target than the college. He planned to set fire to the cycle sheds, the epicentre of the family's shame.

Keith stole his father's car, loaded it with cans of petrol and paper. The cycle sheds were soon aflame, along with the gym, the canteen, and the modern sciences block. There were only sixteen deaths, and Keith was taken away charged with murder and manslaughter. They couldn't stop him laughing.

Danny revelled in the suckings. It had been one of his more successful achievements, but they were an easy family to manipulate.

44

More Interviewing

Narrator, 'You haven't killed me yet.'

Danny, 'Hello Mr Narrator, your time will come.'

Narrator, 'It looks like Emma's family is going through it.'

Danny, 'They are a really nice family. It's a shame in a way that I'm disrupting them.'

Narrator, 'Why are you doing it then?'

Danny, 'I need my suckings, and I'm not here to judge.'

Narrator, 'But you plan to kill them all.'

Danny, 'That's not true, I need their emotional energy. It makes more sense to keep them alive but make them suffer.'

Narrator, 'You are a truly horrible species.'

Danny, 'I agree, we are not nice, but we are what we are. Anyway, I have a present for you.'

Narrator, 'Really?'

Danny, 'Yes, Dolores is still not delivering, so I thought you might need cheering up.'

In walked a totally naked Emma.

Narrator, 'What are you playing at?'

Danny, 'She is all yours. You can do what you like with her. She will give you the best fuck of your life.'

Narrator, 'You are an evil shit.'

Danny, 'You don't have to be offensive. It's what you want. A willing woman. You don't have to worry about getting her pregnant as she is already expecting.'

Emma walked up to him and started unzipping his flies.

Danny, 'Do you want her?'

Narrator, 'No, take her away.'

Emma pulled his cock out of his trousers and was preparing to suck. Danny laughing said, 'You want her, I know you do. It's in your eyes.'

The Narrator tore himself free and said, 'I'm not being dragged into your games.'

Danny, 'But you are.'

Emma grabbed his cock again.

The Narrator, 'You can't play with a young girl's emotions.'

Danny, 'I can and worse. I've sold her unborn baby's soul to the fairies.'

The Narrator desperately wanted to sample her charms, but he summoned up enough will power to walk away. He wanted to know what Danny meant about selling the baby's soul to the fairies. That would have to wait.

45

The Fairy Deal

Fairy Queen, 'So you have a baby's soul for sale?'

Danny, 'Not quite yet but shortly. I was planning to terminate the pregnancy. There is no point going to full term.'

Fairy Queen, 'How will the host feel?'

Danny, 'Does it matter?'

Fairy Queen, 'And what do you want in return?'

Danny, 'The normal.'

Fairy Queen, 'Five ounces of fairy dust.'

Danny, 'Six.'

Fairy Queen, 'Do you know how long it takes to get an ounce?'

Danny, 'Who cares; you have many lifetimes. Just think what you could do with a pure, unadulterated soul. You will be able to conquer other fairy strongholds.'

Fairy Queen, 'It's not all about conquering.'

Danny, 'But that is your plan, isn't it?'

Fairy Queen, 'Possibly.'

Danny, 'You fairies are so predictable.'

Fairy Queen, 'That may be the case, eleven of thirty-nine. Will you ever be number one?'

Danny, 'I'm getting there.'

Fairy Queen, 'I could help you.'

Danny, 'And why would you do that?'

Fairy Queen, 'Every seven years we have to pay a tithe of souls to the devil, and we need help against the marauding goblins.'

Danny, 'What do you need?'

Fairy Queen, 'More souls.'

Danny, 'How many?'

Fairy Queen, 'At least one a month.'

Danny, 'I will need to get a production line going.'

Fairy Queen. 'That's fine, with me.'

Danny, 'What's the deal.'

Fairy Queen. 'One place for every soul.'

Danny, 'And the fairy dust?'

Fairy Queen, 'You push me too hard.'

Danny, 'Fairy dust?'

Fairy Queen, 'OK, but they better be untainted.'

Danny, 'You can count on me.'

46

Mrs Brown gets her Oats

Danny liked having a job to do; it gave his life purpose. He neutralised Mrs Brown's contraceptives. Not that she needed them as Mr Brown had not visited her for a while. She assumed that he was bored with her, which was a shame as she used to enjoy their tussles.

She looked at her naked self in the mirror. Pert tits, flat tummy, shaved fanny, and shapely legs, just how Mr Brown liked them. She assumed that ten years of fucking the same fanny was enough for any man. She wished that she had the courage to initiate sexual congress, but she was chicken until now.

Now there was a burning sensation in her groin. An urge that she had never experienced before. It was basic, primaeval and all-encompassing. She needed to be taken, fucked, and devoured. Mr Brown could do whatever he liked with her.

The heat and the pressure were too much. She burst into his study and leapt onto him, ripping his clothes off in her frenzy. The zip on his trousers was literally ripped off in her effort to get to his prick. Her pent-up sexual desire showed no mercy as his cock was forced into her womanhood.

She rode him until he ejaculated and then rode him until his penis was a bloody mess. She couldn't stop. She needed everything he had, including his life. She rode him until it was too difficult to recognise that the corpse was once Mr Brown. She rode him until the carcass ceased to look human. She just about felt satisfied. She didn't know that she was pregnant, but Danny did. That was two souls on the go. Now for Emma's sister.

47

Emma's Sister

Emma's sister was a star called Jill. She topped her class in every subject. She sang, acted, and played the guitar and the violin. She had already got her place in Oxford and on the Olympic team. She was a genuine star and looked the part. She was a real beauty who could speak three languages.

She was still a virgin and proud of it. She was saving herself for the right man. It was what God wanted. But it wasn't what Danny wanted. He decided that the defloration should be religious.

The local vicar was surprised that Jill had arrived at the church naked. It wasn't her usual dress style. She explained that she had little to offer the congregation except her body. This seemed entirely logical to the vicar. She explained that she would read a prayer and then lay on the altar like a vestal virgin and accept donations.

The first donation took her virginity but failed to get her pregnant. The second donation was also unsuccessful, and the third, fourth, and fifth. Danny was getting restless. It was into double numbers now, and there was no sign of impregnation. He wondered if he had backed the wrong horse when the janitor got the job done on his third attempt.

Danny now realised that this pregnancy malarkey was going to be more challenging than he thought. Anyway, that was three in the bag.

48

Mass Pregnancy

Danny now had three pregnant women to look after. That definitely wasn't his cup of tea. He could control them, but he didn't want to nurse them. He needed help. He decided that a bloke would be best to look after three randy women. They would keep themselves occupied.

He wondered if the Narrator would be interested, but he had previously rejected his present and run off. He hadn't expected that. These humans had huge desires and complex, illogical social rules that seemed to vary with geography, tribe, and ethnicity.

The 'girls', as he called them, wanted to buy baby stuff, but Danny knew that it wasn't going to be necessary. The Fairy Queen only wanted the souls as a weapon against the goblins. One soul provided enough ammunition for at least 1,000 quavers.

Danny planned to collect the souls on the same day, but it was going to be a shocking day in the household. No one seemed to think it unusual that a mother and her two daughters were all pregnant at the same time. A few people wondered what had happened to Mr Brown, but the 'girls' never gave him a thought.

49

The Police Pontificate

It was rare that the Haywards Heath and Burgess Hill police got together. They were brothers in the eyes of the law but also fierce rivals. However, the weirdness in Sussex had attracted the attention of Scotland Yard.

They decided to list the various strange events:

Haywards Heath

- The death of Reverend John in a locked room with his penis made into a necklace and put around Isabella's head

Burgess Hill

- The annihilation of the local pet community (twenty-six cats, eleven dogs, eight budgies, two tortoises, four rats, two gerbils, a clutch of chickens, one salamander and a horse)
- The accidental death or four or five pet owners
- The death of Isabella in a locked room
- The rape of June
- The death of Jim, the neighbour
- The suicide of Jim's wife, Carol, and the death of their two children
- The destruction of Burgess Hill and Doug by a meteorite
- Ivor's apparently accidental death
- June's suicide
- Sexual escapades in Burgess Hill Cinema
- Sexual escapades at the college
- Arson at the college resulting in 16 deaths
- The disappearance of Mr Brown
- Sexual escapades at the local church

The Head of the Hayward Heath police said that they thought it was a

Burgess Hill problem, and his whole team walked out.

They later learnt that Keith had committed suicide in remand by slicing his testicles with an onion peeler and bleeding to death.

The Head of the Burgess Hill police asked for details showing how the various incidents were connected. They created a mind diagram which pointed to an instigator, but there was no apparent suspect.

Inspector Jill Wiseman suggested that there had been several supernatural connotations: the Luke inscription, the death of the reverend, locked room killings, etc. She could see the hand of God in many of the proceedings. She was ignored.

Sergeant Tomlinson wondered if they could identify any future victims of the serial killer. His boss told him that there was no evidence of such a killer but agreed that it was a good question.

With Keith's death, the only living connections left were the Brown family, and the father was missing. A round-the-clock surveillance operation was set up.

50

Soul Collecting

Danny was a fully qualified elf. He was one of the best, although they were all identical, but he had no experience of stealing the souls of unborn children. How do you do it? What do you collect the souls in? How do you know that you have got them? None of the thirty-eight had any guidance to offer.

He could ask the Fairy Queen, but he didn't want to appear weak. The elves needed to maintain their hard-earned veneer of superiority. It might be critical in future council meetings.

Danny decided to consult the key reference guides. The Brothers Grimm outlined the following:

'A mother had her child taken from the cradle by elves. In its place they laid a changeling with a thick head and staring eyes who would do nothing but eat and drink. In distress, she went to a neighbour and asked for advice. The neighbour told her to carry the changeling into the kitchen, set it on the hearth, make a fire, and boil water in two eggshells. That should make the changeling laugh, and if he laughs it will be all over with him. The woman did everything just as her neighbour said. When she placed the eggshells filled with water over the fire, the changeling said:

'Now I am as old
As the Wester Wood,
But have never seen anyone cooking in shells!'

And he began laughing about it. When he laughed, a band of little elves suddenly appeared. They brought the rightful child, set it on the hearth, and took the changeling away.

In folklore, supernatural creatures are often as susceptible to trickery as humans.' (Public Domain)

Well, he wasn't going to bother with all that changeling rubbish. He just wanted the souls. This was the twenty-first century. Danny then consulted the following references:

- *Croker, Thomas Crofton, Fairy Legends, and Traditions. 1825.*
- *Douglas, George. Scottish Fairy and Folk Tales. 1901.*
- *Gregory, Lady Augusta. Cuchulain of Muirthemne. 1902*
- *Kirk, Robert and Lang, Andrew, The Secret Commonwealth of Elves, Fauns, and Fairies. 1893.*
- *Wildes, Lady Francesca Speranza, Ancient Legends, Mystic Charms, and Superstitions of Ireland. 1887.*
- *Yeats, William Butler, Fairy and Folk Tales of the Irish Peasantry. 1888.*

Danny was even more confused when he read about the Grim Reaper. He uses a scythe. Danny assumed that he uses it to cut the connection between the physical world and the spirit world, but how do you actually collect the soul? He didn't like these sorts of conundrums. He didn't like exhaustive thinking. It's not what elves do.

He felt that he had no choice but to consult the Fairy Queen. The thirty-eight agreed with him.

51

There are too many Interviews

Narrator, 'Why have you asked for a meeting? I can't forgive you for that last stunt.'

Danny, 'Hello, my friend.'

Narrator, 'I'm not your friend. You are a cold-hearted killer.'

Danny, 'That's not very nice. I thought we were buddies. I thought you were investigating my world, but your mind is fixed and closed.'

Narrator, 'You are not what I thought you were going to be.'

Danny, 'You have watched too many Disney films. We may be called the "Good People" or the "Little Folk", but we are far from being compassionate and generous wish-givers. We are devious, cunning, tricky, scheming little creatures that have to survive like most others. The Darwinian rules affect us like any other species. We have the additional burden of having to hide our existence.'

Narrator, 'Why are you telling me all this?'

Danny, 'I thought we agreed that I was going to kill you. It's not a big deal. You are going to die anyway.'

Narrator, 'I want a few more years yet.'

Danny, 'You shall have them if you do a job for me.'

Narrator, 'OK, that's encouraging.'

Danny. 'I want you to make something for me.'

Narrator, 'Go on.'

Danny, 'I need a glass container with a hinged stopper. There needs to be a light in the container. From the neck of the container, I need a sheet that will cover a bed.'

Narrator, 'What's it for?'

Danny, 'That's my business. I need to make sure that you understand the requirement. The sheet will cover the bed on a frame. At one end of the sheet, there will be a bottle or whatever makes sense. The

97

bottle has a light in it and a lid that I can shut. Ideally, I need three of them. Do you understand?'

Narrator, 'I believe so. What do I get in return?'

Danny, 'Firstly, I guarantee not to kill you in the next twenty years providing you behave, and secondly, you will get some fairy dust.'

Narrator, 'Can I trust you?'

Danny, 'No, we are not honourable creatures, but I will honour this deal as I need you.'

Narrator, 'And why would I want fairy dust?'

Danny. 'You will find out, and you will want more.'

Narrator, 'You mentioned that I could meet a fairy.'

Danny, 'There is one with us now.'

Narrator, 'Where?'

Danny, 'She will become visible shortly. Do you want the Pre-Raphaelite version or as they really are?'

Narrator, 'How about both?'

Suddenly there was a beautiful Tinkerbell-like winged creature in front of him. It was a text-book fairy with gossamer wings, wand, and silken clothes. She wore a crown because she was a Fairy Queen. Seeing her made him feel happy.

Then the change. In front of him was a short, wrinkled old hag. There were no wings, a wand, nor even a smile. Instead, there was the look of a conniving, sneaky witch with cruel, malicious intent. The Narrator was now even more certain that he should never have got involved with the "Fair Folk". It was a path that he should never have ventured down.

Fairy Queen, 'It has been a long time since I've seen a ploughman. I had forgotten how bad they smell and how ugly they are.'

Danny, 'I've got used to the smell.'

Fairy Queen, 'What is it based on?'

Dany, 'It's a unique combination of milk, shit, urine, and turnips. Some of them have additional flavourings based on beer and curry.'

Fairy Queen, 'What is this curry?'

Danny, 'You don't want to know. The Fair Folk should keep away from it.'

Fairy Queen, 'And will your mechanism do the job?'

Danny, 'I believe so.'

Fairy Queen, 'It could revolutionise the way we do things.'

Danny, 'Yes, my queen.'

Of course, she wasn't his queen. They all knew that.

Fairy Queen, 'Next time we meet, you should have the goods?'

Danny, 'Of course.'

52

The Lack of Narration

You may have noticed that there has been a distinct lack of narration for a while. There are numerous reasons for this. Firstly, I'm not getting paid. We have crossed the twenty thousand words mark, and no sign of any money. Not even a promise.

Secondly, my life has been put in danger. Danny has made it clear that he plans to kill me. It doesn't help you sleep at night. I've bought a fierce dog that terrifies me. I've fitted burglar alarms. I even got a gun. I've no idea how to use it, but it makes me feel safer.

Thirdly, there have been so many deaths. I feel like I have blood on my hands. I'm sure that the police will link the crimes to me. I'm totally innocent but guilty by connection. I can't tell the police anything as they would lock me away for years.

To be honest, I have questioned my own sanity. This is clearly an implausible story. If it were true, then human civilisation would never be the same again. But having said that, there have been fairy stories throughout man's history.

Now I'm being dragged in further. This simple device surely is needed for evil works. If I make it, I may live; if I don't, I may not last the month.

So readers, what do you think? Some of you would have given up by now. There is action. There is some eroticism. I was sorely tempted to fuck Emma. She wouldn't have minded, but I have principles, or perhaps I *had* principles. Making this device may be the equivalent of crossing the Rubicon. If Emma were offered again, I would probably weaken. Is that just me being weak, or is that the way humanity is?

Anyway, few ploughmen have met a fairy queen, and there is a slight chance of a plot after all this time!

Editor, 'I thought the Narrator was the author. That's the impression I got from the introduction. I should know, I'm the editor.'

Author, 'Stop being boring.'

53

Three Pregnant Ladies Pontificate

Jill, 'Mum, I've been thinking that it is strange that the three of us are pregnant at the same time.'

Mrs Brown, 'It is strange, especially as I was on the pill. Anyway, I still can't forgive you. My little girl, allowing dozens of parishioners to fuck her in the church of all places!'

Jill, 'It seemed the right thing to do at the time. Now I can never go back to that church.'

Emma, 'What about me, aren't you ashamed of me?'

Mrs Brown, 'Of course. I have two daughters who are whores.'

Jill, 'Well, who got you pregnant?'

Mrs Brown. 'It was your father, of course.'

Emma, 'How do we know that, now that he has gone missing?'

Mrs Brown, 'What are you suggesting?'

Emma, 'I saw you with Dad. You were like a savage beast.'

Mrs Brown, 'That is not true.'

Emma showed her some photos she had taken on her smartphone. What could Mrs Brown say; the evidence was there.

Mrs Brown, 'OK, I fucked your father to death.'

Jill, 'There is some mysterious force that is manipulating us. We are all doing things out of character. Look at Keith.'

Mrs Brown, 'Are we still being manipulated?'

Danny had lost control while he was with the Fairy Queen. Now that he was back, their numbness returned. He was quite keen to offer Emma to The Narrator again to see how strong he was.

54

Surveillance

Police Inspector, 'Give me your report.'

Duty Officer, 'For three days there was no activity whatsoever. It appeared that all three women were sleeping. It hasn't been confirmed, but it would seem that all three of them are pregnant.'

Police Inspector, 'You are saying that the mother and her two daughters are all pregnant?'

Duty Officer, 'That would appear to be the case. Most of the time, they are naked, so it is fairly obvious.'

Police Inspector, 'Naked?'

Duty Officer, 'Yes Sir, naked as a jaybird, whatever that means. Call me crazy, but sometimes there does seem to be another inhabitant.'

Police Inspector, 'What are you saying?'

Duty Officer, 'Occasionally, I catch a glimpse of a shadow.'

Police Inspector, 'A shadow of what?

Duty Officer, 'It looks to me like a dwarf.'

Police Inspector, 'Really?'

Duty Officer, 'Yes, there is nothing on camera, and it's more a feeling. Yesterday the three women woke up and were shouting at each other. It got quite aggressive with wild gesticulations. Then suddenly it went quiet, and the three women went back to sleep again.'

Police Inspector, 'What strange behaviour. Is there enough evidence to intervene?'

Duty Officer, 'Not really.'

Police Inspector, 'You could try knocking on the door to check that they are OK.'

Duty Officer, 'Yes, Sir, I will do that.'

55

The device

It took a while for the Narrator to find someone to build the required device. It was made more difficult in that he had no idea what it was for.

In the end, it was quite professional looking. He thought that Danny would be pleased with the work. He needed to contact him to let him know that it was ready.

56

Time for the Midwife

Danny had decided that the time had come for the soul extraction. He could sense the new life developing in the three bodies. It was best to extract the souls before they got too comfortable in their human forms.

The Narrator had delivered the devices. Danny was wondering how he was going to install them. It was a challenge for him due to his diminutive size. He had considered getting the Narrator to help, but that would probably be a step too far.

Danny had been working on the unborn spirits, telling them that he was their father and that they were in danger. They should head towards the light, at the earliest opportunity. Anyway, souls were pre-programmed to head towards the light.

He fitted the frames on the beds and covered the naked women with the sheets. He turned the lights on and then caused a large explosion in the kitchen. This encouraged the souls to flee towards the light. Danny shut the jars, and he had his treasure.

Just then, the front door burst open and in came two burly coppers. They struggled to understand what was going on. There was smoke pouring from the kitchen, and there were three naked women lying on beds, fast asleep.

Danny had teleported out to the fairy glen. It was a far cheaper means of travel than petroleum-based vehicles.

All three women had stillbirths that night. They were in protective custody, still fast asleep. Danny wasn't sure what to do as he was hoping to get them impregnated again. Perhaps the police could help.

57

A Soul for a Soul-Mate

Danny handed over the three souls to the Fairy Queen. It was a strange-looking affair as he had the three souls in milk bottles, which were much larger than her. And she handed over some fairy dust in a jar much smaller than a thimble. Both were happy with the deal. He knew that the Narrator would have serious regrets, but that was his problem.

Fairy Queen, 'So when will I get the next delivery?'

Danny, 'I have the girls and a plan to get them pregnant. I'm not sure how quickly I can harvest souls after pregnancy.'

Fairy Queen, 'You make me laugh. You have asked one of the questions discussed in the *Abomindom*, the Book of the Fay.'

Danny, 'Fair enough, but I need to know the answer.'

Fairy Queen, 'Let me educate you.'

Danny, 'I don't need education, I just need an answer.'

Fairy Queen, 'If you are going to be a soul trader, you need to know. Different folk have different beliefs. I will elucidate.'

Danny, 'I don't need elucidation, I just want an answer.' Danny was a humble, no-nonsense sort of elf. He knew that the Fairy Queen could and would talk for hours, and you still wouldn't have your answer.

Fairy Queen, 'You need to know, so listen. Firstly, there is a huge debate about where souls come from. These are the key points:
- Does God create souls?
- Is there another entity that creates souls?
- Have souls always existed since the creation of the universe?
- Are new souls being created or not?
- Are the souls being recycled through a process of reincarnation?

- Is there a plane of existence where souls wait for a human body?
- Where does the soul go when the body dies?'

Danny, 'I know all of that, but you haven't answered my question.'

Fairy Queen, 'You are in a hurry. What are you going to do with the time you save by not listening to me?'

Danny, 'I've got work to do.'

Fairy Queen, 'But you are almost eternal, you *have* time to waste.'

Danny, 'My women need to get impregnated again.'

Fairy Queen, 'You will listen, and I will answer your question about ensoulment. There are four possible times:
- At conception
- Between conception and birth
- At birth
- After birth

'Let's look at conception. Spiritually, there is a strong argument for this. The soul enters the body when the sperm and ovum unite.'

Danny, 'That all sounds a bit technical for you, sperm and ovum?'

Fairy Queen. 'They are not terms we would use, but I was using language that you might have come across. We don't live in the human world like you.'

Danny, 'What do you call them?'

Fairy Queen, 'Stinger and Egg.'

Danny, 'Why stinger?'

Fairy Queen, 'When fairies have sex, every one hundred and twenty-five years, it can be quite painful. Female fairies are a bit like felines in that when the penis is removed, it hurts the female. The pain, or sting as we call it, encourages impregnation. Also, like cats, female fairies can store sperm from many admirers.'

Danny, 'The whole process sickens me.'

Fairy Queen, 'You don't know what you are missing. I've got to the stage where I even enjoy the pain. There is nothing quite like a big todger up your petticoat.' She had a big grin on her face.

Danny, 'Have we finished?'

Fairy Queen, 'No, the human Bible says, "Indeed, I was born guilty, a sinner when my mother conceived me." This suggests spirituality, and therefore, there is a soul from the point of conception. The Christian church takes the view that the body is not really human without the soul.

Danny, 'This is all very interesting, but it doesn't answer my question.'

Fairy Queen, 'I warn you, don't get me annoyed.'

Danny, 'I'm not frightened; I'm an elf. Your magick doesn't work on me.'

Fairy Queen, 'Are you so sure, Eight of thirty-nine?'

Danny pondered on the fact that he had jumped three places. He was always surprised that the other elves never seemed to mind, but they were all the same.

'Thank you, Fairy Queen,' he said.

Fairy Queen, 'It was our deal.'

Danny, 'What has happened to the souls of the three elves?'

Fairy Queen, 'Stupid elf! The children of the Fay don't have souls. Don't you remember the days of the Repugnance when there was a revolt in Heaven? God ordered that the gates of Heaven should be closed shut. Those who remained in Heaven became angels; those in Hell became demons, and those in between became fairies.'

Danny, 'What about the elves?'

Fairy Queen, 'Your stupidity amazes me.'

Danny, 'I just appeared, like my three new brothers who have just arrived at Ynys-witrin. We know what we know, and that is it.'

Fairy Queen, 'Aren't you curious?'

Danny, 'Not until recently. So what are elves?'

Fairy Queen, 'You are a fairy, a child of the Fay.'

Danny, 'Then why am I called an elf?'

Fairy Queen, 'There are many types of fairy, *many* types. There is a view that once we were all angels that failed to make the grade. We were not godly enough to stay in Heaven and not evil enough for Hell. So here we are.'

Danny, 'So why do you pay a tithe to the Devil?'

Fairy Queen, 'The reason is lost in time, but he expects it, and we are too cowardly to say no.'

Danny, 'Do you have to pay a tithe to Heaven?'

Fairy Queen, 'You are cleverer than you look.'

Danny, 'That has been said before. Does that mean that we are agents of his demonic master?'

Fairy Queen, 'Such flowery words. Do you have the urge to do good or bad?

Danny, 'You know the answer.'

Fairy Queen, 'Then you have your answer. Strangely the different types of fairy have different types of evilness.'

Danny, 'What I don't understand is that in the human world, fairies are seen as good.'

Fairy Queen, 'That's simply good marketing; we had to adapt. But really, we are into baby stealing, murder, enslavement, enchantment, etc. The list goes on and on. What we are doing today is hardly good behaviour.'

Danny, 'I never really thought about it before. I just do what I do.'

Fairy Queen, 'How many humans have you killed or should I say caused to be killed?

Danny, with a smile on his face, said, 'Thousands.'

Fairy Queen, 'Back to conception. It doesn't make sense when you look at microbiology.'

Danny, 'Microbiology?'

Fairy Queen, 'At the point of conception, we are talking about two single cells combining. It's hardly a human. Where would the soul reside?'

Danny, 'This is all beyond me.'

Fairy Queen, 'Fair enough. Others believe that when the sperm and ovum unite, there is a flash in the astral world, and a soul that is ready to be reborn may select that body. Apparently, these souls are sitting there, waiting for a type of life that will help develop them. They choose the life they want.'

Danny, 'That sounds nonsense to me.'

Fairy Queen, 'So the next option is that the soul arrives after conception but before birth. Aristotle believed that conception was an extended process: "The conception of the male finishes on the fortieth day and that of the woman on the ninetieth." This view has mostly been rejected.'

Danny, 'I can't talk to the soul until a few weeks after impregnation.'

Fairy Queen, 'You can talk to the souls?'

Danny, 'Yes, in this case, I guided them into the bottles.'

Fairy Queen, 'Are you absolutely sure?'

Danny, 'I can talk to them now.'

Fairy Queen, 'What are they saying?'

Danny, 'They don't like where they are. They have gone from a lovely warm home where they are fed, and they can hear and feel their mother's heart, to somewhere cold and frightening.'

Fairy Queen, 'I've never thought of them as living.'

Danny, 'They trusted me. I told them that I was their father. That should teach them a lesson.'

Fairy Queen, 'So you are saying that the soul arrived after conception?'

Danny, 'I'm not sure. I couldn't talk to them at first.'

Fairy Queen, 'Well, the argument that it happens at birth or after birth is irrelevant then.'

Danny, 'I guess so.'

Fairy Queen, 'Danny, I think you have taught me more than I have taught you.'

Danny, 'Most questions are answers that live in the shadows.'

58

A Present for the Narrator

Danny handed over the present to the Narrator.

Narrator, 'What is this tiny little thing?'

Danny, 'It's fairy dust.'

Narrator, 'You are joking.'

Danny, 'Have you ever heard me tell a single joke?'

Narrator, 'OK, what does fairy dust do?'

Danny, 'It's a bit like having a genie but not as powerful. It helps make things happen. If you said that you wanted wealth, you would find that small things would steadily make you richer, but you probably wouldn't win the lottery.

'If you wanted a new car, it would happen in a way you would expect. However, I need to warn you. Fairy magick is never simple. There are always consequences. My advice is that you should not use it.'

Narrator, 'Are you going to use it?'

Danny, 'Of course, but I'm experienced in its use. If you do decide to use it, then try not to be too greedy.'

Narrator, 'Thank you for the present then. I'm assuming that the device worked.'

Danny, 'It worked brilliantly. Can you get three more made please?'

Narrator, 'When do you need them?'

Danny, 'In the next few weeks.'

Narrator, 'I will get that done.'

Danny, 'I've got to go now.' And he vanished.

The Narrator decided that he would test the fairy dust that very night.

59

A Policeman's Lot is Never a Happy One

Police Inspector, 'So where are we now?'

Officer Newman, 'As you know, we were assigned twenty-four-hour surveillance duties. On the day in question at 19.35, there was a large explosion in the house. Officer Cage and I broke the front door in to find smoke pouring out of the kitchen and three naked women.'

Police Inspector, 'What caused the explosion?'

Officer Newman, 'A loaf of bread, Sir.'

Police Inspector, 'A loaf of bread?'

Officer Newman, 'Yes Sir, the forensic team believe that the bread just spontaneously exploded.'

Police Inspector, 'So, it was toast then?'

Officer Newman laughing said, 'That's quite funny, Sir.'

Police Inspector, 'It may be, but this whole situation is far from funny. Do you really expect me to believe that a loaf of bread just burst into flames?'

Office Newman, 'No Sir, but it has taken the fire brigade two days to put the loaf of bread out.'

Police Inspector, 'I saw the report. It doesn't make sense. What about the ladies?'

Officer Cage, 'There were three naked women on single beds fast asleep.'

Police Inspector, 'I would have thought that the explosion would have woken them up.'

Officer Cage, 'You would have thought so Sir, but it didn't, and they still haven't woken up.'

Police Inspector, 'But that's almost ten days now. Are they in a coma?'

Officer Cage, 'No Sir, we have been told that its normal sleep.'

Police Inspector, 'I've never heard of normal sleep being everlasting.'

Officer Newman, 'Can I mention something that I left off the report?'

Police Inspector, 'You can, but I just want to discuss something further regarding the ladies.'

Office Newman, 'Yes, Sir?'

Police Inspector, 'Who took the photos?' He put a selection of photos on the table, which all depicted the naked women. That was bad but what was worse was the different positions they were posed in, some were downright pornographic.

Officer Newman, 'It wasn't us, Sir.'

Police Inspector, 'There will be an investigation.'

Officer Cage, looking worried, 'Of course, Sir.'

Police Inspector, 'OK, what was this additional piece of information? Before you tell me, I should point out that deliberately leaving out key information from your report is a disciplinary matter.'

Officer Newman, 'I understand that, Sir. What I saw was three milk bottles floating through the air and possibly a shadow holding them. Then they just disappeared.'

Police Inspector, 'Three milk bottles floating?'

Officer Newman, 'Yes, Sir.'

Police Inspector, 'Officer Cage, did you see the bottles?'

Officer Cage, 'Yes, Sir. Do you want us to change our report?'

Police Inspector, 'No, I don't think I do. What's also strange is that the three women had stillbirths at exactly the same time.'

60

Some More Narration

At last, they have agreed to pay me for some narration. So you will get some narration. Actually, it's probably going to be some of my observations.

This is supposed to be entertainment. It started off about a family in Hayward's Heath experiencing some strange events. We got a long diatribe about each character, which I thought was a poor way of introducing characters. It was more like a textbook. Overall, it was pretty amateurish, but look at the author: he never went to university; he has never had any literary training, and he collects comic books. What a tosser.

I complained about the lack of a plot. So guess what happened? Most of the characters were killed off, and a meteorite destroyed a large chunk of Sussex. Right, complaining about the lack of a plot doesn't mean constant, childish action. We needed some subtlety. We wanted a sincere literary accomplishment. Why spend all that time creating paper-thin characters and then killing them off?

Then the book became porn. We had one sexual act after another. I know that sex sells, but no one is going to buy this nonsense. Anyway, there is good porn and nasty porn. This, I'm afraid, is on the wrong side. It has stretched what's acceptable to the limit with chapter titles like 'Emma Drops her Knickers' and 'Did you enjoy the Rape?' This is disgusting filth and is unacceptable in today's climate. This book deserves to be burnt. The author is worse than a tosser.

As you know, I have been complaining about the lack of a plot. I'm now also complaining about categorisation. When you buy a book, you want to know roughly the sort of area it's going to cover. Well, after the celestial body hit Earth, it started to become a detective story, and then it became a pure fantasy. All that rubbish about fairies and souls. Who fucking cares when the soul arrives? It just went on and on.

I'm also a bit fed up with some of these small chapters. What's that all about? I'm just grateful that I got some money out of this ponce of an author.

61

Author's Comment

No one seems to think that authors have feelings. This book has been brewing for several years. It has been a labour of love. It's not an autobiography, but nevertheless, it does contain a lot of me in it. The first part of the book is true, but then it becomes pure fantasy.

I accept the criticism about the plot. There are two types of writer. Those who plot everything well in advance and those who just write and see what happens. Well, it's fairly evident that I'm in the second category. But normally I get there in the end.

But how dare he call me a tosser? I'm paying that mercenary bastard a decent fee. I thought that shit-face was a friend. Well, he is no friend of mine, and he won't get any acknowledgement in this book now.

Anyway, I think his days are numbered. The writer has the ultimate power.

Editor, 'Can we clear up your relationship with the Narrator?'

Author, 'Fuck off!'

62

The Narrator gets his end away

The Narrator wondered what to do with the fairy dust. Should he go for money? Should he go for fame? As a child, he always thought that when you meet a genie, your first wish should be to wish for an unlimited number of wishes. But there was always a catch.

He reviewed his life. He was happy with it. The only area that needed a boost was his sex life. That night when his wife was asleep, he sprinkled the fairy dust on her fanny and made his wish.

His wish came true almost immediately. His wife sat up, grabbed his cock through his pyjamas and starting tossing him off. (Author, who is the tosser now?) The Narrator came fairly quickly, but then she carried on tossing him off. He asked her to stop, but she just carried on and on.

The Narrator tried to remove her hand, but it was steadfast. He had never experienced such a grip before. The skin on his penis was getting stretched and sore. She totally ignored his complaints, and her fingers tightened. He became worried when blood appeared.

(Author, 'Is this enough plot for you?')

Then it happened: the Narrator and his penis separated. His wife had tossed the penis entirely off his body.

(Author, 'I bet you are not laughing now.')

63

Editor's Update

Editor, 'I've got to be honest, we are not happy with the way this book is going.'

Alan, 'What exactly is your problem?'

Editor, 'Well, some of the points made by the Narrator are reasonable.'

Alan, 'What do you fucking mean?'

Editor, 'There is no point in getting upset, I'm here to help.'

Alan, 'Sorry; what are your suggestions?'

Editor, 'I've listed them below:
- Sort out the plot
- Decide what category the book fits into
- Reduce the amount of sex; some is OK, but it's far too black for our liking. We are a family publisher

Cut out Chapter 62; we want the role of the Narrator to carry on.'

Alan, *'Jawohl, Mein Führer.'*

64

The Narrator's Dream

The Narrator was relieved that the events in Chapter 62 were all a dream. He decided that he was going to save the fairy dust for later.

(Author, 'Is that chapter short enough for you?')

65

A Medical Kidnapping

Danny's women were still fast asleep in a secure hospital. They had a twenty-four-hour guard and CCTV. The Police Inspector wanted them in a totally safe environment.

But there wasn't a safe environment from a determined elf on a mission. Danny teleported into the room then teleported himself and his three breeders back to the flat only to find it under police protection. He had to teleport out again.

The guard on duty phoned the Police Inspector to say that the women had disappeared and that he was sending the CCTV film to the police station.

The Police Inspector and Officers Newman and Cage started to review the CCTV Film.

Officer Newman provided commentary that was going to be added to the film:

- The three women in question were fast asleep in single beds in a secure hospital
- The windows and doors were locked
- There were two sets of security doors to go through
- There was a full CCTV operation in place
- The CCTV film has not been doctored in any way. No external body has been involved in its creation
- There were security guards in place, and the CCTV cameras were manned
- The content of this film was manually viewed, and statements will be available at a later date.

Now for the activities:

- Suddenly, a man appeared in the room

120

- The man and the three women in question disappeared
- The man is less than two feet tall with a long beard. Almost gnome-like in appearance.
- There was no flash nor any physical activity relating to the disappearance. They were there and then they weren't.

Police Inspector, 'What do you make of that?'

Officer Newman, 'Just like Star Trek: it was teleportation.'

Police Inspector, 'Hard to argue with that.'

Officer Newman, 'I can only suggest that the film has been manipulated in some way.'

Police Inspector, 'That's not the case as I have further information. The team at the house where the girls were found had visitors. A short, elderly gentleman and three women suddenly appeared in the house and then immediately disappeared. There is some proof of this as one of the women's medical gowns was left behind.'

66

Danny has a Problem

Danny's life was getting complicated. He had three women stuck in limbo who needed to be impregnated, and he had nowhere to go.

He had also realised that he had been filmed. The cameras were visible once you were in the room. He even knew that he had been spotted at the house. The other thirty-eight were not going to be happy. Then he was extinguished.

Narrator, 'Hi, I thought that it was essential to jump in at this stage as we have nearly run out of characters. See my analysis below:

Name	Current Status
Narrator	Still alive
Dolores	Still alive
Doug	Dead—killed by a meteorite
June	Dead—Suicide
Isabella	Dead—Accidentally sucked to death by Danny
Old Irishman	Alive
Ivor	Dead—Drowned in the bath
Danny	Extinguished
John	Dead—Genitalia removed
Polly	Alive
Jim	Dead—Suffocated by a vagina
Carol	Dead—Suicide
Emma	Alive but in limbo-land
Mr Brown	Dead—Fucked to death
Mrs Brown	Alive but in limbo-land
Keith	Suicide—Bled to death
Jill	Alive but in limbo-land
Fairy Queen	Still alive

So, discounting me and my wife, we only have the old Irishman, Polly, and the three women in limbo-land who are effectively dead as only Danny knows where they are. The Fairy Queen is still a potential player.

67

Polly has a bit of Irish

Polly had always thought it funny that when her husband was fucking June, she was fucking June's lodger. She knew about June and actively encouraged it as she had her hands full with Michael. She didn't think that June knew about them. Anyway, it was all a bit academic now as the whole family was dead.

Now she lived with Michael, and it was good. What she didn't know was that Michael was an angel that had been sent to investigate a blip in the human worldview. He had got there early and correctly identified the presence of Danny.

The problem was that he had a penis. Most angels are androgynous but lack the interest or the inclination to have sex. Their libido had either never existed or had been neutered. When an angel was allocated a task on Earth, their sexuality was switched back on. For some, it was too much to bear. For Michael, it was impossible to cope with. He had been consumed by lust.

And Polly was the sort of girl to respond to his needs, which was unfortunate as Heaven had been trying to contact Michael for the last few weeks.

As there had been no contact, a second representative was being allocated.

68

The Clean-up

Laylah was assigned:

Phase One

Officer Newman, 'Sir, I have some startling news.'

Police Inspector, 'What's that?'

Officer Newman, 'The film has gone blank.'

Police Inspector, 'What about the copies?'

Officer Newman, 'All blank, Sir.'

Police Inspector, 'Do we still have the witness statements?'

Officer Newman, 'What statements?'

Police Inspector, 'What are you talking about?'

Officer Newman, 'Sorry, Sir, things have gone a bit blank.'

Police Inspector, 'Like something else which I have forgotten.'

Phase Two

Three beds in the secure hospital were suddenly re-occupied. Emma, Jill, and Mrs Brown had been returned from limbo-land and were awake. Their memories had been wiped, and they had even forgotten that they had been pregnant.

Phase Three

Michael had been found, and Polly's memory of him had been wiped. Michael was sent back to Heaven in disgrace.

Phase Four

The Fairy Queen had been warned about her activities, but she couldn't care a toss. Heaven had no jurisdiction over her.

Phase Five

Laylah out-trumped the editor and Chapter 62 was reinstated. The Narrator has been castrated. Please now ignore Chapter 64.

There wasn't a load more that Laylah could do. But as her libido had

125

been turned on, she was determined to get some action. She quite fancied the look of the Police Inspector. He would know how to handle a naughty girl.

69

Laylah cocked up

It wasn't surprising that Laylah didn't really understand twenty-first century technology. She was actually a BC type girl.

Phase One

Officer Newman, 'Sir, I have some more startling news.'

Police Inspector, 'What's that?'

Officer Newman, 'The blank film that was sent to Forensics as one of the lads thought that they might have been some tampering have discovered something really odd.'

Police Inspector, 'What's that?'

Officer Newman, 'It contains images of the three women being abducted from our secure hospital by a hobbit. It has a commentary by myself with some input from you.'

Police Inspector, 'I don't remember that, do you?'

Officer Newman, 'No Sir, but the film is being sent over now.'

Police Inspector, 'Let me know when it arrives.'

Officer Newman, 'I will have it in a few seconds.'

Police Inspector, 'OK. let's review the content now.'

The two officers of the law couldn't believe what they saw. It was clear proof that someone or something was manipulating them.

Police Inspector, 'How come the images were still there if an entity had cleared it?'

Officer Newman, 'It is notoriously difficult to delete data from any digital system. The data is marked as deleted, but it stays there until it is overwritten.'

Police Inspector, 'I see. Let's take lots of copies and distribute them. I will try and get permission to make the image public. That should stop any future interference.'

Phase Two

Emma, Jill, and Mrs Brown were shown the film. They couldn't believe what they saw, but it triggered off some strange memories. Jill wondered what had caused some minor but noticeable stretch marks on her body.

A review of paper records showed that there had been three stillbirths. This caused Emma to cry. She wasn't sure why, but she had been feeling depressed. An internal examination confirmed what they had been through.

A second film showed the three of them being returned by an angel. They knew that it was an angel because of the large white wings.

The officers asked Forensics to confirm the authenticity of the film.

The Police Inspector had been confronted by one unusual event after another. He was grateful that he was enjoying a romantic interlude. He had always been a confirmed bachelor, but now he was getting the shagging of his life. He thought that he might be in love with this strange, enigmatic woman.

Phase Three

Michael didn't know that an angel could fall in love. Polly was now the reason for his existence. Did he want to spend eternity in Heaven without her or a brief period on Earth in her arms? There was no doubt in his mind.

He returned to Earth, which almost certainly meant the loss of his wings, and he would become mortal. When Polly saw him, her memory immediately returned. Polly put the kettle on, and they both had tea. There was no sign of Sukey.

Phase Four

The Fairy Queen formally complained to the Fairy Ombudsman about Laylah's behaviour. It, in turn, complained to the standing celestial body for cooperation between Heaven and Hell; Laylah's record was formally admonished, and the Fairy Queen's tithe was officially reduced. That sort of interference was not going to be tolerated.

Phase Five

The Chairman of the Celestial Committee for Cooperation between Heaven and Hell trumped Laylah, and consequently, Chapter 62 is to be ignored, and Chapter 64 has been reinstated. The editor started to wonder who was in charge. Then he remembered that it was his wife.

70

Danny makes his return

Of course, it wasn't Danny, but he was one of the thirty-nine. The elves had a contract with the Fairy Queen, which had to be fulfilled. They were now behind schedule.

Danny (the editor wanted to call him Danny 2, but as they were all the same, why did it matter?) was planning to kidnap the three women again. As far as he was concerned, they belonged to him.

He had established a tepee in the New Forest as his base camp. Only an elf would see that as an ideal hideaway. His first challenge was how to get them impregnated again.

He decided to use the fairy dust to turn the girls into sirens. The three girls were sitting on their beds, happily chatting away when suddenly they started moaning in a very suggestive way. They stripped off, exposing some of the most beautiful bodies the world had ever seen.

Officer Newman, 'Sir, something is happening at the hospital.'

The Inspector had been daydreaming about the new angel in his life. Suddenly, defending the realm against organised criminals had lost its lustre.

Police Inspector, 'They seem to be naked.'

Officer Newman, 'Yes Sir, I've seen them naked before, but somehow they seem different. Mrs Brown's sagging breasts have uplifted themselves.'

Police Inspector, 'And her bald patch has gone.'

Officer Newman, 'And Emma's breasts have grown larger and are more curvaceous.'

Police Inspector, 'You seem to be somewhat obsessed with breasts.'

Officer Newman, 'But have you ever seen three better sets of tits before?'

The Police Inspector was thinking about the pair he had at home, but he had to agree that the three sets on show were perfect.

Officer Newman, 'And what about Jill's fanny? That was worth a few pints any time.'

Police Inspector, 'I don't believe that we should be making those sorts of comments.'

Then he realised that he had the biggest hard-on that he had ever experienced.

Officer Newman, 'Sir, I have to report that my penis has involuntarily extended itself and could I be relieved?'

Police Inspector, 'Relieved?'

Officer Newman, 'Temporarily relieved from duty, Sir.'

Police Inspector, 'I suppose so.'

Officer Newman, 'Thank you, Sir.'

Then the Police Inspector noticed the crowds of men trying to get into the hospital ward holding the girls. They looked as if they meant business. Business of the carnal sort.

Police Inspector, 'Officer Cage, we need to get more security organised to protect the girls.'

Officer Cage, 'Yes, Sir, but a lot of those men who were trying to break in were either policemen or medical staff.'

Police Inspector, 'I can't believe the complete lack of standards nowadays. Why would all of those men belittle themselves?'

Officer Cage, 'Can't you feel the urge, Sir?'

The Police Inspector had noticed that Officer Cage had uncaged his manhood and was teaching it to dance.

Editor's Note

A LARGE SECTION OF DESCRIPTIVE TEXT HAS BEEN REMOVED. THAT DESCRIBED IN DETAIL THE SORDID HAPPENINGS WHEN THIRTY SEX-MAD MEN ENCOUNTERED THREE SEX-MAD BEAUTIFUL, WILLING WOMEN AS IT WAS UNNECESSARY. THE READER COULD IMAGINE WHAT WAS GOING ON WITHOUT DESCRIBING JUST HOW MANY PENISES ENTERED HOW MANY VAGINAS.

It is surprising, but the act of conception can take place as quickly as twenty minutes after the act of copulation. Danny extracted the girls one by one as they got impregnated. He felt a bit sorry for Mrs Brown as she had to experience a considerable number of copulations before impregnation was achieved.

Editor's Note:

Neither the author of this book nor the publisher condones this type of behaviour. They would like to confirm that they have full respect for a woman's body.

Editorial Committee:

This is just another example of how women are being debased for no apparent reason. Is this pathetic cheap collection of words really going to help sell this book? I don't think so! We need to improve our standards, and we can start by removing this crap from the bookshelf.

From Danny's perspective, he had his three impregnated women safely in his tent. Now he needed the extraction device from the Narrator. So far, he couldn't make contact with any of the multicellular foetal souls.

Private Enterprise

Copies of what has been called 'The Bugs Hole Orgy' are now available for sale.

71

Non-Critical Narration

The editor had warned the Narrator that if he still wanted his fee, then he should focus on narration rather than continually criticising the author. The editor agreed that the author might be a tosser, but that was not the issue. If you are paid to be the Narrator, then narrate.

The Narrator couldn't really argue and decided to narrate.

So dear reader, where are we? I'd better update you in case you have lost the plot. The following is a well-written list that will clarify things for you:

- Danny is dead, so a new Danny appeared
- All Dannys are the same, so it doesn't really matter
- Plot problem: If all the Dannys are the same, why was the original Danny trying to go up the order? Why did he want to be the top Danny?
- The new Danny has taken on the job of delivering souls to the Fairy Queen
- He has recaptured the three girls. Actually, it's a mother and two daughters
- He got them pregnant by converting them into sirens and organising a mass orgy at a secure hospital
- The editor had to intervene as the scene was getting far too graphic. This was another example of unnecessary porn. We didn't need to know that the police had raging hard-ons
- The ravished, impregnated 'girls' were teleported to a tepee in the New Forest
- The sexual activities and the teleportations were all captured on film

As most of the characters had been killed off, some of the earlier

132

characters were reintroduced. There was Polly, who was the wife of John, the vicar who had been having it off with June. Both John and June are now dead.

Polly was having an illicit affair with June's lodger's todger. We originally referred to him as the old Irishman. It appears that his name was Michael, and somewhat miraculously, it turns out that he was really an angel sent to sort out some anomalies. The primary anomaly being Danny.

Michael and his penis were enjoying Polly's company, and specifically her vagina. That's probably a bit unfair as they were in love.

Another angel called Laylah was despatched to sort out the mess but made things worse. She is now having it off with the Police Inspector.

- So where are we going?
- What is Danny going to do with the three girls?
- What is going to happen to Michael and Laylah?
- Will the Fairy Queen get her souls?
- What are the police going to do?
- When will this author have a proper plot?

72

A pee in a tepee

It wasn't easy looking after three pregnant women in a tepee in the New Forest. This new Danny wasn't that experienced in the management of women under canvas.

Although they were under his control, they still demanded the basic essentials: water, food, lipstick, and shoes. He wasn't quite sure what lipstick was. What was strange was that they all wanted a pee at the same time. They didn't want to pee in the tepee, or near the tepee, unless it was late at night, then peeing by the tepee was OK.

He wondered how long he would have to wait until the souls appeared. Did they arrive at the time of conception, after conception but before birth, during birth, or after childbirth?

(Narrator, This has all been covered in Chapter 57. It was agreed that extraction could take place once you could communicate with the souls. Anyway, I thought that all Dannys were the same?)

Danny decided to wait until he could communicate with the souls. He needed the Narrator to make some more devices for him but wondered how co-operative he was going to be.

(Narrator, I would be willing to help in exchange for some more fairy dust. After my last wish, I lost my todger. Next time I will wish for its return.)

Danny was pleased to hear that after a telepathic conversation with the Narrator, he was willing to deliver three more devices in exchange for some more fairy dust. He was also going to provide food, water, shoes, and lipstick.

Danny realised then that he was a very clever elf.

73

The Police Commissioner

Police Commissioner, 'Inspector I have watched the films in detail, even the graphic sexual activities that took place in the hospital ward. I didn't know that a woman could handle more than one organ at a time.'

Police Inspector, 'Yes Ma'am, that was a bit of a shock.'

Police Commissioner, 'You understand the implications of these films?'

Police Inspector, 'No Ma'am. I would appreciate your guidance.'

Police Commissioner, 'There will be a considerable increase in people buying new spectacles. You need excellent eyesight to see the intimate details.'

Police Inspector, 'Yes, Ma'am, I'm sure that is the case. What about the supernatural acts?'

Police Commissioner, 'I've been told that all of those are natural nowadays. When I was courting, you never expected or allowed anything up the old shitter. It was just not done.'

Police Inspector, 'I understand, Ma'am. I was actually referring to the hobbit and the disappearance of the three women.'

Police Commissioner, 'I ignored all of that crap; it was clearly nonsense. Now back to the ward scene. It looked like one of the girls was sucking on a penis. Why would she do that?'

Police Inspector, 'I believe that it is a sign of affection, Ma'am.' He had received a lot of affection recently.

Police Commissioner, 'I see. Do you think my husband would like that?'

Police Inspector, 'It's awfully hard to say, Ma'am. We need to discuss the hobbit and the other unusual events. At the press conference, they will want to question you about it.'

Police Commissioner, 'Surely that wasn't real?'

Police Inspector, 'I'm afraid that it was, Ma'am. It's definitely been confirmed as real.'

Police Commissioner, 'Even that funny little man with the large leather belt and floppy green hat?'

Police Inspector, 'Yes, Ma'am.'

Police Commissioner, 'But there are implications!'

Police Inspector, 'Exactly, Ma'am.'

Police Commissioner, 'Well, what are they?'

Police Inspector, 'I thought that it was *your* job to assess the situation and inform the public.'

Police Commissioner, 'If you want to keep your job, you had better prepare a statement for me.'

Police Inspector, 'I have, Ma'am.'

Police Commissioner, 'OK, take me through it.'

Police Inspector, 'Yes, Ma'am'

Statement

During the months of May, June, July and August 2020, there have been several unexplained events and deaths, including the following:

- The death of Reverend John Smith in a locked room. His genitalia had been removed.
- The extermination of numerous pets in Burgess Hill which included twenty-six cats, eleven dogs, eight budgies, two tortoises, four rats, two gerbils, a clutch of chickens, one salamander and a horse
- The death of five pet owners linked to the above
- The death of Isabella Mason in a locked room in Burgess Hill
- The death of Jim Cogan, a Burgess Hill resident
- The suicide of Jim Cogan's wife, Carol, and the murder of their two children
- The death of Doug Mason and his son Ivor
- The suicide of June Mason
- A series of sexual offences in Burgess Hill Cinema and College
- The death of sixteen individuals at Burgess Hill College due

to arson
- The disappearance of Mr Brown
- The disappearance of Mrs Brown and her two daughters and several strange subsequent movements
- The suicide of Mrs Brown's son

Many of the deaths seem to focus around the Mason family. All four members of the family are now dead, but the mystery continues.

As part of the investigation, it would appear that some supernatural events had taken place:

- It took two days to put out a loaf of bread that was on fire
- Three milk bottles were seen floating through the air
- In a secure room, a short, bearded man teleported in, took three female patients, and teleported all of them out
- They then teleported into another location, were seen, and immediately teleported out
- The above teleporting was filmed, but then the films were blanked out, and all memories of the event amongst the staff were removed
- The original films were then restored clearly showing the small man and the teleportations
- Paper records showed that the three patients had all experienced stillbirths, but had no memory of it
- The three female patients reappeared, accompanied by an angel
- Then there was an unprompted and inexplicable orgy
- Then the little man appeared again and teleported himself and the three patients out again
- There were several other sightings of the short, bearded man.

End of Statement.

Police Commissioner, 'This is going to cause a stir.'

Police Inspector, 'Yes, Ma'am; please feel free to change it. You have two hours until the press conference.'

74

A Fairy Ring

The Council met in the fairy ring near British Camp on the Malvern Hills. It was hard to be specific about the exact location, but the attendees knew where they were going. Some had never been there before, but they knew its location. Every little person knew the location.

From British Camp, you walk southward via Millennium and Hangman's Hills, before descending via the Silurian Pass towards Castlemorton Common. The walk then climbs steeply to Swinyard Hill and then back northward via Giant's Cave. Somewhere in this ring, you will find the circle.

In the circle sat the Grand Fay Council with representatives from all of the clans, dreamworlds, and marders. It included the following:

- The Asrai
- The Pixi
- The Elfi
- The Mersi
- The Bansheei
- The Leprechauni
- The Browni
- The Gremli
- The Impi
- The Famili
- The Impi

Many other spirits and ghosts tended to lurk around the area. The dreamers cast their spells, and the uninvited would be misentangled, some would never be seen again except in a dream.

A spell of covenant was cast. What was secret would remain secret.

Her most magnificent Fayden of the Garand Fay Council stood to address the assembled and said, 'Fellow councillors I call this Melde in order to address the wrongs of exposure. I call the elf One of Thirty-Eight to address the Council.

Danny number one stood up, ready to defend The Elfi.

Danny, 'I submit that our actions did not lead to exposure as outlined by The Council. We have no case to defend.'

Fayden, 'One of Thirty-Eight, the evidence against you is overwhelming:

- You used fairy-fire on a loaf of bread. It took the ploughmen two days to put the fire out
- Your teleportation skills resulted in three milk bottles floating through the air. This was seen by several ploughmen
- Your teleportation of three ploughwomen was filmed on more than one occasion
- The kidnapping of the three ploughwomen, their forced impregnation and subsequent stillbirths goes against our faylaws
- There were many sightings of your kind.

Danny, 'Some of this was caused by angelic interventions.'

Fayden, 'Yes, we know that. There appears to have been two angels involved. One was sent to repair the damage your kind has done.'

Danny, 'What could we do when agents of Heaven were interfering?'

Fayden, 'Your kind went too far. The issue now is, what do we do about it?'

75

The Ring Of Truth

Police Commissioner, 'Order, Order, Order!'
There was a crowd of three hundred sitting in the hall and a few hundred outside watching monitors. She found it all a bit intimidating. She wished that she had spent more time on her hair as everything is exposed on TV.

Police Commissioner, 'Ladies and gentlemen, fellow colleagues, thank you for attending this press conference. I can tell you now that the content will surprise you, and that it will challenge the way we view the world.'

There was an immediate reaction from the audience. There was a sense of anticipation and excitement.

Police Commissioner, 'Order, Order, Order. Ladies and gentlemen, I plan to read a statement that will generate hundreds of questions. Before I answer them, I plan to show some films to validate the statement. I will then take questions.'

The statement was made.

There was an immediate uproar. It was a mixture of laughter, anger, aggression, joviality, disbelief, incredulity, doubt and scepticism. No one believed that a Police Commissioner could come up with this sort of rubbish. Then the films were shown.

There was still doubt, but a lot less. The films were shown a second time.

Police Commissioner, 'Order, Order, Order. Ladies and gentlemen, please be calm. I'm ready to take questions.'

Reporter 1, 'Do you expect us to believe this?'

Police Commissioner, 'You have heard my statement, and you have seen the films. I also have here signed affidavits from all of those involved.'

Reporter 1, 'Regardless, it is just not possible.'

Police Commissioner, 'Are you accusing my officers of lying?'

Reporter 2, 'You must admit that it doesn't seem possible?'

Police Commissioner, 'I do admit that, but these are the facts. That is the truth.'

Reporter 3, 'Could someone have faked all of this?'

Police Commissioner, 'It's always possible, but these events occurred over a four-month period. Faking is not really a viable alternative to the truth.'

Reporter 4, 'You are expecting us to believe that the supernatural exists?'

Reporter 5, 'And goblins?'

Police Commissioner, 'I never called them goblins. I don't know what the creature is.'

Reporter 6, 'What's happened to the three women?'

Police Commissioner, 'I'm glad you asked that. They are the victims here. We have picked up some dust from the ward, and it suggests that the 'creature' came from the New Forest in Hampshire. We already have search parties looking for them.'

The questions continued, but few were happy with the answers. Humans are strange; they will often accept the most insane conspiracy theory and reject clear unadulterated facts.

The press had a field day with some great headings:

- *What has the Police Commissioner been gobbling?*
- *Police Pixie dust provokes Police Commissioner*
- *A fairy nice time was had by all*
- *A policeman's lot is not fairy nice*
- *It was a fairy cop*

76

Polly's Kettle turned Black

Polly was having a nice cup of coffee in a little café on the high street. It was a lovely summer day with blue skies, puffy white clouds, and just a hint of a breeze. It was the sort of day that appeared on TV advertising ice cream and foreign holidays.

She sat there enjoying the hustle and bustle of people shopping, of people on their way to lunch and of people just chilling out. She had always been a people watcher. She had this dream of retiring in a little flat over a shop where she could watch the world go by.

As she sipped her coffee, she was offended that someone had sat down at her table. There were other empty tables. Why would they sit here? It was a damned cheek. It wasn't the British way of doing things. She contemplated moving to another table when the intruder said, 'Hello Polly.'

Polly scrutinised the enemy. She was an attractive blonde. A very attractive blonde with piercing blue eyes and a strangely enigmatic but understanding smile. She had a figure to die for. Her beauty was almost intimidating, but somehow, she reminded her of Michael. Her Michael.

Then it dawned on her. This must be Michael's wife. She had been waiting for the lightning bolt. Whenever things were going well in her life, there was always a lightning bolt.

Polly, 'Do I know you?'

Laylah, 'Perhaps you do.'

Polly, 'I'm not sure what you mean.'

Laylah, 'I know.'

Polly, 'Why are you disturbing me?'

Laylah, 'It's what I do.'

Polly, 'I'm sure that there are other people that want to be disturbed.'

Laylah, 'But they are not sleeping with Michael.'

Polly, 'Are you his wife?'

Laylah laughed and said, 'No.'

Polly, 'Who are you then?'

Laylah, 'What do you know about Michael?'

Polly, 'I know that I love him.'

Laylah, 'We all love him.'

Polly, 'How do you know him?'

Laylah, 'I've never met him.'

Polly, 'Then why do you love him?'

Laylah, 'Because he is love.'

Polly, 'I don't understand.'

Laylah, 'I know, but you don't know who you are playing with.'

Polly, 'Playing?'

Laylah, 'Michael is more than you realise. Check his back, and I will return.'

Laylah got up and quickly disappeared into the crowd.

Polly wondered what was going on.

77

Tepee Tales

Danny wondered how long he would have to wait. Just how long does it take for souls to enter the young ones?

He wasn't equipped to look after three pregnant women. He was in control, but he had to enter the human world to get shoes and lipstick on a regular basis. He had to teleport into department stores overnight and secure the required goods.

It was a small tepee, and there really wasn't enough room for over a thousand pairs of shoes, a lipstick mountain, and three beds containing pregnant women.

Then he heard noises and saw lights. There was a troop of men marching towards the tent in a long line. He hadn't expected this and immediately teleported back to the hospital. It was the only place he could think of. Perhaps he wasn't a clever elf after all.

78

The Fairy Challenge

Fayden realised that they could spend a lifetime blaming The Elfi, but the real challenge was deciding what to do about it.

Fayden, 'Fellow Fay, what options do we have?'

Eternal Star-Dreamer of the Pixi, 'Have we fully defined the problem?'

Fayden, 'In simple terms, the existence of the Fay has been exposed. There have even been pictures of the elf on the ploughman's TV.'

Eternal Star-Dreamer of the Pixi, 'So what is the challenge?'

Fayden, 'We need to convince the ploughmen that the Fay do not exist. The recorded events were faked. It was just one big con.'

Princess Antion of the Impi, 'We need to destroy all of the evidence, the films, the police statements, the pregnant women, the memories. Everything.'

Fayden, 'What about the players?'

Princess Antion of the Impi, 'Yes, you are right. Kill the police involved, all witnesses and every ploughman involved in this fiasco.'

Slumberknee of the Browni, 'We must hide our existence. Otherwise, we will go the way of the dodo.'

Fayden, 'What about the angels?'

Daykill of the Gremli, 'Shit on the angels.'

Fayden, 'I'm not sure if that will help our cause.'

Daykill of the Gremli, 'Fuck them, that's what I say.'

Hinderbottom of the Bansheei, 'The angels could reverse time.'

Fayden, 'They would only do that in extreme circumstances.'

Eternal Star-Dreamer of the Pixi, 'Surely this *is* quite extreme.'

Fayden, 'Is it extreme enough for them?'

Eternal Star-Dreamer of the Pixi, 'We could ask them.'

Fayden hated talking to the angels. They were far too condescending. She would rather shit on them. Perhaps Daykill had the right attitude after all.

Pinkypale of the Mersi, 'We could do what we normally do?'

Fayden, 'And what's that?'

Pinkypale of the Mersi, 'Nothing, we do nothing. Just let it fade away.'

Fayden, 'That is often the best policy. Inaction is a sound military tactic.'

The debate continued late into the night. There was anger, there were stabbings; rough sex; blame; recriminations; spitting, and everything you would expect from a Melde, but in the end, an action plan was developed:

- Discuss the option of a time-reversal with the angels (It was thought that this option was unlikely)
- Determine what the angels are doing on Earth
- Locate the films of the elf and destroy all copies
- Terminate the three pregnant women
- Terminate any police officials involved in the fiasco
- Terminate all other witnesses
- Destroy all witness statements
- Eliminate any of the Fay who have failed to act within the rules
- Contemplate terminating the angels involved

It was decided that the original Danny should be allocated the task. It appeared that there had only ever been 39 elves. When an elf is extinguished, he comes back as elf number 39 and gradually works his way up. They are telepathic but not identical. Some are bright, but most are stupid, but the bright ones are more dangerous.

The original Danny was activated. He knew what he had to do.

79

The Police Commissioner is in Trouble

Police Commissioner, 'I'm in trouble, and if I'm in trouble, then you are in trouble.'

Police Inspector, 'I understand, Ma'am.'

Police Commissioner, 'The Home Secretary has requested a meeting with me.'

Police Inspector, 'That's not good.'

Police Commissioner, 'I'm not sure what to do as we only spoke the truth.'

Police Inspector, 'Well, there is acceptable truth and the sort that is not so palatable.'

Police Commissioner, 'You are right. I have a pile of the unpalatable stuff.'

Police Inspector, 'Ma'am, I've just had a text to say that the three women have reappeared back in the hospital ward. Two officers have grabbed each woman in an attempt to stop any further teleportations, and they have done the same with the little old man.'

Police Commissioner, 'That's good news; we can stick the hobbit up the Home Secretary's arse.'

But that wasn't part of the Fay plan. When the two police officials entered the lift on the thirteenth floor, they had no idea that their legs would be shooting up their arses. They ended up as a pool of mangled body parts. A human soup that was still warm and steaming.

The lift company, to this day, could not find any explanation why the lift failed. Apparently, it was an act of God!

80

The Police's Troubles Continue

MI5 Officer, 'So tell me exactly what happened here.'

Sergeant Baker, 'I had just finished my supper when three women suddenly reappeared in the hospital ward with the hobbit. I immediately texted the Police Inspector and ordered two officers to grab all four of them to stop any teleportations.'

MI5 Officer, 'How did you know that holding them would stop the teleportations?'

Sergeant Baker, 'I didn't, but it was worth a try.'

MI5 Officer, 'What happened next?'

Sergeant Baker, 'I'm not sure if you will believe me. I don't have any supporting evidence.'

MI5 Officer, 'Please continue.'

Sergeant Baker, 'A giant hand came out of the ground and crushed all six people. It left only dust behind.'

MI5 Officer, 'That is hard to believe.'

But he changed his mind when a giant hand came out of the ground and crushed them to dust.

81

Angel Trouble

Angelic Control, Sector 16, 'Angel Laylah, please come in.'

Angel Laylah, 'Yes Angelic Control, I'm reporting in.'

Angelic Control, Sector 16, 'We need to update you on recent events.'

Angel Laylah, 'Please go ahead.'

Angelic Control, Sector 16, 'There has been a meeting of the Melde, and as a result, they have formally asked for a time-reversal. This has been refused, and the Fay has initiated a campaign to remove all evidence of their existence. This may cause you some problems'

Angel Laylah, 'Thank you for the update.'

Anyway, she was off to see Polly at the café. She wondered how Polly was going to react when she told her that Michael was an angel. She just left the flat when a tiny arrowhead missed her by a few millimetres. She went to pick it up from the floor, but it stung her. She used a bit of paper to slide it into her bag and carried on to the café.

Polly was already there sipping a cup of coffee. Laylah sat down and ordered a coffee which she had no intention of drinking. Angels were composed of energy; they had no need for physical sustenance.

Laylah, 'How are you?'

Polly, 'Fine.'

Laylah, 'Did you manage to look at Michaels's back?'

Polly, 'I did.'

Laylah, 'And what did you see?'

Polly, 'What's it got to do with you?'

Laylah, 'I know what you saw.'

Polly, 'How do you know so much about Michael?'

Laylah, 'Because I have the same on my back.'

Polly, 'So what?'

Laylah, 'Don't you think that's strange?'

Polly, 'Lots of people have tattoos.'

Laylah, 'But these are magick tattoos.'

Polly, 'Tell me. I can tell that you are dying to tell me something.'

Laylah smiled and said, 'Michael is an angel.'

Just then Laylah felt a huge disturbance. Someone she knew had just been killed. Without any thought, she leapt into the air in full view of the café crowd. It's not often you see an angel with their white wings fully extended.

Polly's coffee had got cold. Anyway, she decided to go home as she had a question to ask Michael.

82

An Update from Danny

Fayden, 'What progress has been made?'

Our Danny, 'Your majesty, the following has been achieved:

The Police Commissioner and the Police Inspector involved in the fiasco have been terminated in an elevator accident

The Hand of Hannibalaster has eliminated Danny, the three pregnant women and eight police officers

The Hand also eliminated an MI5 agent

An attack on one of the angels failed.'

Fayden, 'What do you plan to do next?'

Our Danny, 'I plan to destroy the Haywards Heath and Burgess Hill Police Stations and eliminate some further witnesses. I'm not sure how I'm going to destroy the film copies, but I will find a way.'

Fayden, 'And the angels?'

Our Danny, 'They will be eliminated.'

Fayden, 'You know that it cannot be traced back to us.'

Our Danny, 'Of course. Is there anything else that you want me to do?'

Fayden, 'I will have a few jobs for you later. You could be quite useful to me.'

83

Officer Newman Hits the Dust

Officer Newman was walking home after finishing a night shift. He enjoyed the walk home in the wee hours in the morning. It was peaceful. It gave him a chance to reflect on things, and he thought about the breakfast he was going to eat before his head hit the pillow.

His head was never going to hit the pillow as a giant magpie flew down and bit it off.

Danny was getting down to his last bit of fairy dust.

84

The Police Task Force

The Home Office established a task force to investigate the strange events in Mid-Sussex.

Agent Middleton, 'Give me your overview.'

Officer Cage, 'Yes, Sir. I have been involved since the early days. I produced the following list of issues some time ago.'

He displayed the following on the screen:

- The death of Reverend John in a locked room with his penis made into a necklace and put around Isabella's head
- The annihilation of the local pet community (twenty-six cats, eleven dogs, eight budgies, two tortoises, four rats, two gerbils, a clutch of chickens, one salamander and a horse)
- The accidental death of four or five pet owners
- The death of Isabella in a locked room
- The rape of June
- The death of Jim, the neighbour
- The suicide of Jim's wife, Carol, and the death of their two children
- The destruction of Wivelsfield by a meteorite and the death of Doug
- Ivor's apparently accidental death
- June's suicide
- Sexual escapades in the Burgess Hill Cinema
- Sexual escapades at the college
- Arson at the college resulting in 16 deaths
- The disappearance of Mr Brown
- Sexual escapades at the local church
- The suicide of Keith

This, however, was the official statement:

Statement

During the months of May, June, July and August 2020, there have been several unexplained events and deaths, including the following:

- The death of Reverend John Smith in a locked room. His genitalia had been removed.
- The extermination of numerous pets in Burgess Hill which included twenty-six cats, eleven dogs, eight budgies, two tortoises, four rats, two gerbils, a clutch of chickens, one salamander and a horse
- The death of five pet owners linked to the above
- The death of Isabella Mason in a locked room in Burgess Hill
- The death of Jim Cogan, a Burgess Hill resident
- The suicide of Jim Cogan's wife, Carol, and the murder of their two children
- The death of Doug Mason and his son Ivor
- The suicide of June Mason
- A series of sexual offences in the Burgess Hill Cinema and College
- The death of sixteen individuals at Burgess Hill College due to arson
- The disappearance of Mr Brown
- The disappearance of Mrs Brown and her two daughters and several strange subsequent movements
- The suicide of Mrs Brown's son
- Many of the deaths seem to focus around the Mason family. All four members of the family are now dead, but the mystery continues.

As part of the investigation, it would appear that some supernatural events had taken place:

- It took two days to put out a loaf of bread that was on fire
- Three milk bottles were seen floating through the air
- In a very secure room, a short, bearded man teleported in, took three female patients, and teleported all of them out
- They then teleported into another location, were seen, and

154

immediately teleported out

- The above teleporting was filmed, but then the films were blanked out, and all memories of the event amongst the staff were removed
- The original films were restored, and they clearly showed the small man and the teleportations
- Paper records showed that the three patients had all experienced stillbirths but had no memory of it
- The three female patients reappeared, accompanied by an angel
- Then there was an unprompted and inexplicable orgy
- Then the little man appeared again and teleported himself and the three patients out again
- There were several other sightings of the short, bearded man.

Since then, the following has happened:

- The Police Commissioner and the Police Inspector were killed in an inexplicable elevator accident
- The three women and the hobbit returned to the hospital
- The above plus eight officers were turned to dust
- Then an MI5 officer and Sergeant Baker were turned to dust
- An angel was spotted leaving a café on Haywards Heath High Street
- A witness spotted Officer Newman's head being bitten off by a giant magpie.'

Agent Middleton, 'Clearly most of this is fabricated rubbish. My job is to end all of this hysteria.'

Officer Cage, 'Yes, Sir.'

85

Michael Meets his Match

Immediately after sex is often a dangerous time for men. Powerful chemicals released after orgasm cause the male to drowse. The post-orgasmic sleep can be the best ever. It's vital for the male to reach deep sleep before the woman can say your name.

If they say it and you haven't entered the land of nod, then you are in for a long chat. It's worse if your lover says things like, 'I wondered' or, 'Have you thought about' or, 'If only.'

Michael could sense that a question had been lingering all day. The time for its birth was almost upon him, and he wasn't quite asleep.

Polly, 'Michael, love.'

Michael knew that it was almost there, and he knew what the question was going to be. Well, he *was* an angel.

Michael, 'Yes, my dearest.'

He was intrigued to see how she was going to approach it.

Polly, 'I was wondering the other day what it would be like in Heaven.'

Michael now knew that she was going for the long curvaceous route followed by a short sharp question.

Michael, 'Yes, I've often wondered myself, but it can't be any better than lying here with you.' He gently caressed her nipple.

Polly, 'You are so sweet, but really, what do you think it's like?'

Michael's side-track did not work. 'Probably calm and peaceful.'

Polly, 'Well you should know, you *are* a fucking angel. Aren't you?'

Michael released his wings from the tattoo (it was the very latest wing technology) and stood in front of her. Naked and Angelic. Polly was naked and angry.

Polly, 'What have you got to say for yourself? You come down here and seduce us humans, for your pleasure. I hope you don't expect me to give birth to the next messiah. Fucking angels, they get on your tits.'

That was true; he had been on her tits.

86

Paid for Narration Moment

For a brief period of time, I thought that a plot was developing. We had some interesting characters. This author kills them off before they are fully developed. I'm not sure if he would understand what a fully developed character would look like if you stuck one up his arse. It's probably full of shit anyway.

During my last narration, page 121, I asked the following:

- What Is Danny going to do with the three girls?
  They are all dead.
- What is going to happen with Michael and Laylah?
  We are still not sure
- Will the Fairy Queen get her souls?
  There is little chance of that as the girls are dead.
- What are the police going to do?
  Most of them are dead.
- When will this author have a proper plot?
  Let's not be too hopeful.

To be fair, I do like the sections on the fairies. It does provide some insight. Those sugary, sweeter-than-life goody-goodies turn out to be nasty little buggers. I've quite enjoyed that.

I've also quite enjoyed the police investigations. They are not particularly accurate, but they are reasonably amusing. And I want to see what happens with the angels.

Now for the shitty parts. How can anyone find having a pee in a teepee even vaguely amusing? That's just childish gutter humour that even five-year-olds would find immature. And then 'Polly puts the kettle on'! I ask you, is this book aimed at adults or imbeciles?

87

The Home Office does its Best

Agent Middleton, 'I've told you that my job is to tidy everything up. Do you understand?'

Officer Cage, 'Yes, Sir.'

Agent Middleton, 'As part of the tidy up process I want you to do the following:

- Destroy all copies of the films in police possession
- Remove all copies you can find on-file
- Destroy all paper statements
- Destroy all police records relating to these events
- Destroy the HR records for the Police Commissioner, the Police Inspector and all of the policemen who died, including Officer Newman
- Destroy any other physical evidence we are holding
- Remove all related diary information
- Destroy all records relating to the victims
- Destroy any medical evidence we have, including DNA samples and fingerprints
- Destroy all related missing-person records

Do you understand?

Officer Cage, 'Yes, Sir, but surely we are tampering with the evidence?'

Agent Middleton, 'Do as I say.'

Officer Cage was hesitant, but he was approaching pensionable age. That was more important to him than ethics. And the job was done.

Danny was struggling to maintain the persona of Agent Middleton. The things he had to do.

88

Polly Wings it

It was a shock, and strictly Michael had been deceitful, but angels never lie. Polly liked stroking the feathers on his wings. Michael found it handy having a partner who was keen to maintain them. On Earth, they were subject to a range of pests: fleas, nits, and stinging nettles. It's hard to believe that a stinging nettle could take root on an angel's wing.

Polly liked varnishing the ribs and lubricating the supports. There was a lot of pressure on the angel's back. Anyway, a good old polish certainly got the gander up. And Michael had become a bit of an expert on satisfying her needs.

Her needs were being satisfied for the fourth time that day when there was a knock on the door. Michael completed the satisfaction process, dewinged, put a towel around himself and went to answer the front door. Before he opened it, he could sense the presence of another angel. He knew that it was Laylah.

He telepathically asked her what she wanted. She said that her lover had been killed and that they were both in danger. He decided to let her in. They had met before, but they didn't really know each other as they were in different choirs and there were an awful lot of angels.

(Author's note. Angels are divided into the following:
- The first hierarchy contains Seraphim, Cherubim and Thrones.
- The second hierarchy contains Dominions, Virtues and Powers.
- The third and final hierarchy contains Principalities, Archangels and Angels.)

Michael, 'Come in.'

Laylah, 'Thank you.'

Michael 'Can I get you anything?'

Laylah, 'Could I ask for a favour?

Michael, 'Of course.'

Laylah, 'Is there anything growing on my wing?' She released them from her tattoo and there on the bottom of the right wing was a baby stinging nettle. Michael denettled her, and they sat down after she dewinged.

Michael, 'What happened?'

Laylah, 'My lover, a Police Inspector, was killed in an inexplicable elevator crash.'

Michael, 'You suspect foul play.'

Laylah, 'I know that it was elf-play if you can call it play. Horrid little creatures. Why did God make them?'

Michael, 'What do you plan to do?'

Laylah, 'It may be more about what they plan to do to us or me.'

Michael, 'Go on.'

Laylah. 'As I was leaving my house yesterday, an arrow was shot at me. Fortunately, it missed. I picked it up, and it stung my fingers.' Since then, I have done some research on it. It contains Qeres.'

Michael, 'Are you sure?'

Laylah, 'I don't know much about it, but I'm sure that arrowhead was covered in it. I know that it is the only thing on Earth that can kill an angel. That's why I came straight here.'

Michael, 'Qeres is actually a perfume used by the Egyptians during their burial rites. It's exceedingly rare as the recipe has been lost.'

Laylah, 'Why is it so deadly to angels?'

Michael, 'No one knows. It is also deadly to any human that has the nephilitic gene.'

Laylah, 'What's that?'

Michael, 'It's a kidney disease. If you google it, you will get lots of mumbo jumbo crap about the hunt for the recipe, Satan, Hitler, Dr Mengele and Synaesthesia. However, it is a fact that Qeres can kill an angel.'

Laylah, 'So what do we do about it?'

89

The Last Cage

Officer Cage was delighted with the quality of his work. He had done a cracking job of destroying the evidence. It was a lot easier eliminating it than obtaining it. He was convinced that he would have made a great undercover agent.

He did spend an inordinate amount of time looking out for giant magpies. They should be fairly easy things to spot. His fear increased in the evening when the dog demanded a walk. He didn't feel that he could tell the wife that he couldn't go in case a giant magpie ate him.

He remembered the rhyme his grandmother had taught him:

One for sorrow,
Two for mirth,
Three for a funeral
And four for birth

So according to the rhyme, he should be safe.

The annoying thing was that he saw it coming. It was just a speck in the sky. As it got nearer, he realised that he would have to hide from this giant avian killer. What he hadn't noticed was the monstrous giant vole that crept up on him from behind and swallowed him whole.

A witness thought that he might have been a shrew, but it was a vole.

90

Danny's on a Roll

Fayden, 'So what further progress has been made?'

Our Danny, 'Your majesty, since our last meeting the following has been achieved:

- The following records have been destroyed: All films, paper statements, all relevant police records, key HR records, all physical evidence, all diary information, all victim records, fingerprints, DNA samples and missing-persons data.
- Officers Newman and Cage have been consumed.'

Fayden, 'What about the two police stations?'

Our Danny, 'I had to destroy the records first.'

Fayden, 'And no progress regarding the angels?'

Our Danny, 'Not yet but I have plans.'

Fayden, 'Well done, you have been busy. When can I expect finality?'

Our Danny, 'Before Dipdown, my majesty.'

Fayden, 'I will keep you to that.'

91

It's really hot now

In some parts of the world, there is a considerable amount of warning. Elsewhere there are monitors that constantly track any activity. In the case of Burgess Hill, it was totally unexpected.

No one, absolutely *no one,* ever expected a rupture of the planetary crust in Burgess Hill. It was unheard of in the Sussex Downs. It's not as if the tectonic plates were converging on this small Sussex town. A brush fire, a plague or even a UFO encounter were all possibilities but never a major volcanic eruption.

Linda had been somewhat shocked to see the meteor destroy WH Smith in the Martlets Shopping Centre a few months ago. She had considered that a once-in-a-lifetime experience. But now she was watching lava rolling down the High Street. She wondered how the parking warden was going to handle that.

Linda became slightly concerned when she detected the smell of sulphur in the little room, but she shouldn't have worried as Bert, her husband caused it.

Magma poured out of the rupture and created a classic volcano. Gillian was concerned that it was going to block her view of the Downs. There were strict Green Belt regulations in place, and as far as she was concerned, this volcano was an unauthorised structure.

Vents were pouring out noxious gases. Ben, part of the Neighbourhood Watch scheme, wasn't having that and wrote a stiff letter to the Home Office. He hadn't fought the Hun in the Second World War for nothing and he wasn't going to be intimidated by a few thousand tons of hot steaming gases. In fact, he was far too young to have been in the war, but the sentiment was right.

The local population, well those that had survived, were extremely impressed by the shooting cinder bombs. They were also impressed by the pyroclastic flow. It consisted of molten volcanic ash that incinerated everything flammable in its path including the Asda supermarket, the local bus depot, a Skoda showroom, a BT switching centre and the local bowls club. The bowls team decided to go down with the club.

This river of magma trundled along to Haywards Heath and continued until it reached the police station. It seemed quite happy to end its journey there filling the building with silica and an earthy smell that will probably take years to clear.

Danny's work had been done. He was surprised by how much power he could wield.

92

Polly couldn't put the kettle on

Polly couldn't put the kettle on now. It wasn't easy when you had been burnt to a cinder. It wasn't lava that did her in. It was volcanic gases. It is an interesting fact that volcanic gases were directly responsible for approximately 3% of all volcano-related deaths of humans between 1900 and 1986. Some volcanic gases kill by acidic corrosion; others kill by asphyxiation.

Anyway, she was dead. This did not go down that well with the local angel population.

Revenge was in the air, and so was copulation. Michael and Laylah had discovered the joys of mid-air sex. They had joined the mile-high club. Both of their lovers had been killed by the dastardly deeds of a despicable, desperate elf, but they realised that they were in love with sex and not their human companions. The flighty, flippant angels would soon forget even the names of their lovers. That was always the case with those who lived forever.

Their carefree bonking provided a perfect target. One arrow laced with Qeres was all it took. The archery skills of the Elfi were renowned. Check out *Lord of the Rings* if you don't believe me. One arrow through two hearts and that was the end of a very intimate romance.

However, two dead angel bodies on Ditchling Common caused an uproar in the scientific community.

93

Me again

A good author knows that you have to keep the players down to a reasonable number. Otherwise, readers find it hard to follow the plot.

"What plot?" do I hear you say?

Well, this was the original list of players I put together:

Name	Current Status
Narrator	Still alive
Dolores	Still alive
Doug	Dead—Killed by a meteorite
June	Dead—Suicide
Isabella	Dead—Accidentally sucked to death by Danny
Old Irishman	**Really an angel, but now dead from an arrow shot**
Ivor	Dead—Drowned in the bath
Danny	**Extinguished, but returned**
John	Dead—Genitalia removed
Polly	**Dead—Volcanic gases**
Jim	Dead—Suffocated by a vagina
Carol	Dead—Suicide
Emma	**Dead—Crushed by a giant hand**
Mr Brown	Dead—Fucked to death
Mrs Brown	**Dead—Crushed by a giant hand**
Keith	Suicide—Bled to death
Jill	**Dead—Crushed by a giant hand**
Fairy Queen	Still alive

Any changes to the above have been outlined in bold. So, the only survivors are Dolores, the Fairy Queen and I. (I always think me sounds better, and it might even be right in this case). And of course, Danny returned.

But to be fair, some new players were added

Name	Current Status
Laylah	Dead—killed by an arrow
Officer Newman	Dead—Eaten by a magpie
Officer Cave	Dead—Eaten by a vole
Police Inspector	Dead—Elevator accident
Police Commissioner	Dead—Elevator accident
Fayden	Alive
MI5 Officer	Dead—Crushed by a giant hand
Sergeant Baker	Dead—Crushed by a giant hand

So if we ignore the Narrator and the Fay Folk, we have no one left. That is no way to run a novel. Readers want to identify with the principal characters. If I weren't getting paid, I would be off.

94

Danny's Done

Fayden, 'I was a bit surprised to see large chunks of Angleland covered in a volcano.'

Our Danny, 'Yes, Your majesty, it was a great success.'

Fayden, 'Did you have to kill 30,000 ploughmen?'

Our Danny, 'They were just collateral damage.'

Fayden, 'That was a lot of collateral damage.'

Our Danny, 'It was, but so what?'

Fayden, 'It just raises other issues. And if we are talking about other issues what about the two dead angel bodies?'

Our Danny, 'What about the bodies? My job was to kill them, and I did it.'

Fayden, 'True, but Heaven is not happy.'

Our Danny, 'What's that got to do with us?'

Fayden, 'Point taken. I think your mission has been completed.'

Our Danny, 'Can I have some more fairy dust? I've used my private supply up on the mission.'

Fayden, 'Yes, I will get that organised.'

Our Danny, 'What about my contract with the Fairy Queen to supply souls?'

Fayden, 'That stands; a contract is a contract.' Danny was hoping that the contract would have been cancelled as he was a very tired elf.

95

Angel Control is on the Case

Angelic Control, Sector 16, 'God Control, we have a report of two angels down.'

God Control, 'Please provide details.'

Angelic Control, 'Angel Laylah, who was on assignment, has been terminated along with Angel Michael 15, who had gone rogue.'

God Control, 'How were they terminated?'

Angelic Control, 'That is not known, your holiness.'

God Control, 'Where are the bodies?'

Angelic Control, 'Again we are not sure, but we can only assume that the ploughmen have them.'

God Control, 'This is extremely serious.'

Angelic Control, 'Yes your holiness.'

God Control, 'What are your plans?'

Angelic Control, 'We need your guidance, your holiness.'

God Control, 'I understand.'

96

Ministers Get Involved

The Chief Secretary to The Prime Minister, 'The PM has asked me to investigate this nonsense.' He was addressing the civil servants in the Home Office

Chief Secretary, 'Have you all read this?'

Private Report on Inexplicable Events in Mid-Sussex

During the period May to September 2020, there has been a significant number of unexplained events and deaths, including the following:

- The death of J. Smith in a locked room.
- The extermination of numerous pets and five of their owners
- The death of Isi Mason in a locked room
- The death of J. Cogan, the suicide of his wife and the murder of their two children
- The death of Doug and Ivor Mason and the suicide of June Mason
- A major arson attack at Burgess Hill College killing 16
- The killing of the entire Brown family
- The fact that it took two days to put out a loaf of bread that was on fire
- The fact that three milk bottles were seen floating through the air
- The fact that in a very secure room, a short, bearded man teleported in, took three female patients, and teleported all of them out (There were numerous other examples of teleportation).
- The doctoring of films and memories
- Paper records showed that the three patients had all

experienced stillbirths but had no memory of it

- The local Police Commissioner and Police Inspector were killed in an inexplicable elevator accident
- Three women, an unknown creature and eight officers were turned to dust
- An MI5 officer and a policeman were also turned to dust
- An angel was spotted leaving a café on Haywards Heath High Street
- A witness spotted a police officer's head being bitten off by a giant magpie.
- Another witness spotted a police officer being eaten by a giant vole
- There was a deliberate destruction of police records relating to these events
- The dead bodies of two fallen angels were found and are in secure storage
- And of course, they suffered two major incidents: a meteorite and a volcano.

Chief Clerk, 'Mr Secretary, I have to report that the two angel bodies have disappeared.'

Chief Secretary, 'That's very convenient. What proof of any supernatural involvement do we have?'

Chief Clerk, 'Very Little, Mr Secretary. There are no films, no witness statements and no records at all.'

Home Office Consultant, 'What about photos of the angels?'

Chief Clerk, 'They appear to have disappeared.'

Home Office Consultant, 'What do you mean disappeared?'

Chief Clerk, 'We remember taking the photos but they have all gone. There aren't any.'

Chief Secretary, 'I actually saw them being taken on a digital camera. You are telling me that not one photo exists?'

Chief Clerk, 'Yes, Sir.'

Chief Secretary, 'That doesn't make sense.'

Chief Clerk, 'No, Sir.'

Chief Secretary, 'At first I thought that this was a big con, but something is going on. I want a team set up to carry out a thorough investigation. It must have a full forensics capability.'

Chief Clerk, 'Yes, Sir.'

Chief Secretary, 'Can you also provide a full breakdown of the death toll?'

Chief Clerk, 'Yes, Sir.'

97

God Control

God Control, 'Your supreme godliness, we have retrieved the bodies of the two dead angels and devalued the photos that the humans had taken of them.'

God, 'Devalued?'

God Control, 'Yes, your supreme godliness, the photos are devalued as they are blanked out. They now have no value.'

One of the problems of knowing everything is that it is hard to sift through the billions of data items received every second. God employs thousands of angels in God Control to manage this. Otherwise, God gets headaches.

God, 'How were my angels killed?'

God Control, 'By Fay archery using arrows dipped in Qeres.'

God, 'But there is no more Qeres, and I had the recipe deknown.'

God Control, 'You are right your supreme godliness, but that appears to be the case.'

God, 'I will not have this. Find me the one who is responsible.'

God Control, 'We know who it is, your supreme godliness, but it is a long story.'

God, 'Give me a name.'

God Control, 'Yes, your supreme godliness, it's one of the elves.'

God, 'Which one?'

God Control, 'Does it matter, your supreme godliness, as they are all the same?'

God, 'I remember now. There are 39 of them that exist in a continuous extinguishment loop. One of my more creative ideas. All rather droll.'

God Control, 'Agent Angel Michael 15 was sent to investigate and eliminate the elf problem, but he was distracted.'

God, 'It was fanny, wasn't it?'

God Control, 'I'm afraid that you are right, your supreme godliness.'

God, 'Which fanny was it?'

God Control, 'I'm just checking the records now, your supreme godliness. I have them:

It was a mortal called Polly. The copulation record is as follows

Date	Erection Achieved	Semen Transferred	Position
2/5	Yes	Yes	Missionary
2/5	Yes	Yes	Doggy
2/5	Yes	Yes	Corkscrew
2/5	Yes	Yes	Pretzel Dip
3/5	Yes	No	Missionary
4/5	Yes	Yes	Missionary
4/5	Yes	Yes	Flat Iron
4/5	Yes	Yes	Wheelbarrow
5/5	Yes	Yes	Cowgirl
5/5	Yes	Yes	Stand and Deliver
6/5	Yes	Yes	Magick Mountain
6/5	Yes	Yes	Reverse Cowgirl
6/5	Yes	Yes	Missionary
6/5	Yes	Yes	Doggy
6/5	Yes	Yes	Ballet Dancer
6/5	Yes	Yes	Caboose
6/5	Yes	Yes	Snow Angel
6/5	Yes	Yes	Wrapped Lotus
8/5	Yes	Yes	Missionary
8/5	Yes	Yes	Doggy
8/5	Yes	Yes	The Snake
8/5	Yes	Yes	The Lazy Man
8/5	Yes	Yes	The Spider
8/5	Yes	Yes	The Om
9/5	Yes	Yes	Missionary

9/5	Yes	Yes	Table Top
9/5	Yes	Yes	Upstanding Citizen
9/5	Yes	Yes	Spock
10/5	Yes	Yes	Missionary
10/5	Yes	Yes	Doggy
10/5	Yes	Yes	Valedictorian

God, 'What's a snow angel?'

God Control, 'It's where the female lies on her back and her partner straddles her facing away. The female lifts her legs and wraps them around their back to elevate her pelvis so they can enter her. I understand that it is quite a tricky manoeuvre, your supreme godliness.

I can provide photos or video of them in that position if you want. I also have samples of the semen if required.'

God, 'That won't be necessary, but it will be necessary to punish Polly.'

God Control, 'Punishment has already been inflicted. She was asphyxiated by volcanic gases. She currently resides in the other place. If further punishment is required, I could request a transfer.'

God, 'That won't be necessary, but I want that elf.'

God Control, 'Agent Angel Laylah was sent to sort out the problem and resolve the Michael 15 issue. She failed.'

God, 'Was it cock this time?'

God Control, 'Yes, your supreme godliness. She fornicated with a police inspector. Do you want to see the records?'

God, 'Not really, but how many fornications were there?'

God Control, 'Our records show that there were over 300.'

God, 'She was a lusty little bitch, wasn't she?'

God Control, 'Yes, your supreme godliness.'

God, 'I give our agents genitalia so that they fit in on Earth and they can't wait to fuck around. They are angels for fuck's sake. Well, we need to punish that police inspector.'

God Control, 'He was liquidised in an elevator accident, your supreme godliness.'

God, 'I don't remember doing that.'

God Control, 'It was the Fay, your supreme godliness.'

God, 'Not that fucking elf again?'

God Control could tell that God was getting angry as that was the only time he swore, and an angry God was not a good thing.

God Control, 'It was, your supreme godliness.'

God, 'Where is he now?'

God Control, 'Just tracking him now, your supreme godliness.'

God Control knew that something awful was going to happen.

'Your supreme godliness, we have found the offending being.'

Then there was the smell of ozone in the air, and a loud blast and the little village of World's End on the edge of the Burgess Hill volcano was evaporated by the largest lightning bolt recorded in the northern hemisphere.

Linda had initially been shocked to see WH Smith in the Martlets being destroyed by a meteorite. As far as she was concerned, it was a once-in-a-lifetime event. That was until an enormous volcano grew out of the Asda car park. That was an even greater once-in-a-lifetime event, but the lightning bolt that destroyed World's End topped it all. She was saddened by that fact that her best friend, Teresa who lived in the area was not answering the phone. As far as she was concerned, there had been far too many 'once-in-a-lifetime' events.

98

Sussex has had enough

The Chief Secretary to The Prime Minister, 'Sir, I need to tell you that an enormous lightning bolt has evaporated a small village in Sussex called World's End.'

Prime Minister, 'At least the name is appropriate. Is it one of ours?'

Chief Secretary, 'I'm afraid so.'

Prime Minister, 'Do I need to go there?'

Chief Secretary, 'I would advise against it, Sir. That area of Mid-Sussex was hit by a meteorite, then had a major volcanic eruption and has now experienced an enormous lightning bolt.'

Prime Minister, 'That's a bizarre set of coincidences.'

Chief Secretary, 'I put it down to satanic forces.'

The PM then realised that he needed a new Chief Secretary.

Prime Minister, 'Surely you are joking?!'

Chief Secretary, 'I know that you think I'm mad, but I will send you the file. It is one inexplicable event after another.'

Prime Minister, 'I will read it with interest.'

The Chief Secretary knew that meant the PM was not going near it with two or three barge poles stuck together.

Chief Secretary, 'In the meantime, we are evacuating most of West Sussex.'

Prime Minister, 'You can't be serious.'

Chief Secretary, 'We have little choice as the local population—well what is left of it—are streaming out of the area. We have a serious refugee problem.'

Prime Minister, 'You are being serious, aren't you?'

Chief Secretary, 'Yes, Prime Minister. The following is taking place:
  • The motorway network is being used to transport the

survivors out of West Sussex
- The army is establishing temporary housing in East Sussex, Kent, and parts of London
- Gatwick Airport has been closed and is under military control
- Food and clothing stocks are being organised
- The London to Brighton Railway Line is closed, mainly because great chunks of it are missing
- Government science officers are investigating the phenomena
- The DOE is determining what they can do with the magma and other volcanic outpourings
- Construction teams are in place to repair the road and rail networks, but they can only consider minor activities at this stage
- Burial parties have been organised.
- The Anglican Church is providing a team to fight Satan.'

Prime Minister, 'Well done, Benson.'

Chief Secretary, 'And Sir, I believe that you need to put out a statement. Something like, "This is not retribution from God because of the activities of Brighton's inhabitants". Most of our party believe it is.'

99

Which Danny?

As we know, God works in mysterious ways. He is infallible, and consequently, he must have wanted to kill another elf and not our Danny. It doesn't matter much as all Dannys are the same.

Our Danny felt the extinguishment of one of the Dannys. It pushed him up the list, but then he couldn't see any reason for caring. Why was six of thirty-nine better or worse than twenty of thirty-nine? It just didn't matter. In this case, our Danny felt relieved as he suspected that he should have been the target.

Danny evaluated the current situation. He had completed all of the tasks allocated to him. He patted himself on the back mainly because no one else was going to. Anyway, it had been fun. He now understood just how much power he could wield with the help of fairy dust. And he had an ample supply.

He was, however, conscious that he now had a few enemies:
- God and the angel choirs
- The residents of Mid-Sussex
- UK Government and specifically the local police forces
- The ploughmen in general
- Probably the Fay Council
- Possibly some of his fellow elves

But did it matter? He was evil and eternal. He could, if he wanted to, become the top fairy.

100

A Note from the Author

There has been some criticism from the Turd. Sorry, that's my new name for the Narrator. He was a friend once. We even went on holiday together to Dagenham. I wanted to go to Grimsby, but he said that we should go to the home of the Ford Escort. I could understand where he was coming from, but the tour of one of the largest council estates in England was not a great success. But Alf Ramsey came from Dagenham.

Anyway, the Turd has never written a book. What right has he got to be so condescending? OK, he has got a degree, and a MA and is a Doctor of Literature, but he hasn't written a book. OK, he lectures on Twentieth-Century American writers and has published two volumes of poetry, but he is not a novelist.

You can see where I am coming from. He is not qualified.

Anyway, I've been through his list of players on page 155 and analysed it further:

The Dead:
- Carol
- Doug
- Emma
- Sergeant Baker
- Isabella
- Ivor
- Jill
- Jim
- John
- June

- Keith
- Laylah
- MI5 Officer
- Michael (Previously the Old Irishman)
- Mr Brown
- Mrs Brown
- Officer Cave
- Officer Newman
- Police Commissioner
- Police Inspector
- Polly

The Living:
- Danny
- Narrator
- Dolores
- Fairy Queen

The Narrator and his wife are not part of the story. It was never intended that they would be. I would accept that the Narrator has participated in the story to a minimal extent, but now that I realise just how big a shit he is, I have excluded him from now onwards. And his wife is going to die from an ingrowing toenail that is going to pierce her heart.

So we are down to Danny and the Fairy Queen.

However, if you go back to page 26 and specifically this paragraph:

'June and her sister May fixed a date for tea. They were actually coming round to give us the babysitting money. I should point out that June wasn't born in June and May wasn't born in May. It was a bit annoying that Dolores spent more on the tea than we were going to receive for babysitting.'

You will notice that June had a sister: May. The Narrator forgot her. Not so smart, is he?

101

May Day

It had not been a good year for May. It all started with the supernatural occurrences. She had bullied June into organising an exorcism which ultimately resulted in the death of the reverend in Isi's bedroom. May had always thought that June was too familiar with the vicar and also his son.

There had been two or three occasions when she had come around to find all three of them getting dressed. She had heard things like, 'Quick get it up her as the old battle-axe will be here soon', and, 'God, God, that's so fucking good, it's good for a father and son to share sometimes.'

Anyway, the father has left us; God bless his soul. (Of course, we know that it wasn't the case).

May wasn't happy when her sister decided to move to Burgess Hill. She saw it as a backward move. It was a step down the ladder in the social hierarchy, but June was never interested in the important things in life. Then Isi died mysteriously in her room followed by the attempted rape of her sister and death of the entire neighbouring family.

May found it hard to believe that a meteorite had hit Burgess Hill and that Doug had been killed. She immediately went to her sister's, to provide some comfort. She wasn't a lot of comfort and especially when she said, 'At least he didn't die alone, and 'I bet that girl didn't expect that.' It was the last thing June wanted to hear.

The death of her nephew was another blow, but then she never really liked him. He wasn't the sort you *could* like. She couldn't believe that she had to go to yet another funeral.

June could cope with the loss of her husband as the man was a waste of time. The vicar dying was a bitter blow, and the loss of her two children was almost too much to bear although she had to agree that Ivor wasn't particularly likeable. What she couldn't cope with was her sister saying, 'I told you so' and, 'I told you that you needed an exorcism,' and, 'You should never have married that man'. That's why she committed suicide. She couldn't stand her sister's rantings.

May found that the suicide of her loving sister was a real blow. Who was going to look after her dog when she went on holiday with that nice Mr Franklyn? Where would she go for her Christmas dinner? Who would she borrow money from now? It was a tragic shame.

May was further surprised by the volcanic eruption and the lightning bolt. She was now being evacuated to Croydon. It appeared that she would be spending the night in the Fairfield Halls.

Narrator's Note, 'Why did we have to go through all of this? What has it added to the story?'

Author's Note, 'Just wait and see, you cruddy pile of shit.'

The Publisher could see that their relationship had broken down. He had the skills to see this as he had received training in human interactions and psychology. Publishers are normally incredibly wise and intelligent people.

102

Fay Day

It was another Fay Day where once again the Fay Council met in the fairy ring near British Camp on the Malvern Hills. For some, it was a play away day, but for Fayden it was not a hay day but the day of days. Somehow, she was reminded of Edgar Allan Poe:

"Those who dream by day are cognizant of many things which escape those who dream only by night."

The wind was blowing hard, telling all that she was in charge. She knew every crack and cranny of these hills and more. The day of days had come, one predicted by the score. Fay reflected that once there were twenty of the Fay Brethren but alas there was only eleven now. They had lost:

- The Unicorni
- The Gnomi
- The Goblini
- The Spriti
- The Elementi
- The Sylphi
- The Dragoni
- The Nympi
- The Fauni

By lost she meant that they had ceased to exist, or they had left the Fay Council. The Goblini were now deadly enemies and attacked fairy camps for food. The food being any magickal being. Serious magick was being used to protect this ring.

The Dragoni simply left this dimension. Their like would never be seen again, which was the pittiest of pities.

So we were left with:

- The Asrai
- The Pixi
- The Elfi
- The Mersi
- The Bansheei
- The Leprechauni
- The Browni
- The Gremli
- The Impi
- The Famili
- The Impi

An earlier debate had identified several misdemeanours committed by The Elfi, but no action had been taken. Since then, the crimes against the Fay Laws had escalated.

Today's debate focuses on the future of the Elfi. Could the Council allow the Elfi to exist? Did they have the right to extinguish them all permanently?

Two fairy lords had been appointed:

Lord Elderberry of the Enchanted Eleonores for the Defence (Elderberry), and

Lord Rufus Randytoad of the Roundheadians (Rufus) for the Prosecution

In the dock were Thirty-Nine Elves. The Court decided to call the defendants Danny as they were all the same.

The Case for the Prosecution

Lord Rufus, 'Fellow Fay, today is a solemn event in the history of the Fay People. We are gathered here today to investigate and make a judgement on a whole Fay Race: The Elfi.

The following indictments have been made against them:
- That they did expose themselves and the Fay Folk to the ploughmen
- That they, through actions or inactions, caused the death of Fay Folk
- That they deliberately assassinated two Angel Folk

- That they used elemental powers beyond the requirement to achieve their goals, namely fast-flying space stones and fire mountains.
- That they used elemental powers without the permission of the Fay Council
- That the disruption to the ploughmen has caused unnecessary aggravation for the Fay Folk

Before we focus on the indictments, we need to agree that the Fay Council has the right to put the Elfi on trial.'

Fayden of the Grand Fay Council, 'Please continue, Lord Rufus.'

Lord Rufus, 'I would argue that the Fay Council has the right to put the Elfi on trial based on precedent. When The Goblini worked against the wishes of the Fay Council, they were scorned.'

Fayden, 'And they are still scorned. Eating fairies is a totally unacceptable behaviour.'

Lord Rufus, 'Quite so, your majesty. However, it does set a precedent that the Council has the power of scorning. Here we are looking at going one stage further—permanent extinguishment.

'My second argument is that the Elfi has no hierarchy or management structure. Consequently, there are no controls or balances. Individual elves can do what they like.

'Thirdly there is no retribution. If an elf commits an illegal act, they are simply extinguished and re-born. They have no incentive to follow the laws of the Fay.'

Fayden, 'It is my belief that each elf is the same.'

Lord Rufus, 'That has been said, your majesty, but the evidence doesn't back it up. We believe that this is untrue.'

Fayden, 'Does that mean that we should punish individual elves rather than the whole race?'

Lord Rufus, 'The extinguishment encirclement makes this exceedingly difficult. I see no benefit in prolonging their race and request a vote giving The Fay Council the right of permanent extinguishment.'

The vote was cast by dropping small stones into one of two ploughman's skulls.

Yes Skull
- The Asrai

- The Mersi
- The Bansheei
- The Gremli
- The Famili

No Skull
- The Impi
- The Impi
- The Leprechauni
- The Pixi
- The Browni

Some of you may wonder why The Impi appears twice. That is because the ancient Impi lived in the north and were really Ice-Impi. Their newer brothers lived in the rain forests of the south and were really Tree-Impi. The problem was that they both claimed The Impi name and so both races were allowed on the Council with identical race names. Compromise had always been the order of the day.

Fayden now had the casting vote. She dropped her stone into the yes skull. This meant that the Council had the power. She believed in the Council as every increase in its power was an increase in hers.

Lord Rufus, 'Thank you, Council members. We now need to review the crimes of The Elfi. Some had been documented at a previous meeting:
- You used fairy-fire on a loaf of bread. It took the ploughmen two days to put the fire out
- Your teleportation skills resulted in three milk bottles floating through the air. This was seen by several ploughmen
- Your teleportation of three ploughwomen was filmed on many occasions
- The kidnapping of the three ploughwomen, their forced impregnation and subsequent stillbirths goes against our faylaws
- There were many sightings of your kind.'

Lord Rufus went on, 'The Elfi were warned that this sort of behaviour would not be tolerated, but it continued:

- Two ploughmen were killed in an inexplicable elevator accident
- Further sightings of elves at the hospital
- Eleven ploughmen were turned to dust in public view
- Two further ploughmen were turned to dust on another occasion
- A witness spotted a ploughman's head being bitten off by a giant magpie.
- Another witness spotted a ploughman being eaten by a giant vole
- The use of Qeres, a banned substance
- The killing of two angels

'Then we come to the elemental crimes:

- Flying space stones
- Fire Mountains

'These elemental actions destroyed a large Fay settlement under Burgess Hill. There was a Fay community under every ploughman community named after a hill. It didn't matter whether the hill existed or not. I rest my case.' And a rest was called. A soup of boiled donkey brains was distributed to one and all.

Fayden wasn't too sure how she wanted this to go. Some of Danny's actions could be directly linked back to her.

103

May's Fay Day

Few people knew that May was a changeling. As discussed before, Fay culture has been sanitised. Before Disney and the Pre-Raphaelites, fairies were terrifying little shits. Based on the contents of this book, they are certainly not the most pleasant of creatures.

Anyway, we need to investigate some of their less-friendly behaviours:

- Drowning of mortals. This appears to be one of their favourite pastimes
- Abduction of young women to become brides. This is simply rape and sexual enslavement
- Abduction of new mothers to serve as nursemaids
- Sexual abduction of young men
- Abduction of babies. They usually leave a changeling in its place which typically is sickly and soon dies
- Murder, especially of children
- General enslavement
- Soul collecting

The general rule is that you shouldn't piss off a fairy. At best, they are temperamental and at worst, spiteful, vindictive, and malicious. Their punishment is typically wholly out of proportion to the alleged crime.

Narrator, 'I'm wondering who is saying this? Is it the author? Sometimes we are in the first person, then the third.

'Anyway, I'm thinking of pissing off a fairy.'

Fairy Queen, 'I would advise against that. We may be spiteful, vindictive, and malicious, but we have good reason to be. I think the author is making a good attempt.'

Danny, 'I agree. I've warned that fucking narrator before. If I weren't on trial, I would eviscerate him.'

May, 'What does eviscerate mean?'

Author, 'It really means disembowel.'

Fairy Queen, 'I prefer disembowel.'

Author, 'Fair enough.'

Danny, 'I agree. I've warned that fucking narrator before. If I weren't on trial, I would disembowel him.'

Narrator, 'Well I'm sorry that everyone feels that way. I'm also not happy with the lists. The author should be using the Queen's English, not producing list after list. Look at my analysis:

Page No	List Name
3-5	List of characteristics for 1972
6	List of Haywards Heath Attractions
9	List of Adam Strange's Characteristics
11	List of Characteristics of my Ex-Wife
15-16	List of Isi's Characteristics
41	List of Anomalies regarding the Vicar's Death
44	List of Dead Pets
46	List of Unknowns regarding Isi's Death
49	List of Queries regarding Jim's Death
50-51	List of Deaths
61-62	List of Emma's Tourette symptoms
84	List of Strange Events
86-87	List of References
96	List of where Souls might come from
97	List of Ensoulment Times
109	List of events relating to the hospital abduction
111	List of Players and their status
121-122	Story Update
125-126	Statement of Events
127	List of Fairy Races
128	Evidence List against The Elfi
135	Fairy Action Plan
140	List of Danny's Achievements
142-144	List of Strange Events and Statements
147	List of Actions for Officer Cage

Fairy Queen, 'Why did you waste so much time putting the list together?'

Narrator, 'Well, the reader has paid for a novel not a sequence of lists, and to make it worse, some are duplicated. Look at pages 125 and 159.'

Editor, 'I agree; there are far too many lists.'

Author, 'Tell me which ones you want removed.'

Danny, 'I like them. Repetition is a good technique. It helps the reader follow the plot.'

Narrator, 'What plot?'

May, 'I thought this chapter was about me?'

Author, 'Sorry, let's carry on.'

It turns out that the real May had been abducted by the fairies and replaced by a pathetic, sickly, gangly, excuse for a child.

May, 'I think that is going too far. I wasn't the healthiest of children, but I wasn't *that* bad.'

Usually, the changeling dies, but Mary has survived. In fact, she has survived eleven heart attacks and a few bouts of cancer.

May, 'That's not true, I did have one heart attack and one case of skin cancer.'

Author, 'I was just trying to show how sickly you were.'

May, 'Piss off.'

104

May's Visit

May, being of fairy origins, was allowed to address the Fay Council. It was strange seeing the Fairy Council in the fairy ring with a giant human standing next to them.

Fayden, 'May the Changeling, you have the ears of the Court. I understand that you want to provide evidence against the Elfi on behalf of the ploughmen.'

May, 'I do, your magnificence.'

Fayden. 'You may proceed, but we have no obligation to take your evidence into account. What happens to ploughmen is of little consequence to the Fay.'

May, 'Of course, your magnificence.'

Fayden, 'You may start.'

Narrator, 'I sense another list coming.'

May, 'The list of crimes committed by Danny is as follows:
- The killing of Reverend John in a locked room with his penis made into a necklace and put around Isabella's head
- The killing of five pet owners
- The killing of Isabella Mason in a locked room
- The killing of the entire Cogan family
- The Killing of Doug Mason
- The killing of Ivor mason
- The suicide of June Mason
- The death of sixteen individuals at Burgess Hill College due to arson
- The killing of the entire Brown family
- The killing of two police officials in an inexplicable elevator accident

- The killing of eight policemen and three women in a hospital
- The killing of two further officers
- The killing of a police officer by having his head being bitten off by a giant magpie.
- The killing of another officer by being eaten by a giant vole

I make this a total of 48 human beings.

Now we need to add the major events:

- The meteorite killed at least 3,000
- The volcanic eruption killed a further 30,000
- The lightning bolt killed 400

That is a grand total of 33,448.'

Fayden, 'The bolt was nothing to do with us, but what are you saying?'

May, 'Danny has committed serious crimes against humanity.'

Fayden. 'And your point is?'

May, 'Humanity deserves retribution.'

Fayden, 'I'm really not interested. Ploughmen have killed millions of the Fay. They are currently destroying our world and your world, and they don't care. They have killed millions of their own kind. I say, let them die. Now begone with you.'

105

The Case for the Defence

Lord Elderberry of the Enchanted Eleonores, 'My salutations to Lord Rufus. It is my intention to defend The Elfi and prove that their actions were of critical value to The Fay.

Firstly, I need to remind you of the indictments that have been made against my clients:

- That they did expose themselves and the Fay Folk to the ploughmen
- That they, through actions or inactions, caused the death of Fay Folk
- That they deliberately assassinated two Angel Folk
- That they used elemental powers beyond the requirements to achieve their goals, namely fast-flying space stones and fire mountains.
- That they used elemental powers without the permission of the Fay Council
- That the disruption to the ploughmen has caused unnecessary aggravation for the Fay Folk

Secondly, if I go back to a previous council meeting, the following actions were approved:

- Discuss the option of a time-reversal with the Angels
- Determine what the angels are doing on Earth
- Locate the films of the elf and destroy all copies
- Terminate the three pregnant women
- Terminate any police officials involved in the fiasco
- Terminate other witnesses
- Destroy all witness statements
- Eliminate any of the Fay who have failed to act within the

195

rules
- Contemplate terminating the angels involved

'In terms of a defence, The Elfi did everything they could to remove any evidence of their existence. The following records have been successfully destroyed: All films, paper statements, all relevant police records, key HR records, all physical evidence, all diary information, all victim records, fingerprints, DNA samples and missing-persons data.

'In fact, let's review the Elf's performance:

Action	Status
Discuss the option of a time-reversal with the Angels	Not approved
Determine what the angels are doing on Earth	Achieved
Locate the films of the elf and destroy all copies	Achieved
Terminate the three pregnant women	Achieved
Terminate any police officials involved in the fiasco	Achieved
Terminate other witnesses	Achieved
Destroy all witness statements	Achieved
Eliminate any of the Fay who have failed to act within the rules	Not required
Contemplate terminating the angels involved	Achieved

'My fellow members of the Council, you must admit that the tasks allocated to Danny have been successfully completed. In terms of the methodology, the use of elementals may seem to be excessive, but the entire area needed to be cleansed.

'Danny had no knowledge of any Fay community under Burgess Hill. There is no directory of Fay establishments.

'The Elfi have been key members and supporters of the Council and have attended every meeting since its inception. They have powers that are unique to them.

'The Elfi are willing to accept additional controls.'

Elderberry's defence was not that energetic as he knew that the Elfi

196

would win. There was absolutely no way that the Council would vote against them.

'My fellow Council Members I rest my case.'

It was time for the vote. The skulls were prepared.

- Yes Skull—The Elfi are guilty and should be punished
- No Skull—The Elfi are not guilty and should be exonerated.

The No skull received every vote. Danny was free to continue.

Fayden, 'My fellow Council members, thank you for coming to a quick decision, but things are not good. I can feel that we need a well-constructed plan to weave our way through the next few moon cycles.'

106

Fayden has her say

Fayden, 'So Danny, you got away with it.'

Danny, 'Yes, your majesty.'

Fayden, 'You know of course that there was no chance of your race being found guilty.'

Danny, 'I had suspected that, but I was worried.'

Fayden, 'What have you learnt?'

Danny, 'Detail, I need to focus more on detail. The ploughmen are much more sophisticated than they used to be.'

Fayden, 'And what else have you learnt?'

Danny, 'I'm not sure what you mean.'

Fayden, 'In that case I will tell you. You have learnt not to piss your Queen off. You have learnt to get my permission first. You have learnt to consider your actions before you jump in, haven't you?'

Danny, 'Yes, your majesty.'

Fayden, 'And you will carry out my orders, won't you?'

Danny, 'Yes, your majesty.'

Fayden, 'And you are going to calm down your activities for the next hundred years, aren't you?'

Danny, 'Yes, your majesty.'

Fayden, 'It strikes me that May the Changeling is a bit of a pain.'

Danny, 'And you want to be pain-free?'

Fayden, 'I think you have got my drift.'

107

Angelic Killings

Fayden was not looking forward to a meeting of the Celestial Committee for Cooperation between Heaven and Hell. There was only one item on the agenda: The use of Qeres and the assassination of two angels.

Her plan was to deny any knowledge of anything to do with angels. But there were rumours that God may attend. That made lying exceedingly difficult. The meeting was always held in Heaven as God refused to travel.

There were only going to be six attendees at the meeting: God, Satan, Fayden and an advisor each. Lord Elderberry of the Enchanted Eleonores was Fayden's advisor and principal fixer. They were waiting for the entrance ceremony to start.

The ceremony started with the ceremonial ringing of the Great Celestion, a massive bell that promoted peace. Fayden never understood how the din it caused could be regarded as peaceful.

Then the Celestial Trumpeters added to the racket. Fayden quite enjoyed their sound. It was the traditional welcome to Heaven. It was the welcome that new souls experienced.

Then the flower girls danced around covering the path in white rose petals. God liked his flower girls naked as he wanted to see their breasts bouncing around. God often thought that breasts were his most beautiful creation.

Satan was bored stiff. He spent most of his time picking his nose with long, gnarled fingernails. He flicked the results of his nasal mine over his shoulder. When the steaming hot, smelly bogies landed on the ground, they caused minor explosions as the bad collided with the good. Fayden wished that good and bad were that easy to define.

Satan was also interested in the flower girls. He was much more carnal, he just wanted to stick his long, gnarled cock up every one of their cunts, and then he wanted to rip their heads off. Well, even Satan had to have a hobby.

There was one terrible occasion when the timing was wrong, resulting in Satan getting his way. It made a right mess of the white petal display. It also made the recruitment of flower girls a lot more difficult. God punished Satan by making him spend a week working in a charity shop in Tunbridge Wells. That certainly taught him a lesson: charity starts at home. He ended up establishing a chain of satanic shops in Hell.

They followed the normal human rules: the employment of toothless old hags who couldn't count and didn't even know how to operate a till, chronically slow service, the re-keying of data two or three times due to keying errors, the constant need to call for the manager and the smell of lingering farts amongst the clothing stock. It was a unique version of Hell that humans were awfully familiar with.

They were still queuing, waiting for the Almighty. They could see him in the distance being carried on a litter by six strong men. God liked his litter men naked. He liked to see their penises swing back and forward. He never really liked the look of penises that much, but then who does? He much preferred breasts.

Satan had finished with his nasal extractions and had moved onto his ears. Large blocks of salty wax were being flung across the floor. Fayden had to duck on one occasion to avoid his Satanic Majesty's cerumen deposits. They could cause lasting damage to anyone not of hell. They were hugely prized by the wilderwomen.

Things only got worse when Satan started removing the contents of his arse. They don't have toilet paper in Hell. Satan's associates chip away at his turd-encrusted bowels on a regular basis. Demons fight for the privilege as they taste surprisingly good.

Lord Elderberry of the Enchanted Eleonores was a gentleman, or rather a gentlefairy. He used his cloak to protect her from the shitstorm. A small piece of satanic shit could sting a fairy and probably kill a human. It was to be avoided. By now, Fayden had had enough. This drawn-out procedure was the norm, and there was still more to come.

God had stopped to bless the trees and the grass, and the flowers and the bees, and the grasshoppers and the baby rabbits. Blessings was one of the things he did. It was expected of him. Anyway, he liked to keep Beelzebub waiting. He often wondered who Fayden was. She was a bit too small for his liking.

Further trumpeting heralded the entrance of the One and Only. Doves and dragonflies were released which always surprised Fayden as the doves regularly attacked the dragonflies, but Heaven was nothing but consistent. Nothing has changed in millennia, and there were no signs of any future change.

Loud chimes announced the imminent arrival of the God-Head.

God, 'Welcome my children.' He put out his hand for the ceremonial kiss. Satan and his advisor spat on it, and Fayden and Lord Elderberry of the Enchanted Eleonores couldn't reach his hand. God didn't seem to notice, but not noticing wasn't unusual for God.

The small party walked to the conference room. Fayden was always surprised that no allowance was made for their size. There were large seats or no seats. The two Fay stood, as was normal.

God moved into boom mode and said, 'Lucifer, why did you kill my angels?'

Lucifer, 'Yahweh, it wasn't me.'

God, 'Are you sure? The arrow was covered in Qeres.'

Lucifer, 'None of the denizens of Hell killed those angels.'

God, 'Fair enough. Let's finish the meeting and have a pint.'

Lucifer, 'Sounds good to me.'

They walked off.

God, 'Do you know why those little ones are here?'

Lucifer, 'Fuck knows.'

Fayden, 'I guess that was a result.'

Lord Elderberry of the Enchanted Eleonores, 'I think it was. You handled it brilliantly.'

They both laughed a fairy laugh, but Fay had her reservations.

108

The New Chief Secretary

Prime Minister, 'Ladies and gentlemen, thank you for meeting with me.'
The following were in attendance:
- The New Chief Secretary
- The Home Secretary
- The Head of the National Crime Agency
- A SAS representative
- The Archbishop of Canterbury
- The Head of MI5
- UK Head Scientist

Prime Minister, 'Firstly I would like to welcome my new Chief Secretary, Stella Weller.'

She was an attractive woman with a slim figure but with curves in all the right places. God would have appreciated her assets. There was a fine pair of legs and a fine brain. She knew how the politics of Westminster worked. And she worked it to her advantage. Well, it was the survival of the fittest.

Prime Minister, 'Stella replaced my previous Chief Secretary because he had an aberration. He believed that the problems of Mid-Sussex were down to satanic forces.'

Everyone in the room laughed except the archbishop.

Prime Minister, 'I believe that you have all seen the dossier but let's recap where we are:

During the period May to October 2020, there has been a significant number of unexplained events and deaths, including the following:
- The killing of a vicar in a locked room
- The killing of five pet owners
- The killing of Isabella Mason in a locked room

- The killing of the entire Cogan family
- The Killing of Doug and Ivor Mason
- The death of sixteen individuals at Burgess Hill College due to arson
- The killing of the entire Brown family
- The killing of two police officials in an inexplicable elevator accident
- The killing of eight policemen and three women in a hospital who were turned to dust
- The killing of two further officers who were also turned to dust
- The killing of a police officer by having his head being bitten off by a giant magpie.
- The killing of another officer by being eaten by a giant vole
- Numerous examples of teleportation
- The frequent appearance of a short dwarf-like creature at many of the crime scenes
- The deliberate destruction of police records relating to these events
- Angelic appearances
- The disappearance of two dead angel bodies that were held in secure storage
- Forced impregnation of women
- Levitation experiences and unnatural fire
- The destruction of Burgess Hill by a meteorite, unprecedented volcanic activity and lightning bolts.'

Prime Minister, 'We know that all of these events can be explained by standard scientific methodologies, don't we?'

Archbishop of Canterbury, 'I tell you it is the work of Satan himself.'

Prime Minister, 'Thank you, Archbishop.'

Chief Inspector Morris, Head of the National Crime Agency, 'Mr Prime Minister, I must point out that most of these cases have been thoroughly investigated by the local police forces.'

Prime Minister, 'And where is the evidence?'

Chief Inspector Morris, 'As you know, Prime Minister, we have little evidence; many of the witness memories have even mysteriously faded.'

Prime Minister, 'I asked for a forensic investigation. What do we have?'

Chief Inspector Morris, 'The investigation was carried out, and we have the following:

- The dust collected from the hospital contains mostly human remains and the remains of one alien body
- We have witness statements relating to the death of Reverend Smith
- We have some newspaper reports relating to the Cogan and Mason deaths
- We have a fair amount of evidence relating to the arson attack at the Burgess Hill College
- We have a report that says that the elevator in which two people died is and was in perfect condition
- We have proof that police records were destroyed
- We have witness statement from a café in Haywards Heath of an angel visitation
- We have numerous witness statements that two angel bodies were collected and put into secure storage. No one saw them disappear
- We have some medical records that detail the stillbirths for the women who had been teleported into hospital
- We have a giant feather from a magpie, but it was not found at the scene of the murder of Officer Newman
- We have the meteorite and the volcano.'

Prime Minister, 'Some questions. What are your views regarding the alien body found in the dust?'

Chief Inspector Morris, 'It is not human although it does contain human DNA.'

UK Head Scientist, 'Can I jump in? Its DNA structure is much older than humans. In the order of a million years or so. It's both primitive and very advanced. We are still working our way through its gene structure. It will generate decades of work.'

Prime Minister, 'Summarise your findings for me.'

UK Head Scientist, 'It's not human.'

Archbishop of Canterbury, 'Told you. It is the devil at work.'

Prime Minister, 'Thank you, Archbishop.'

Prime Minister, 'How big is this magpie feather?'

Chief Inspector Morris, 'It's outside, Sir. Shall I get it brought in?

Prime Minister, 'Yes please.'

It's not every day you see a magpie feather over six foot long. They didn't see it for long as it disappeared in front of their eyes.

Prime Minister, 'Did you see the size of it? Where did it go?'

Chief Inspector Morris, 'It went the way of all evidence.'

Prime Minister, 'What about the photos?'

They quickly looked in the dossier to find a set of blank photos. Danny had done his job. May next.

Prime Minister, 'We can't just sit here all day, we need some form of action plan.'

109

May's Days are Numbered

May was not stupid even though she looked stupid. It was part of the curse of being a changeling. She knew that her days were numbered. She felt that she had done the right thing, but the right thing for the cause was not necessarily the right thing for her.

It wasn't that easy disappearing in the human world. But in the Fay world, she was up against magickal tracking techniques that could even invade your dreams. She realised that hiding was almost impossible without some supernatural help. Ignoring the Fay world, the only sources of magick were:

- Human Lore
- Ceremonial Lore
- Witch Lore
- Angel Lore
- Demon Lore

Human Lore hardly existed in the twenty-first century. The days of Merlin and the druids are long gone. Ceremonial Lore was also human-based and was focussed on the world religions, especially the Judeo-Christian varieties. Today it appears to be mostly ineffectual.

Both angel and demon lore was not really available to your average human. Well, there wasn't a shop or online service that you could go to. This left witch lore. The trouble nowadays was that effective witches were few and far between, and many of them secured their power from the Fay world. There was one witch that might help her: Jonas.

Jonas was a male witch. He wasn't a warlock, a sorcerer or even a wizard. They all had their powers and their place in the arcane world. Jonas was proud to be a witch. He wasn't born a witch, and he never planned to be a witch. He didn't even have witchcraft thrust upon him.

He caught witchcraft from a dirty old hag that was dying in a rat-infested bog.

For a long time, he had no idea that he was a witch. It was a series of little things that came to his attention: his ability to talk to frogs; his inclination to only wear black; his preference for silver over gold; his ability to cure headaches and the common cold; his fascination with the moon; his ability to attract animals and, most significantly of all, his ability to summon the spirits of the dead.

Whenever he thought of a dead person, he or she would appear. They would tell him things in exchange for favours. At first, he was seriously frightened; as time went on, he became terrified, and after more experience, he became horrified to the point where he was petrified. The rational part of his brain realised that he was going to have to cope with this or go mad.

Slowly, very slowly, he moved from petrified to shocked, and then to alarmed, and finally, he reached a state of uncomfortable panic. How would you like it? You are in the bath, and the spirit of Hattie Jacques appears.

The dead taught him how to use his powers. He was now a powerful grey witch. He could never understand the blackness and whiteness of black and white witches. Greyness was much less decisive. He could swing either way. Regardless, he had power, lots of power. There were few in this world or the next that could resist him. Then a giant magpie bit his head off. That surprised May and surprised Jonas even more.

May realised that she was alone, but not alone as she heard the noise of flapping wings and the unmistakable sound of a corvid on the prowl.

A giant black-and-white bird smashed through the French doors of her lounge, but May was ready. As soon as the magpie was in the room, it was confronted with its own reflection in the mirror. It is one of only a few non-mammal species that can recognise itself in a mirror test, and as it preened and admired itself, May gave it the saucepan test. It failed the test as the sizeable cast-iron stewing pan restructured its head.

May enjoyed calling the police to let them know that she had withstood an avian attack of monstrous proportions, but the evidence had disappeared before they arrived.

110

Danny's Head Hurts

Danny was not feeling that good. It is not every day that you are hit with a heavy cooking utensil. He wasn't sure if it was a traditional saucepan or a frying pan, or even a skillet. It was quite heavy so that it might have been a wok.

Clearly, May was better prepared than Jonas. Those witches have too high an opinion of themselves. He wondered if Fayden would approve of his termination of the witch. Anyway, it was too late now.

Danny went through his list of killing techniques in his mind:

- Alcoholic poisoning
- Air crash
- Apparent suicide
- Archery accident
- Bee stings
- Being burnt
- Being devoured by wild animals
- Being hit by a saucepan
- Being boiled alive
- Being quartered
- Being tied to the mouth of a cannon, which is then fired
- Blown-up
- Breaking wheel
- Buried alive
- Car crash
- Carbon monoxide inhalation
- Crucifixion
- Crushing

- Death by a thousand cuts
- Death by sawing
- Decapitation
- Dehydration
- Disembowelment
- Drowning
- Drug overdose
- Electrocution
- Falling from a height
- Falling into an acid bath
- Flaying
- Food poisoning
- Forced feeding
- Gunshot
- Hanging
- Hit by a train
- Impalement
- Jumping into 50 tons of molten iron
- Jumping into a live volcano
- Jumping into a steamroller's path
- Keelhauling
- Knifing
- Lethal injection
- Pesticide Poisoning
- Poisoning
- Puncturing your heart with an electric drill
- Sawing in half
- Shooting yourself in the head with a nail gun
- Shoving a red-hot poker down your throat
- Snakebite
- Starvation
- Stepping into a tiger's den
- Strangulation
- Stoning
- Suffocation
- Sword wound

- Vicious attack on the coccyx
- Wrist cutting

Over the last thousand years, Danny had used most of these techniques. They all had their merits. Danny quite enjoyed the long, slow deaths. He liked to see the life gradually fading away. On the other hand, there was a lot of excitement in a short, sharp termination. The look of surprise on a ploughman's face was always a delight.

Danny quite enjoyed killing the young as it wasn't just a physical killing but also robbing them of their future. He enjoyed their loss of hope. He also liked to tease the victim, pretending that there was some hope of salvation and then mercilessly killing them at the last moment. Life or rather, death was good.

So what delights did he have in store for the changeling? He decided to keep it reasonably simple but agonising. She was never meant to live anyway.

111

The Church Musters its Forces

A secret subsection of a secret subsection of The Church of England Parochial Church Council met to discuss the disturbing paranormal events. They also invited a representative from the Roman Catholic Church as they had more experience in these matters. A government minister, who didn't want to be named, also attended.

Bishop Docherty, 'As you know, publicly we don't hold with supernatural powers, but clearly, there has been a serious breakdown between the spiritual realms. My team have come up with the following conclusions:

- The Fay has got a dedicated hit team
- They assassinated Reverend John Smith, a dedicated and conservative man of the cloth
- It was some form of ritual murder as his penis and testicles had been cut off and placed around a young girl's neck. The vicar's body was found with a large cactus sticking through his flies.
- On the wall written in blood was the message,
  'Luke 17:2 It were better for him that a millstone was hanged about his neck, and he cast into the sea, than that he should offend one of these little ones.'
- We can only assume that Mr Smith was onto something and they took him out to keep him quiet
- We are not sure why the Mason and Cogan families were eliminated one by one. Again, we suspect that they knew too much
- Then there were further ritual killings—15 people were turned to dust

- The magpie and vole attacks were a deliberate attack against the church. They were more or less saying that they can do what they like.
- The Fay assassin was spotted although all records were destroyed. The Team believe that there has been a fair amount of mind-warping.
- The forced impregnation of the three women smacks of satanic involvement
- The fact that angels have been involved also suggests that Heaven is on the case except a reliable witness says that two angels were assassinated. God would never allow that.
- Then the angel bodies disappeared from secure storage

'Most of the above could have been 'patched up,' but the destruction of Burgess Hill by a meteorite, unprecedented volcanic activity and lightning bolts has made it all rather complicated.'

Deacon Bell, 'So what we are saying is that at least three forces are at work:

- The Fay
- Hell
- Heaven.'

Bishop Docherty, 'It certainly looks that way. There is far too much evidence just to ignore it as a coincidence. Things are going on that we need to understand.'

Descon Bell, 'Evil things.'

Bishop Docherty, 'Yes, to put it mildly. Mass murder, rape, ritual killings, black magick, genocide, mind-control and who knows what else.'

Deacon Bell, 'Where is our favourite white witch? He normally attends these meetings.'

Bishop Docherty, 'He has been magpied.'

Deacon Bell, 'Not Janus?'

Bishop Docherty, 'I'm afraid so; he is headless.'

Deacon Bell, 'Are they coming for us?'

Bishop Docherty, 'Possibly.'

Unknown Minister, 'I can organise a security detail.'

Bishop Docherty, 'They will be of little use against the powers of evil.'

Deacon Bell, 'If they can take Janus out, then we have little hope.'

Bishop Wilson, 'There is always hope; that is the basis of our faith.'

Deacon Bell, 'I agree with you, Madam Bishop, but how do we defend ourselves?'

Bishop Wilson, 'God will show us a way.'

Bishop Docherty, 'I'm sure that he will, but we still need a plan.'

112

God has his Beer

God always enjoyed his pint with Lucifer. He always said it as it was. Although he was the angel of lies and deceit, he was still honest.

Lucifer, 'You know after breasts, your second-best invention was beer.'
God, 'I think you may be right. So tell me why you killed those two angels?'
Lucifer, 'It wasn't me, boss.'
God, 'Then who was it?'
Lucifer, 'The only options are humans or the Fay.'
God, 'But humans love angels. I made them that way.'
Lucifer, 'In that case you have your answer. It's those runts.'
God, 'Those tiny wee creatures? How could they take out two senior angels?'
Lucifer, 'You know. They used Qeres.'
God, 'Yes, I forgot. I will decimate them.'
Lucifer, 'You should and you must, but we need a plan.'

113

Plans, damned Plans, and no Sign of Statistics

I'm back. Time for some more narration. It's my attempt to guide you through this quagmire. I think the whole story has become a bit stilted. Well, let's see where we are.

Firstly, May is trying to avoid being killed. I'm not sure why they are trying to kill her. Being a changeling is not really her fault. I don't rate her chances, but perhaps the author will surprise us.

The Government—and specifically Stella Weller—is putting a plan together. You can't accuse them of being particularly active. And what sort of plan could they formulate to fight magickal forces? But then humanity has succeeded in the past.

The Church is also putting a plan together. They have more experience in fighting the dark forces but are they now a spent force?

Lucifer has possibly convinced God that a plan is needed regarding the Fay rather than just random action. You can never tell whether God has listened or not.

Fayden is reasonably sure that there are challenges ahead. She feels that they need to carefully tread the path between Heaven and Hell and those ploughmen. Despite her meeting with God, she knew that retribution regarding the two dead angels was on its way.

So for once, the author has constructed a plausible plot. The clashing of four plans should be interesting, although I have my doubts.

Book wise, we have probably crossed the halfway point, although I'm not sure how he is going to drag it out to 80,000 words. More lists probably. Is it time to try and guess the end of the book?

I predict one of the following:

- A calamitous war between Heaven and Hell on Earth
- A similar war between The Fay and humanity

- The End of Danny
- Danny does something amazing
- Magick is used to put everything back to normal.

The chances of a great ending are a thousand to one.

114

God gets it Wrong

If God could drink what he liked and not get drunk, then what was the point in drinking? A drunken God was not a good idea. A drunken, vengeful God was even worse.

God knew that Beelzebub killed those angels. Even if he didn't, it was time to teach him a lesson. It had been a long time coming: a few hundred thousand years. He called a meeting of the War Council, the first one in living memory.

The attendees were Azrael, Camael, Gabriel and Michael, and of course, God.

God, 'My warrior angels, leaders of the legions, I have decided to declare war on Hell...'

Azrael, 'Excellent my lord; can I ask why? We have been at peace for many millennia.'

God, 'I don't need to justify my actions.'

Azrael, 'Of course not, my lord, it was just curiosity. I will go and organise death and destruction immediately.'

God, 'Stop, we need to plan this war carefully. And to answer your question, firstly we are avenging Laylah and Michael. Secondly, there was an illegal use of Qeres and lastly it is because Lucifer is far too red.'

Camael, 'Lord, I'm keen to follow your orders. Can I ask you what our objectives would be?'

God, 'Punishment my boy, punishment.'

Camael, 'So it's just a smack on the bum. You don't want us to conquer Hell?'

God, 'Let's see how it progresses.'

Camael, 'We outnumber them 2:1, it should be a walkover.'

Gabriel, 'Camael, you might be a bit optimistic. Our forces have not fought in an exceedingly long time. Their weapons have not been used in anger since the birth of humanity.'

Michael, 'Our might will not be denied. I say attack now. Let's catch them totally unawares.'

God, 'Last time we did that they fought us to a standstill.'

Michael, 'That's because they had better weapons than us.'

God, 'And has anything changed?'

Michael, 'No, lord; I see where you are coming from.'

God, 'I'm wondering if we should get some human assistance. They have had a lot more military experience than us. Much more.'

Gabriel, 'But that would mean them coming to Heaven.'

God, 'Well a lot of them do you know. Anyway, we could meet half-way. Gabriel, I want you to meet with Bishop Docherty to discuss a possible alliance.'

Gabriel, 'Yes, my lord.'

God, 'Michael, 'I would like you to review our forces and plan for the attack.'

Michael, 'Of course, your majesty.'

115

Lucifer gets it Wronger

Asbeel, one of the fallen angels, 'My demonic majesty, I have grave news.'

Satan, 'And what's that, my angelic fiend?'

Asbeel, 'Our sources above (the word Heaven was banned) indicate that they are planning an attack.'

Satan, 'Not again.'

Asbeel, 'To be fair, my lord, they haven't been that frequent.'

Satan, 'That old fool gets it wrong every time. It's about time he was pensioned off.'

Asbeel, 'And, my lord, there is another development. They are planning to form an alliance with the humans.'

Satan, 'That's quite innovative. They have the numbers and equipment. What are our options?'

Asbeel, 'We could try to beat upstairs to an alliance with the humans.'

Satan, 'I'm not sure why but we've always had bad press with the short-lived.'

Asbeel, 'The other option is The Fay.'

Satan, 'What use are they?'

Asbeel, 'I know that you have never had much time for them, but they do have magickal powers. They could certainly give the humans a few issues.'

Satan, 'OK, Asbeel get me an alliance with Fatwhat.'

Asbeel, 'Yes, my lord.'

Satan, 'And get me Tamiel.'

Asbeel, 'Yes, my lord.'

In the flick of a heartbeat, Tamiel was present and presenting himself.

Tamiel, 'My demonic majesty, how can I be of assistance?'

Satan, 'Them upstairs are planning to attack us.

Tamiel, 'We beat them last time, we will beat them again.'

Satan, 'Last time they thought that they were going to surprise us. You know what upstairs is like, it's a rumour mill.'

Tamiel, 'More like a sieve.'

Satan, 'It will be harder this time. I want you to plan our defence.'

Tamiel, 'Yes, my lord.'

Satan, 'And if you get a chance, we need to kill the old bugger.'

116

May gets it Right

It is notoriously hard to kill a fairy, any sort. There is a view that they are a force of nature and you can't kill nature although the ploughmen were having a good go at it. There is hardly any reference to death amongst the Fay.

But May knew better. She knew because she was half fairy that what kills a fairy is iron or steel. Other metals are fine. The Fay like gold and they love silver. Silver is the colour of the Moon. However, few knew that to kill a fairy, it had to be struck in the heart. Even fewer knew that a fairy's heart was just behind their coccyx.

May had escaped once, but she knew that they would be back almost every night until the job was done. They are persistent little buggers. It just happens that May had a mannequin with a long blonde wig. It is even stranger that she used to display it in the downstairs windows partly to ward off burglars and other undesirables, and partly because it was fun. Neighbours and passing children had got used to it, and some even waved. They never got a wave back.

Now was his chance. She was sitting there by the window. He would teleport into the lounge and simply stab her in the back. Quick and easy. No finesse but the job would be done, and he could have a long-deserved rest. The model had no resemblance to May whatsoever, but to The Fay, the ploughmen and ploughwomen all looked much the same.

The Fay knife struck the fibreglass body of the model to no avail, but May's cold steel knife pierced straight into the flesh above the coccyx into the heart. Danny was dead. This time he was not going to come back. Now there were only 38 elves.

The entire Fay world felt the death. It was such a rare occurrence. Under Fay Lore, May was now freed from their attacks. She could live again.

Author's note to Narrator, 'Stuff that up your jumper!'

117

But then it went wrong

May was ecstatic—she knew that she was safe now. She stood and watched as Danny's body started to fade and then disappear. It was the Fay way.

It was ironic that May's saviour became her curse. That very night, one of the undesirables broke in to steal the mannequin. May rushed downstairs to meet the wrong end of a knife. She bled to death, but no one noticed. The mannequin made a full recovery.

118

Latest Body Count

It's the Narrator again. Quite a short gap this time. If you measured a novel by the number of deaths, then this novel is doing quite well.

Name	Current Status
Narrator	Still alive
Dolores	Still alive
Doug	Dead—Killed by a meteorite
June	Dead—Suicide
Isabella	Dead—Accidentally sucked to death by Danny
Old Irishman	Dead—Arrow shot
Ivor	Dead—Drowned in the bath
John	Dead—Genitalia removed
Polly	Dead—Volcanic gases
Janus	Dead—Death by Magpie
Jim	Dead—Suffocated by a vagina
Carol	Dead—Suicide
Emma	Dead—Crushed by a giant hand
Mr Brown	Dead—Fucked to death
Mrs Brown	Dead—Crushed by a giant hand
Keith	Dead—Bled to death
Jill	Dead—Crushed by a giant hand
Fairy Queen	Still alive
Laylah	Dead—Killed by an arrow
Officer Newman	Dead—Eaten by a magpie
Officer Cave	Dead—Eaten by a vole
Police Inspector	Dead—Elevator accident

Police Commissioner	Dead—Elevator accident
Fayden	Alive
MI5 Officer	Dead—Crushed by a giant hand
Sergeant Baker	Dead—Crushed by a giant hand
Danny	Dead—Stabbed
May	Dead—Stabbed

Now it has gone the other way. There are far too many new characters:

- The Prime Minister
- Chief Secretary to the Prime Minister, soon to be replaced by Stella Weller, Chief Secretary to the Prime Minister
- Chief Clerk
- Home Office Consultant
- God
- Linda
- Lord Elderberry of the Enchanted Eleonores
- Lord Rufus Randytoad of the Roundheadians
- Satan, sometimes called Beelzebub or Lucifer
- The Archbishop of Canterbury
- Chief Inspector Morris
- UK Head Scientist
- Janus
- Bishop Docherty
- Deacon Bell
- Bishop Wilson
- Azrael
- Camael
- Michael
- Gabriel
- Asbeel
- Tamiel

That's 23 new characters since Chapter 96. That's almost one new character for every two pages. It's really not good enough. In my view, this project should be terminated.

Publisher. 'No way! The author had an advance. This baby is going to market.'

Narrator, 'It's going to need a lot of editing.'

Publisher, 'That might be the case, but it's going to be on the shelves at WH Smith.'

Narrator, 'Not at the Burgess Hill branch.'

Publisher, 'They will be back.'

119

God did show us the way

Bishop Docherty presided over the latest meeting of the secret subsection of a secret subsection of The Church of England Parochial Church Council.

The Committee had the same members as last time:

- Bishop Docherty (Catholic)
- Bishop Wilson (C of E)
- Deacon Bell (C of E)
- Unknown Government Minister

Bishop Docherty, 'At the last meeting Bishop Wilson said, "God will show us the way". I need to apologise as I treated the remark with scorn, and I was wrong.

'I need to introduce you to an honoured guest, a very honoured guest.'

Bishop Docherty knocked on an adjacent door and in walked Gabriel with the full-wing effect. To say that the room was awestruck would be a major understatement.

Deacon Bell, 'You are an angel!'

Gabriel, 'Yes, Deacon Bell, I am Gabriel.'

Deacon Bell, 'The one in the Bible?'

Gabriel, 'Yes, that one.'

Deacon Bell, 'You must be at least a thousand years old.'

Gabriel, 'More like a hundred thousand.'

Bishop Wilson, 'You are very welcome.'

Gabriel, 'I appreciate that, Denise.'

Bishop Wilson, 'How did you know my name?'

Gabriel, 'I know everyone's name.'

Unknown Minster, 'You expect me to believe that you are Angel

Gabriel?'

Gabriel, 'I do, John Maldive. It is a pleasure to meet you. You have done some great work helping the poor.'

Bishop Docherty, 'We were meeting to put a plan together to fight the forces of darkness. There have been many strange paranormal events during the last few months.'

Gabriel, 'As Bob Dylan once said, "The Times they are a-Changin'". There is a coming war between Heaven and Hell. God has requested assistance from his flock. We need military assistance and expertise.'

Unknown Minster, 'You want military help from your subjects?'

Gabriel, 'That's correct. We are looking for the following:

- Strategic planning
- Weapons Supply
- Logistical Support
- Training
- Intelligence Support
- Air attack and defence
- Infantry
- Armoured divisions
- And anything else that you think relevant.

Angelkind have not been in battle for a very, very, long time. In fact, before humans existed.

Do we have your support?'

Bishop Docherty, 'I commit the Roman Catholic Church.'

Bishop Wilson, 'I commit the Church of England, the Protestant Movement and the non-aligned churches.'

John Maldive, 'I commit the military power of the Christian democracies, but I will need your presence to obtain it.'

Gabriel, 'I'm sure that I can even get God to make a visit.'

120

Time Moves Very Quickly

Fayden was concerned, very concerned. Usually for her, time moved fairly slowly but things were hotting up. Unlike the ploughmen, they only measured time in days and years. Seconds, minutes, hours, weeks, and months did not exist. They were not real, just figments of imagination created by the ploughmen in their efforts to control their short and complex lives.

To be honest, she wished that they did have additional time units as their clock was a bit like 'when the sun appears over the hill' or 'the first whiskers of evening tide', or, 'when the moon wanes on the third day'. It was awfully hard to work out exactly when a meeting was going to happen.

If you took into account their method of travel, then it became even more difficult. Some of the wild-folk had only just got back home from the last meeting using shanks' pony. Others teleported instantly, although teleporting had to use a line of sight or strong memories in the mind's eye. There had been many disasters with friends fatally arriving in the middle of a tree.

Fayden's concern was not just the concern of being a leader. It was more about possible futures. Every future she scanned led to death and destruction. Not just for the Fay. Human cities were devastated. Heaven and Hell were in ruins. The old order had been shattered. She wondered if she should call a Fleenation. One had never been called in her lifetime, and that was an exceedingly long time.

A meeting of the Fay Council was due, but that would result in days if not weeks of indecisive squabbling. The Fay were not good at decision-making. A strong leader had to recognise this and act for the general good.

She decided to meet with Rufus and Elderberry and if they agreed she would call a Fleenation.

Rufus and Elderberry teleported in, missing the local trees but almost arriving in the same space. That would have been a disaster for them and her. These were the only two that she could rely on.

All three sat down by the table of the Allfree and sipped some mead. Fayden hated the sweet sickly stuff, but it was a necessary precursor to a meeting.

Fayden, 'Good morning, my brave advisors.'

They both responded accordingly, and she continued, 'I've asked for this meeting as I need to make a decision. Before I start, can I ask how you feel?'

Lord Elderberry of the Enchanted Eleonores, 'Your majesty, I have a feeling of dread. My body, my mind and my spirit are all screaming warnings of a terrible future. My gut tells me that there is a strong likelihood of our kind being no more. Evil forces are being aligned against us.'

Fayden, 'When did this start?'

Lord Elderberry of the Enchanted Eleonores, 'With the death of the elf. They cannot die, and it did.'

Fayden, 'So could your worries be directly related to that?'

Lord Elderberry of the Enchanted Eleonores, 'I don't think so, your majesty, it goes deeper. It is time to hide. It's time for us to return to our roots.'

Lord Rufus Randytoad of the Roundheadians, 'Can I jump in, your majesty? I've noticed that some of the werecreatures are already hibernating. Those up north are building fat stocks and growing their fur. It's going to be a very long winter.'

Fayden, 'How do you feel?'

Lord Rufus Randytoad of the Roundheadians, 'I plan to join the werecreatures. Something is calling me to shelter in my ancestral home. For the first time in my life, I have a fear of death.'

A shiver ran down Fayden's back. She felt the same.

Fayden. 'The wind smells different. The earth beneath my feet beckons. The creatures of the field are sleepy. The moon grows cold. The clouds scatter in fear.'

Lord Rufus Randytoad of the Roundheadians, 'You are going to do it, aren't you?'

Fayden, 'Yes, Lord Rufus.'

Lord Rufus Randytoad of the Roundheadians, 'Have you really thought it through?'

Fayden, 'What is there to think about? We know, don't we?'

Lord Elderberry of the Enchanted Eleonores, 'I think we know. No, we *do* know. Our Queen is right.'

Lord Rufus Randytoad of the Roundheadians, 'Then so be it.'

Fayden walked to the corner of the room and took the trumpet off the wall. This was a trumpet that had not been used in a hundred thousand years. This was the trumpet that every Fay could hear everywhere in the world.

One blast was a call to arms, two blasts were to lay down your weapons, and three blasts were to hide.

- By 'hide' it meant to go to the dark secret, obscure places that no one visits
- By 'hide' it meant to hibernate
- By 'hide' it meant to avoid any non-Fay
- By 'hide' it meant to seek concealment
- By 'hide' it meant be armed, be prepared and be ready for a single blast
- By 'hide' it meant to keep out of sight
- By 'hide' it meant only meet in small clandestine groups when absolutely necessary
- By 'hide' it meant use magick to create a covert veil of secrecy.

The Fay would shut themselves off from the world. There would be a complete communications shutdown so that they could weather the storm.

Fayden blew the three blasts. Every Fay heard it. The shutdown was underway. Five blasts would end the hibernation.

121

In Satanland

Satan was luxuriating in a slime bog with his demonesses. He planned to fuck a dozen of them this morning and possibly eat one for lunch. You know how lovemaking can get out of hand, A little nibble here and another one there and suddenly you have got through a complete set of genitals, the odd thigh bone, and a bunch of breasts.

Asbeel, 'Your demonic lordship, I have less than good news.'

Satan, 'You are ruining my mood.'

Asbeel, 'Apologies, your satanic majesty, but two events have happened.'

Satan, Go on.'

Asbeel, 'Gabriel has met with the secret subsection of a secret subsection of The Church of England Parochial Church Council.'

Satan, 'I bet that was fun.'

Asbeel, 'We can only assume that they have formed or are forming an alliance.'

Satan, 'OK, well, Earth is a complex place. What assets can we call upon?'

Asbeel, 'Just the normal:
- The Vampires
- The Werewolves
- The Creatures from the Black Lagoon
- The Republican Party
- Conservative Head Office
- The Anti-Brexiters.'

Satan, 'Start the process of activating them. What's the second point.'

Asbeel, 'The Fay have sounded the horn of Fleenation.'

Satan, 'What does that mean?'

Asbeel, 'They have gone into lockdown.'

Satan, 'What does that mean to us?'

Asbell, 'It means that they are of no use to us as an ally.'

Satan, *'C'est la vie.'*

Asbell, 'Yes, my lord.'

Satan, 'So it's us against the forces of the above and humanity?'

Asbell, 'Yes, my lord.'

122

The PM takes a Lead

The PM called a progress meeting as pressure was building up from the Sussex constituencies. Panorama had carried out a very embarrassing in-depth exposé on "The Sussex Demon". Answers were needed, and they were needed now.

The meeting had the same attendees as before:

- The Chief Secretary, Stella Weller
- The Home Secretary
- The Head of the National Crime Agency
- A SAS representative
- The Archbishop of Canterbury
- The Head of MI5
- UK Head Scientist

There was one new delegate: Bishop Docherty.

PM, 'Welcome to the second meeting of this extraordinary committee. I would like to offer a warm welcome to Bishop Docherty. Since the last session, we have had the Panorama special. The public is demanding action. Consequently, I intend to hand over to Stella Weller and her action plan.'

Stella Weller, 'I have an incredibly detailed action plan.' She threw it on the table. 'But that has been trumped by something unbelievable.' The Archbishop of Canterbury and Bishop Docherty had huge smiles on their faces. Possibly the *hugest* smiles ever seen on human beings. All of their doubts and all of the cynicism that they had experienced over the decades had been wiped out. This was their moment.

The bishop was sure that he heard trumpets as Gabriel entered the room, along with John Maldive, the unknown minister.

The PM's jaw dropped and then dropped a bit more. The SAS

representative went for his gun. The Head of MI5 hid under the table. The room was silent, very silent. No one knew what to say.

The Archbishop of Canterbury and Bishop Docherty got on their knees.

Gabriel, 'Please be calm my children, I am Gabriel. Yes, the one from the Bible.'

PM, 'You mean the one from the Bible?'

Gabriel, 'That very one.'

PM. 'I can't believe it.'

Gabriel, 'Geoff, you have no choice. I'm here. Please feel free to touch me.'

The Archbishop of Canterbury, 'Mr Prime Minister, I can confirm that our angelic friend is who he says he is. There is no doubt.'

The gun was reholstered and the Head of MI5 resumed his seat.

PM, 'Stella is this part of the plan?'

Stella Weller, 'Not exactly, Prime Minister. Gabriel has a message from God and a request. I suggest that I hand over to Gabriel, who can explain.'

Gabriel, 'I know that we have a mixture of believers and non-believers. That is normal. It's partly our fault as the heavenly message has been heavily corrupted over the years.

'Let me give you some history.

'Our God, or another god or even a group of gods, created the universe probably using some form of Big Bang. It's all a bit unclear, and our father doesn't like to talk about it.

'Anyway, our God created a hotchpotch of realms centred around the planet Earth.

'There were competing gods from Mount Olympus, Asgard and several other mythological places. These have mostly disappeared or moved on. Again, this is a taboo subject.

'Our God seemed to be on his own, and perhaps due to loneliness, he created us, angels. His creativity knows no bounds, so he started creating different types of angel, divided into choirs. They included the following: Seraphim, Cherubim, Thrones, Dominions, Virtues, Powers, Principalities, Archangels and Angels.

'Don't ask me about the differences. Some are warriors; others are messengers, healers, watchers, etc.

'Angels, as you probably know, don't have souls. I've never been too sure why that mattered.

'Our God decided to create creatures with souls. That's you lot and possibly all living creatures.'

PM, 'Can I stop you there? What is so special about a soul?'

Gabriel, 'That's a tricky question. Dozens of your philosophers and spiritual leaders have discussed that for centuries. The following definitions have been suggested:

- It is the incorporeal essence of a living being.
- It is a combination of the mental abilities of a living being: reason, character, feeling, consciousness, memory, perception, thinking, etc.
- It may or may not be immortal depending on which religion you choose.

'Thomas Aquinas attributed "soul" (anima) to all organisms but argued that only human souls are immortal.

'Socrates, Plato, and Aristotle understood that the soul must have a logical faculty, the exercise of which was the most divine of human actions.

Hinduism and Jainism believe that all living things from the smallest bacterium to the largest of mammals have souls.

'I could go on and on, but it is not clear. I've never had one to miss. Shall I carry on with the history?'

PM, 'Yes, please.'

Gabriel, 'OK, the following happened a long time ago and is subject to reversioning.'

PM, 'Reversioning?'

Gabriel, 'God often changes history to suit his current needs, or rather, his ego.'

PM, 'We call that changing the manifesto when we get into power.'

Gabriel, 'Quite so.'

Stella Weller, 'It strikes me that God is a bit chaotic.'

Gabriel, 'He is the boss. He does what he wants. He doesn't like advice although he sometimes pretends to seek it. He is changeable, erratic, inconsistent, annoying, irritating, but we love him.'

235

Stella Weller, 'You love him?'

Gabriel, 'We have no choice; we were designed and created to love him. He has always been pissed off that not all humans love him.'

Stella Weller, 'Why didn't he make *us* love him?'

Gabriel, 'He gave you free will. I think he has always regretted that. He retrofitted it onto us angels, so we ended up with no souls but limited free will.'

Stella Weller, 'Was that a problem?'

Gabriel, 'Indirectly, it led to a war in Heaven. Let me continue:
- God created man and decided that the angels should bow down to his latest creation
- Many angels refused to do this
- The gift of free will meant that the angels did not have to do God's bidding, much of which was helping humans
- God then announced that he was going to have a human son and that he would be second in command in Heaven
- Some of the senior angels rebelled, including Satan
- There was a terrible war which God only just won
- Satan and about a third of the angels were cast into Hell by God

'In subsequent battles, there has usually been a stalemate. God is almighty but not that almighty.'

PM, 'So what about this Sussex Demon?'

Gabriel, 'That's an elf. Nothing to do with Heaven.'

PM, 'Do they come from Hell?

Gabriel, 'Again, it gets complicated. The Fay believe, that there was a war in Heaven, and God ordered that the gates should be closed. Those in Heaven became angels; those in Hell became demons, and those in between became fairies. Clearly, it is absolute nonsense.'

PM, 'Clearly.'

He noticed that Gabriel had folded his wings, so perhaps this story was coming to an end. To him, it seemed a worse state of affairs than PMQs. 'So where do they come from?'

Gabriel, 'When God created life on Earth, he created spirit keepers to mind the wilderness. In his wisdom, he created many different types of fairy: elves, gremlins, pixies, goblins, gnomes, etc. Collectively, they are the little folk or as they liked to be called, The Fay.

PM, 'And this Sussex Demon was a fairy?'

Gabriel, 'Yes.'

PM, 'So he wasn't a demon?'

Gabriel, 'That's correct.'

PM, 'So what's a demon?'

Gabriel, 'Geoff, I can see that this is not making sense to you. Let's have another go,' and he drew the following chart on the board:

Type	Division
Gods	
	Judeo-Christian
	Hindu
Angel	
	Seraphim
	Cherubim
	Thrones
	Thrones
	Dominions
	Virtues
	Powers
	Principalities
	Archangels
	Angels.
Devil	
	Angels
	Demons
The Fay	
	The Asrai
	The Pixi
	The Elfi
	The Mersi
	The Bansheei
	The Leprechauni
	The Browni

	The Impi	
	The Famili	
	The Gremli	
Humans		
	Homo Sapiens	
	Vampires	
	Werewolves	
	Witches (and warlocks)	
	Ogres	
	Orcs	
	Trolls	
Spirit		
	Elementals	
	Ghosts	
	The Undead	
	Golems	
History		
	Greek and Roman Gods	
	The Dragoni (Dragons)	
	The Valkyrie	
	Unicorns	

'Demons are creations of the Devil, but they could be classed as spirits.'

PM, 'So why did this fairy attack Sussex?'

Gabriel, 'We are not entirely sure. There must have been a reason, but elves are notoriously fickle creatures. It might just be a simple act of revenge.'

PM, 'He killed 40,000 humans. That is just not acceptable. Anyway, I need to understand why you are here.'

Gabriel, 'Your colleagues have pledged me your support. God has declared war on Hell, and he demands assistance from his human subjects.'

PM, 'And why has he declared war on Hell?'

Gabriel, 'Because he has. It is his right.'

PM, 'What are his objectives?'

The Archbishop of Canterbury, 'We are honour-bound to go to God's aid.'

PM, 'Why?'

The Archbishop of Canterbury, 'Because he is God.'

PM, 'I don't see your logic. God has unilaterally declared war on Hell because he can. We would be condemning countless humans to death and for what?'

The Archbishop of Canterbury, 'For *God*, you cretin! We must go to his aid. He commands it.'

PM. 'I'm not here to do God's bidding.'

The Archbishop of Canterbury, 'Then why are you here?!'

He grabbed the gun from the SAS Officer and shot the Prime Minister in the head.

The meeting ended rather abruptly.

123

Fifty Thousand Words

We are at the 50,000 words mark. I must admit I didn't expect Danny or the Prime Minister to get killed.

I need to go back to one of my hobby horses: lists. Alan plonker Frost just uses text as a preamble to his list-making. My list of lists on page 179 contained about 40 examples. I wonder how many new lists we have had since then:

Page No	List Name
180	List of Danny's Crimes
182	List of Indictments
182	List of Actions requested by the Council
183	List of Danny's Successes
189	List of Meeting Attendees
189 -190	List of Inexplicable Events
190-191	List of Evidence Items
193	List of Magickal Lores
195-196	List of Killing Techniques
198-199	List of Conclusions
202	List of Predictions
209	List of Deaths
209 - 210	List of New Characters
211	List of Committee Members
212	List of Gabriel's Requirement
215	A Definition what 'Hide' means
216	List of Earth Assets
218	List of Meeting Attendees
219-221	List of Historical Events
222-223	List of Entities
225	Another list of lists

I don't want to go on about this, but by now you must see my point. Actually, that is probably not the case. If you are stupid enough to read the book this far, then you are probably a bigger tosser than the writer, and he has reached levels of tosserhood that I previously thought to be unobtainable by a mere mortal.

At least the graphic sex has come to an end.

124

Gabriel goes the Way of all Angels

Stella realised that there would be security bustling around the room in no time at all. It's not every day that the Prime Minister of the UK is assassinated by the Archbishop of Canterbury. The world was not ready for Gabriel yet, so she pushed him into a small ante-room and locked the door.

They could hear the commotion next door, but no one disturbed them.

Stella, 'So what do you angels do for fun?'

Gabriel, 'We are here to serve, not to have fun.'

Stella, 'Don't you have any hobbies?'

Gabriel, 'My hobby is to serve.'

Stella,' Haven't you ever strayed from your service to your lord?'

Gabriel, 'Never. I was the messenger foretelling the birth of John the Baptist and Jesus Christ. I held the hand of Mary. I sit by the right hand of God.'

Stella, 'What about a Murray Mint? Have you tried one of them?'

Gabriel, 'I have no time for fancies, I am Gabriel. I have a mission.'

Stella, 'Just try it.' And she popped it into his mouth.

Gabriel, 'In all my time I have never tried anything so delightful. It is heavenly.'

Stella, 'And you should know.'

Gabriel, 'Could I have another one?'

Stella, 'Of course. It's best to suck rather than crunch.'

Gabriel, 'It's a delight beyond any of my experiences.'

Stella, 'There are a lot more things that you ought to try.'

Gabriel, 'You want to fornicate. You are a harlot.'

Stella, 'To be fair it had crossed my mind. You are exceptionally

242

good-looking, and we are stuck in a hot room with little to do.'

Gabriel, 'I appreciate your beauty and your interest, but angels are beings of light not of the flesh.'

Stella, 'Are you saying that you can't have sex?'

Gabriel, 'I'm not saying that. What I'm saying is that we are higher beings. Pure lustful fornication is not one of our natural instincts.'

Stella, 'That doesn't seem to be the case from the records I've got. Laylah and Michael were fucking everything in sight, including each other.'

Gabriel, 'It's being on Earth, it changes our ways.'

Stella, 'I think it's getting rather hot in here.' She very slowly and provocatively removed her skirt to display a beautiful pair of legs and very skimpy panties. She noticed a slight bulge in his trousers. Women like to check that their ministrations are working.

Gabriel, 'It is getting rather hot in here.'

Stella, 'You are right.' Stella removed her blouse. Gabriel was showing more interest than a well-bred angel should.

Gabriel, 'I think that's enough. Please keep the rest of your clothes on.'

Stella, 'Why would you care whether I keep my clothes on or not? You are not interested in carnal activities. Anyway, I don't believe that you can get it up.'

Gabriel, 'What do you mean by that?'

Stella, 'What I'm saying is that you can't get your penis hard. You can't get an erection. You have never experienced a stiffie.'

Gabriel, 'That's not true.'

Stella, 'Prove it.'

Gabriel pulled a fully erect todger out of his tights. It was a very respectable beastie in terms of length and girth. It was as rigid as a stick of Blackpool rock and similar in size.

Stella. 'And are you saying that your boy has never experienced the joys of a soft, juicy fanny? Gabriel nodded his head. Stella released a set of well-proportioned, firm breasts. Gabriel had never been this close to naked breasts before. He asked if he could touch them, and she nodded.

They were scooped up, fondled, sucked, tweaked, and lovingly caressed. Stella's panties slowly dropped to the floor.

Standing in front of him was a totally naked woman. As far as he was concerned, she was the angel.

Stella bent over, presenting a fine set of buttocks and a very juicy looking fanny. Gabriel relished the slow entry of his throbbing todger into her moist cunt. He could smell her. He could taste her. For the first time in his exceptionally long life, he started to fuck a woman, an exceptionally beautiful woman. Stella thought that it made a nice change from fucking the Prime Minister.

Gabriel used his virgin todger with great abandon. He was using his wings to keep his balance, but Stella was being thrown all over the place. She was being fucked hard by the messenger of God, and she could tell that it wouldn't be long before he sent her a message.

Gabriel felt a huge pressure in his loins. There was an ache that he had never had before that had to be released. A few more thrusts and he should be there. The explosion when it came was legendary. The sheer volume and quantity of spunk was prodigious, and it just kept coming.

Stella had never seen anything like it. There were piles of thick, steamy semen on the floor and walls. It was not dribbling out it was pouring out. Gabriel looked at Stella in dismay and said, 'Was this normal?'

Stella shook her head. She shook it again as she could see no end to this outpouring. It was either a punishment from God or the fact there had been 100,000 years of pent-up production. Stella thought that it was best to leave him to it. It had been a strange day.

125

And there were Others

The archbishop never expected to be standing there with a smoking gun in his hand. He never thought that he could kill anyone. But of course, the PM was an atheist. The world is better without them. 'A curse on them all,' he muttered. He noticed that Stella had quickly bundled Gabriel out of the room, which was quick thinking, especially with shooting going on.

He aimed the gun at the other attendees and shot the Home Secretary, the Head of MI5, and the Head of the National Crime Agency. He suspected that they were all atheists, or possibly agnostics but then if they can't make their mind up, they deserve to die. He excluded the head scientist as he was wearing a cross on a chain.

Now he had to raise the banner for God. It was a call to arms on behalf of the believers. It was a crusade against the forces of evil. The archbishop was determined to lead a multi-national military legion against Beelzebub, the Lord of Flies.

Bishop Docherty was fully supportive of the archbishop's actions. It was a time for great deeds. The weak and the ignorant need to be swept aside in a new holy struggle to claim mankind's rightful place. He had always been fascinated with Lucifer. It was strange that he was never mentioned in Genesis, but many scholars thought that he was probably the serpent in the garden of Eden. However, in the Book of Revelations, he is the Great Red Dragon. But we are coming for you.

The two bishops escaped because they were bishops and beyond approach. Fortunately, or unfortunately, depending on which side of the fence you rest, they left a witness: the head scientist.

Both churches had significant support in the military and police. Many individuals were torn between their loyalty to the Crown and God.

Strings were pulled. Docherty activated contacts he had in the IRA, and the archbishop had a similar relationship with the Freemasons. The Establishment was gearing up to champion the cause of righteousness.

The Church of England had pulled strings to get a prime spot on TV. Gabriel would become a TV star.

126

Sperm Stories

You have probably been wondering what happened to Gabriel. After Stella left, spunk continued to pour out of Gabriel's penis. After a few hours, it was nearly a foot deep in the little room, and it showed no signs of stopping.

Gabriel had no choice but to fly back to Heaven under cover of darkness. The seepage continued spraying large parts of the Earth with ejaculated reproductive seed. There were spermatozoa everywhere. Gabriel was embarrassed, but it wasn't all bad. It was one hell of an orgasm.

God was in stitches when he saw Gabriel's plight. He stopped it with one twitch of his fingers. God, as we know, had always enjoyed the female form and was quite happy to have the odd dip. Mary being one of his conquests.

God had always produced vast amounts of the mucky stuff. He needed somewhere safe to store it as it contained powerful magick. The magick of creation. He needed to keep it somewhere totally safe where it wouldn't be used. He soon realised that Gabriel's testicles would be the perfect place.

God, 'So Gabriel, after all this time, you shot your load?'

Gabriel, 'Yes, my lord.'

God, 'Did you enjoy it?'

Gabriel, 'That and the Murray Mint were heavenly.'

God, 'Murray Mint?'

Gabriel, 'It's a famous human delicacy. I will get you some.'

God, 'So you enjoyed Stella's charms?'

Gabriel, 'I certainly did.'

God, 'And will you be using them again?'

Gabriel, 'I'm not sure.'

God, 'I'm sure.'

127

Sperm Stories Number 2

Some say that a policeman's lot is never a happy one, but it's far worse working in the cleaning fraternity. Let's take an example and look at Edna.

Edna had just had a week off work in Blackpool. That was her annual holiday in a rather dreary B&B. It rained most of the time, but she enjoyed watching the children play in the arcade while she drank her stout. She had always wanted children, but she had spent most of her life looking after her invalid mother. A mother she hated.

Edna never knew her father. She doubted that he ever existed. She was embarrassed that she had never been with a man. At the age of 56, but looking ten years older, the chances of losing her virginity were now rather slim. Anyway, she suspected that it had all dried up.

It was Tuesday morning and time for work. She got up late and had to miss her breakfast, and the bus was late. She was getting grumpier and grumpier. The adverts of sun-baked desert islands on the bus didn't help. Her boss was going to give her a good ticking off for being late and knock a couple of pounds off her minimum wage. That was life.

When she arrived, there was no boss, which was a relief. She clocked in and started her cleaning round.

She was a bit surprised to find four significant bloodstains in the conference room. It took her a while to remove the sticky tape. She wondered why it was there, probably the lads playing stupid games. The tape was covered in lettering, which didn't help much as she couldn't read.

It was a real bugger getting the blood off the walls, ceiling, and carpets. She used her dustpan and brush to shovel up what looked like brains. It was hard, smelly work. Anyway, she would soon have the room looking spick and span.

Then she caught a whiff of another fragrance. She tracked the smell down to the small ante-room. On opening the door, she found what looked like a layer of damp cement about two feet thick across the entire room. The stuff was also clinging to the walls, window, and ceiling. She had never seen anything like it in her life. It had a masculine, salty smell.

She soon realised that this was more than a dustpan job and borrowed a wheelbarrow and shovel from the gardener. In the end, there were sixteen barrow loads. For reasons unknown to her, it made her feel randy. She was going to have a bit of a frig when she got home.

Purely by accident, she tasted the substance. It was delightful, otherworldly, and in fact, life-changing. She felt younger, much younger. Her rheumatism stopped aching, and her eyesight improved. She had found ambrosia, the food of the gods.

That night she lost her virginity to a young man in the flat downstairs. Perhaps her lot wasn't as bad as a policeman's.

128

Sperm Stories Number 3

The national newspapers reported an outbreak of miracles throughout the country:

- A lady of 102 had taken a lover of 46 and had got pregnant
- A lame horse had recovered without any treatment
- An entire cancer ward had been mysteriously cured without the aid of modern medical practices
- A war hero had grown a new arm
- A young female herbalist had grown a penis
- A premier league footballer woke up speaking three new languages
- A dog had grown a third set of legs
- A beekeeper had grown wings and could fly
- An accountant had acquired a sense of humour
- A blind man had acquired both normal and telescopic vision
- A cook could taste colours
- A pauper could accurately predict the winning lottery numbers
- A singer could smell music
- A botanist could change her hair colour at will
- A Minister of the Crown could lie convincingly
- A vicar could dance the Charleston
- A fisherman could breathe underwater
- A tailor could transmute lead into gold
- An office worker could convert water into wine
- A docker could seduce any woman he liked and did
- A fish-and-chip shop owner could convert rats into fish
- A beautician could make a man's penis larger by wishing

- A TV reporter could impregnate any woman
- An advertising executive could talk to the unborn

The only common factor was Gabriel's sperm, or technically God's sperm. One lick was all it took.

129

Too much News

Sometimes there is little to report, and you hear stories about sisters being separated at birth and meeting up after fifty years, or ducks that have nested in a sewer or even the unlikely event of trains running on time. Other times there is just too much going on.

The murder of the PM and several senior police officials shocked the country. Most of the Government stated that they would not rest until the culprit was caught while knowing precisely who the murderer was. But what could they do? Half of the personnel in the military and police had joined the "Crusade Against Satan"—CAS for short. Even badges had been distributed.

The Archbishop and Bishop Docherty were under twenty-four-hour security cover. They were scheduled to meet the Pope next week along with a special friend. Once that had been successfully concluded then the special friend would appear on TV. CAS would then form a mighty military force to defeat Lucifer and his evil cronies.

And the list of miracles continued. No one knew why or how except Edna who had secreted away the barrowloads of congealed sperm. She planned to make her fortune from selling her tonics, but she was too busy fucking the boy downstairs. He couldn't understand how she was looking younger and younger.

130

No news for Fayden

The lockdown had been a success, but the countryside was suffering. Nature had always needed the help of The Fay. Crops were failing; flowers were not being fertilised; no one was directing the bees; birds stopped singing, and the trees stopped caring.

The seasons started to fall apart. The Moon looked duller; the sunset and the sunrise had lost their sheen; the stars twinkled less. Even the ploughmen noticed, but not at first. They put it down to excessive sunspot activity.

The problem with the lockdown was that Fayden had no idea what was going on. There had been a complete loss of news. She decided to consult the runes.

Fayden, Elderberry and Rufus sat around the small pool and practiced their magick. It appeared that the alliance between Heaven and the ploughmen was progressing well. They were confused by the various religious denominations. There were so many different flavours, but the three Abrahamic beliefs had formed an alliance against Lucifer.

Fayden, 'It looks to me that Hell is going to be outgunned and will probably lose.'

Elderberry, 'I don't think Satan will care. He hasn't cared about anything for an awfully long time.'

Fayden, 'How will that affect us?'

Rufus, 'Hard to tell, but it will affect the order of things. If there is no Hell, where do the evil souls go? Do we need evil?'

Elderberry, 'I'm not even sure what evil is. Who is the judge?'

Fayden, 'What if God decides that we are his next target?'

Rufus, 'If he destroys us, then he is destroying the Earth. It doesn't make sense, but then God attacking Hell doesn't really make sense.'

Fayden, 'As someone said, 'God works in mysterious ways'.'

131

A British Broadcasting News Coup

BBC Producer, 'So who is this mystery guest?'

Archbishop of Canterbury, 'I'm saving that information until the very last moment.'

BBC Producer, 'Our rules state that there can be no broadcasting without full disclosure.'

Archbishop of Canterbury, 'Look, young man, I'm the Archbishop of Canterbury, head of the Church in the UK. I don't have to follow your rules.'

BBC Producer, 'Please do not be condescending. I'm a senior producer at the BBC. There will not be a broadcast from this establishment until you tell me the name of your mystery guest.'

The archbishop wished that he still had the gun with him.

Archbishop of Canterbury, 'We shall see.' He made one quick call to the Director-General of the BBC, and the rules were changed, along with the producer.

New BBC Producer, 'I understand that you have a mystery guest.'

Archbishop of Canterbury, 'Yes that is correct.'

New BBC Producer, 'That won't be a problem. Let me walk you through to the studio.'

Archbishop of Canterbury, 'Thank you.'

It was a classic BBC studio with five chairs and a table and multiple camera crews.

BBC Producer, 'Apart from yourself and the mystery guest, can I ask who the other guests are so that we can prepare?'

Archbishop of Canterbury, 'Of course. There will be Bishop Docherty and General Sir Hampton-Smith, the Head of the Church of England Crusade Force.'

BBC Producer, 'Thank you. I've never heard of the Church of England Crusade Force.'

Archbishop of Canterbury, 'Exactly. That is why we have organised this presentation to inform the public. Great things are afoot.'

BBC Producer, 'I'm incredibly pleased to hear that.'

Archbishop of Canterbury, 'Are you a believer?'

BBC Producer, 'Not exactly; I would call myself a lapsed Baptist.'

Archbishop of Canterbury, 'Well you'd better unlapse yourself. The day of judgement is upon us.'

BBC Producer, 'I understand.' Walking away, he signalled to his assistant producer to say, "we have a loon on our hands". 'He has asked for additional lighting to make sure that we capture the "magic of the moment",' he added.

The bishop and the general turned up with their mystery guest undercover. He was hidden in a small room off the studio. At least this time there was no Stella.

The two bishops and the general were sitting around the table. The interviewer, like most in the BBC, was not happy that their standard schedule had been interrupted without any explanation. The archbishop explained that he planned to speak to the nation first rather than just be interviewed.

The interviewer looked at the producer who just shrugged his shoulders.

The programme started, and the archbishop stood up and said, 'Ladies and gentlemen, I bring you great news. Today I can announce that Heaven has declared war on Hell. God has specifically asked humanity for assistance in this great cause.

'There is a battle going on. We have already had some casualties, including my great friend, the Prime Minister. It is the duty of every Christian, every Jew, and every Muslim to take up arms against Lucifer. Now is the time to defeat the beast.

'My dear friend, General Sir Hampton-Smith, is forming the Church of England Crusade Force. His eminence, the Pope, is creating a similar body. A fatwah has been called, and we are expecting similar Jewish and Muslim armed forces to be established.

'We have already had a large number of volunteers from the UK armed forces, and the Government has made firm commitments regarding the release of military assets, including aircraft.

'However, we need more volunteers in this fight against evil.

'Now I know that some of you are laughing in your beer. Who is this old geezer dressed in ceremonial gear demanding that we fight the beast? I tell you that I'm a messenger from God, but I can now announce that we have God's original messenger with us.'

A young man dressed in a grey sheet walked on stage. He was incredibly good-looking with golden-blond hair and a perpetual smile with startling white teeth and sparkling blue eyes.

He removed the sheet to expose a fantastic torso in a skimpy loincloth. And then he opened the most beautiful set of glorious white wings. At that moment, hundreds of thousands of non-believers felt the power of God. They believed.

In his hand, he held a gleaming silver sword which he raised above his head and said, 'I'm Gabriel who sits on the right-hand side of God. I'm his messenger, and the message I bring is: It is now the time to make war against the evil one. We need to crush the Devil and his spawn. I look for humankind to play its part.

'It will not be easy, and many will lose their lives, but the reward is eternal happiness. God will be with you. Join the crusade now.'

He put his sword down and placed it between his legs. He looked simply beautiful.

The interviewer, the producer, the camera team, and the audience were speechless. There were no questions, but of course, there were many.

132

Ye Olde Trip to Jerusalem

There is considerable debate about which pub is the oldest in England. The leading contenders are:

- Ye Olde Man & Scythe, Bolton
- Adam and Eve, Bishopsgate
- Ye Olde Trip to Jerusalem, Nottingham
- The Royal Standard of England, Beaconsfield
- The Bingley Arms, Leeds
- The Porch House, Stow-on-the-Wold
- Ye Olde Fighting Cocks, St Albans
- The Old Ferry Boat Inn, Holywell.

Anyway, four friends are supping away in the Ye Olde Trip to Jerusalem as they usually do on a Saturday night. They were watching the TV when the angel appeared.

Bob almost spilt his beer, a serious crime where he came from. Alfred sat there with his mouth wide open. Madge was a bit more expressive and said, 'Fuck!'

And Doris said, 'You can say that again.'

And again, Madge said, 'Fuck!'

Bob, 'Is it real?'

Alfred, 'You can do a lot with puppets nowadays.'

Madge, 'He is not a puppet you div.'

Doris, 'I'm sure that it is TV trickery.'

Madge hated the pompous twat, but then she was Alfred's latest wife. Stuck-up bitch.

Alfred, 'It certainly looks real.'

Bob, But then so does *Dr Who*.'

Madge, 'Nice body. I wouldn't mind a bit of that.'

Bob, 'Watch it, you have got your Adonis.'

Madge, 'I want one that works.'

Doris, 'He is a fine-looking fellow and those wings!'

Alfred, 'Well, are you joining up?'

Bob, 'I think my fighting days are over.'

Doris, 'I might sign up. Eternal happiness is not a bad deal.'

Bob, 'What does that mean: Eternal happiness?'

Alfred, 'It means happiness eternally.'

Bob, 'You mean fishing?'

Alfred, 'Or fucking.'

Doris, 'Watch it, I won't have that sort of talk.'

133

Lucifer becomes a TV fan

Lucifer, 'So what is this?

Asbell, 'It's a TV, my lord.'

Lucifer, 'TV?'

Asbell, 'Yes, it's a television, my lord.'

Lucifer, 'So is it a TV or a television?'

Asbell, 'TV is an abbreviation for television, my lord. The humans use it for communication and for entertainment.'

Lucifer, 'And why is it here?'

Asbell, 'I thought that you might like to see Gabriel, my lord.'

Lucifer, 'He is in the TV?'

Asbell, 'Not exactly. An image of him will be displayed on the TV.'

Lucifer, 'Show me.'

Asbell, 'Yes, my lord.'

He switched on the TV and re-played the programme.

Startled, Lucifer said, 'I don't believe it. That's Gabriel. I haven't seen my brother for thousands of years.'

Asbell, 'Nor me.'

Lucifer, 'What's he doing in the box?'

Asbell, 'I will turn the sound up.'

Lucifer was even more startled and said, 'He talks as well.'

Asbell, 'Yes, my lord.'

Lucifer, 'So why are you showing me this?'

Asbell, 'I will play it again. It might be a good idea if you listen to what he is saying, my lord.' Asbell played it again, and Lucifer listened this time.

Lucifer, 'It sounds like they are being serious. What can the humans do to us?'

Asbell, 'We are not sure how they can get to Hell to do any damage, my lord.'

Lucifer, 'What else is on TV?' Asbell handed him the TV clicker. Lucifer became a huge TV fan. In fact, he became obsessed, totally obsessed.

So far, his favourite films were:

- *Angel Heart* (1987)
- *Bedazzled* (2000)
- *Childhood's End* (2015)
- *Constantine* (2005)
- *End of Days* (1999)
- *Exorcist: The Beginning* (2004)
- *Fallen* (1998)
- *Grimm* (2011–2017)
- *Hellraiser* (1987)
- *Legend* (1985)
- *Love Letters of a Portuguese Nun* (1977)
- *Lucifer (TV series)*
- *Pan's Labyrinth* (2006)
- *Rosemary's Baby* (1968)
- *Storm of the Century*
- *Supernatural* (2005–2020)
- *The Devil's Advocate* (1997)
- *The Exorcist* (1973)
- *The Omen* (1976)
- *The Passion of the Christ* (2004)
- *The Prophecy* (1995)
- *The Witch* (2015)
- *The Witches of Eastwick* (1987)

He found most of them somewhat depressing. It wasn't the films. They were excellent. It was the fact that the devil in almost every one of these films was much more creative than he was. Most of the time, he couldn't be bothered. Even now he didn't really care whether Hell was destroyed or not, but he had to show willing in support of his supporters.

It wasn't long before TVs multiplied throughout Hell. Now there was no escape from the soaps. Death was no longer a barrier to watching *Coronation Street*, or *I'm a Celebrity Get Me Out Of Here*.

134

Gabriel gets a Mobile

Gabriel loved his mobile. He liked the way it fitted into his hand. He liked the fact that it contained all of his appointments. He loved the games, especially the shooting ones. He even liked his Facebook page. He was slightly surprised just how rude humans could be, but those that were ended up with huge blisters on their tongue. Some of these blisters were over a foot long and were incurable.

He also got quite a few rude e-mails. He wasn't an aggressive angel, but humans needed to understand their place. Rude e-mailers found that their fingers gradually fused together. That certainly slowed their typing down.

The only person he regularly rang was Stella. He wanted more sex but wasn't sure if the spunk spray would happen again. Anyway, he thought he would risk it.

135

Edna turns a Penny

Edna had shagged the poor lad in the flat below to death. Well, that wasn't entirely true. He lives but only just. He was the nearest thing to a zombie that Edna had ever seen.

Anyway, there were lots of other fish in the sea. The break also gave her the chance to focus on her new business. She had taken Gabriel's rock-hard spunk—not that she knew what it was—and divided it into small cubes. She was going to sell it as both a magic youth portion and an aphrodisiac.

She gave away about 1,000 packets, and the resulting reaction became an immediate sensation. The demand was immense, which pushed the price up. Her supplies were limited; in fact, limited to one ejaculation, not that she knew that.

There were lots of unexpected side effects: multiple births, hair gain, weight loss, the development of tiny wings, multi-coloured poo, and urine, talking in strange tongues, bouncier breasts, extremely long nipples, massive erections, many cures, improved memory, new teeth, old teeth repairing themselves, better eyesight, levitation, mind-reading, telekinesis and several things that a decent publication couldn't print.

Many Government Departments took an interest. Samples were procured for analysis but mysteriously disappeared.

Edna was starting to feel the heat, took the money and the remaining stocks and did a runner. She went somewhere warm and sunny, where the young men were warm and weak.

136

A State of Emergency

Archbishop of Canterbury, 'Well how did that go?'

Bishop Docherty, 'As well as can be expected.'

Archbishop of Canterbury, 'What does that mean?'

Bishop Docherty, 'About half the population, are fired up and are ready to join the crusade. The other half think that it is a cynical plot by the Establishment to suppress the common man.'

Archbishop of Canterbury, 'I blame that on the atheists. We need a root-and-branch strategy to track them down and eliminate them.'

Bishop Docherty, 'Are you being serious?'

Archbishop of Canterbury, 'I certainly am. We should track down atheists, agnostics, Humanists, Sheffield Wednesday supporters, Buddhists and communists and put them to the sword.'

Bishop Docherty, 'Sheffield Wednesday supporters?'

Archbishop of Canterbury, 'I hate them, kill them all.'

Bishop Docherty, 'You seem quite passionate about it.'

Archbishop of Canterbury, 'It is what God wants; check with Gabriel. He has a smartphone now.'

Bishop Docherty, 'Hi Gabriel, how are you today?'

Gabriel, 'Off to fuck Stella.'

Bishop Docherty, 'That sounds genuinely nice. I hope you enjoy yourself. Before you go, can I ask you a question?'

Gabriel, 'That *was* a question.'

Bishop Docherty, 'You know what I mean.'

Gabriel, 'OK.'

Bishop Docherty, 'I understand from the archbishop that God wants certain types of humanity eliminated.'

Gabriel, 'Yes, that is true.'

Bishop Docherty, 'Can you tell me which ones?'

Gabriel, 'Of course. I put the list on my smartphone. I've just found it. The following are to be terminated as a matter of urgency:

- Atheists
- Agnostics
- Humanists
- Sheffield Wednesday supporters
- Communists

Bishop Docherty, 'And what would be the justification?'

Gabriel, 'God doesn't need any justification. It is his will.'

Bishop Docherty, 'But our God is a loving God.'

Gabriel, 'What makes you say that?'

Bishop Docherty, 'It's in the Bible.'

Gabriel, 'Try Exodus 4: 21–14.30: God horribly punished the Egyptians for not freeing the Israelite slaves even though God hardened the Pharaoh's heart so that the Pharaoh would not free them.

'Try Exodus 34: 6–7: God punishes the children and grandchildren for the sins of their father and grandfathers.

'Try Leviticus 25: 44 – 46: God taught that slavery is acceptable

'Try Numbers 31: 1–18: God commanded the Israelites to commit genocide and rape

'I could go on and on, but our God has a mean streak.'

Bishop Docherty, 'So you are saying that these are God's wishes?'

Gabriel, 'I am, now please excuse me as I've got to go and exercise my penis.'

Bishop Docherty, 'Well Archbishop, it appears that you are right.'

Archbishop of Canterbury, 'I know that it's harsh, I know that it sounds medieval, but that is what God wants. If we want a new age, we need to do as he commandeth. Don't you agree, General?'

General Sir Hampton-Smith, 'I do your Excellency, but how do we identify them?'

Archbishop of Canterbury, 'Good point, the Sheffield Wednesday supporters shouldn't be a problem, and we can identify quite a few of the Humanists and communists. We need to see what Gabriel says about the rest.

'I think that we need to call a state of emergency and the Crusaders should take over.'

Bishop Docherty, 'I have my concerns, but God's will is God's will.'

137

The Humanist Resistance

President of UK Humanist Group, 'Fellow Board Members, I have some genuinely concerning news. A little birdie has told me that a State of Emergency may well be enacted.'

Director of Communications, 'That's interesting, but how does that affect us specifically?'

President, 'It's highly likely that the Archbishop of Canterbury may well head the Government.'

Director of Communications, 'Surely that's not likely.'

President, 'He has the support of the Conservative Party, the police and most of the military. It is looking highly likely.'

Director of Communications, 'And the concern is?'

President, 'They intend to follow God's wishes, and he wants the following eliminated:
- Atheists
- Agnostics
- Humanists
- Sheffield Wednesday supporters
- Communists.'

Director of Operations, 'How are they going to identify the above?'

President, 'Well there is our web site for a start, and then there is our membership list.'

Director of Communications, 'Are you sure that this is a serious threat?'

President, 'Who knows?'

Director of Communications, 'Should we destroy our records?'

President, 'Probably a bit too early.'

Director of Communications, 'Well one thing is definite.'

President, 'What's that?'

Director of Communications, 'No one is going to miss The Sheffield Wednesday supporters.'

President, 'Very funny. However, we need to put some plans in place.'

However, it was too late. The SAS Crusader team arrived and shot everyone in the room, and then they took the membership list.

138

The new Prime Minister

Bishop Docherty, 'So, Archbishop, did you ever expect to be the Prime Minister?'

Archbishop of Canterbury, 'I always thought that I had a unique destiny. Now I have the power to satisfy God's wishes. I have suspended most of our legislation.

'I've ordered a hit team to take out the Humanist UK HQ and the UK Atheism Group. The Sheffield Wednesday supporters are next. I plan to crucify as many as I can get my hands on. That will teach them a lesson.'

Bishop Docherty, 'Isn't this going to alienate the general population?'

Archbishop of Canterbury, 'It doesn't matter. We are on a mission.'

Bishop Docherty, 'What are your future plans?'

Archbishop of Canterbury, 'This is my list:

- Eliminate atheists, agnostics, Humanists, Sheffield Wednesday supporters and communists.
- Eliminate Homosexuals of all sorts
- Eliminate Cross-dressers
- Eliminate Fetishists
- Eliminate Nymphomaniacs
- Eliminate Paedophiles
- Eliminate Sodomists
- Eliminate Transvestites
- Eliminate Pornographers
- Eliminate Strippers
- Eliminate Prostitutes
- Eliminate Union Leaders

- Eliminate Drug Dealers
- Eliminate Drug Takers
- Eliminate Buddhists
- Eliminate Rapists
- Eliminate Mormons
- Eliminate Blasphemers.'

Bishop Docherty, 'There seems to be a lot of elimination.'

Archbishop of Canterbury, 'That's just the start.'

Bishop Docherty, 'Do you have any non-elimination plans?'

Archbishop of Canterbury, 'Of course, the following are being progressed:

- All schools, colleges and universities will be run by the church
- Additional bishops will be appointed to the House of Lords
- Only churchgoers will have the right to vote
- Witch hunters will be appointed in every town
- Public hanging to be introduced for a range of crimes
- Pubs to be closed
- Alcohol sales to be banned
- Motorways to be closed to private car owners
- All foreign travel banned
- Sunday schools to become compulsory
- Church weddings only
- Adultery to be a hanging offence
- Blasphemy to be a hanging offence
- Every house must have a state-issued Bible
- Formal clothing rules to be introduced
- Juries to be banned
- Judges to be replaced by religious leaders
- Certain books to be banned
- TV programmes and films to be censored
- Newspapers to be state-owned and censored
- All theatres to be closed
- Unauthorised public meetings to be banned
- Certain religious groups to be banned
- Certain prisoner types to be eliminated

- Mobilisation for the Crusaders
- All mail and e-mails to be monitored and censored
- All telephonic conversations to be monitored
- All social media technologies to be banned
- Free speech to be suspended

'I'm sure that there are things that I've forgotten, but it is a good start.'

Bishop Docherty, 'But you are just creating a police state.'

Archbishop of Canterbury, 'That may be so, but it's what God wants.'

Bishop Docherty, 'But that can't be the answer for everything.'

The Archbishop of Canterbury pushed a button, and Bishop Docherty was taken away for reconditioning. The archbishop had always had his suspicions about the bishop's commitment to the will of God.

139

You Fornicate at your Peril

Stella arranged to meet Gabriel on top of Bredon Hill. It was a lovely summer day. One of those days when it was hotter than you wanted it to be. Stella looked sumptuous, wearing only a short dress and a pair of sandals. She was ready for action.

Stella had been thinking about the meeting all week. Her heart was throbbing in anticipation, and her loins were throbbing in expectation. She was really excited. It is not every day that you fuck an angel, especially one as handsome as Gabriel.

She could see his majestic frame in the distance. Giant flapping wings supported on a torso fit for a god, or the nearest thing to a god. As Gabriel got nearer, she was surprised how noisy they were and how much wind they caused. She had to put her arm over her eyes to protect them against the flying dust.

When he landed, Stella just stood there and admired him. Strong firm muscles, perfectly formed arms and legs, the face of a man but with the innocence of a child. He looked far from innocent when he removed his loincloth though. Standing to attention was a proud, erect penis throbbing and ready for action.

When two lovers are ready for action, then there is no reason to wait.

Gabriel, 'Take off your dress.' There were no hugs or kissing or foreplay, just a direct order. Stella obeyed and stood there, starkers. Gabriel suddenly recognised the power of the vagina. She looked stunningly beautiful, and part of him just wanted to stare, but the animalistic part wanted to fuck her and to fuck her hard.

Gabriel, 'Get on your hands and knees.'

Stella obeyed. Gabriel walked behind her with his wings fully stretched. He pulled her buttocks apart and entered her without a word.

Stella was already wet with anticipation. He started thrusting. There was no subtlety. His cock simply demanded serious flesh-on-flesh fucking.

He could feel his balls tighten, but he wanted the experience to last. He grabbed Stella by the breasts and flew up into the air. Stella was both terrified and electrified as she was fucked in mid-air.

Gabriel came and screamed his delight. His whole body just revelled in an orgasmic bout of pure pleasure. It was a truly remarkable experience. Fucking a beautiful woman a mile up in mid-air, was everything he thought it would be. Then he let Stella go.

He shouted, 'Go the way of all whores.'

He thought about Deuteronomy 22: 23–24: "If there is a betrothed virgin, and a man meets her in the city and lies with her, then you shall bring them both out to the gate of that city, and you shall stone them to death with stones, the young woman because she did not cry for help though she was in the city and the man because he violated his neighbour's wife, so you shall purge evil from the midst of you."

Or

Deuteronomy 22: 28–29:

"If a man meets a virgin who is not betrothed and seizes her and lies with her, and they are found, then the man who lays with her shall give the to the father of the young woman fifty shekels of silver, and she shall be his wife, because he has violated her, he may not put her away all his days."

Stella had different thoughts as she was flying naked through the chill air. She landed unconscious on a large bramble bush.

It just happened that Gaye and Earnest were picking blackberries. Both were surprised by the flying Stella.

Earnest, 'You don't see that very often.'

Gaye, 'You certainly don't. Quite a pretty thing.'

Earnest, 'She is, isn't she? I haven't seen one of those for an awfully long time.' He was pointing at her fanny.

Gaye, 'You better not touch it. You don't know where it's been.'

Earnest, 'You are right, but I might just give the breasts a squeeze.' And Earnest did. Stella's erect nipples and firm but curvaceous breasts were a real pleasure to fondle.

Gaye, 'What do you think?'

271

Earnest, 'Very nice, very nice indeed.'

Gaye, 'Do you think they are safe to touch?'

Earnest, 'I think so. I might risk a quick fondle of the fanny.'

Gaye, 'Are you sure? You know how dangerous they can be. My grandfather touched one in the war and caught syphilis. Then the whole neighbourhood in Peebles caught it. Very dangerous.'

Earnest, 'I will use a stick first and see how that goes.' Earnest found a small stick and prodded Stella's vagina. 'It seems to be full of sticky stuff,' he observed.

Gaye, 'Sticky stuff?'

Earnest, 'Yes, I'm not sure what it is…'

Gaye, 'Do you think some bees were storing their honey in there?'

Earnest, 'Could be, I will give it a taste.' Earnest licked the end of the stick. 'It tastes surprisingly good; try some.' Gaye did and was equally impressed.

Gaye, 'My tinnitus has stopped for the first time in twenty years.'

Earnest, 'And you know what? My bad back feels a lot better.'

In no time at all, the two geriatrics were scooping the spunk out of Stella's fanny. They hadn't fully realised that they had taken thirty years off their lives.

Earnest, 'You know what, as it's just lying there, I might fuck that fanny.' He pulled out his prick. It was the first time it had been rigid in twenty years.

Gaye, 'No, you won't. I've got my own little hidey-hole that you can use.' And she pulled her rubber knickers down and presented him with a well-used resting place. He was still tempted to fuck the other fanny on show, but then Stella started stirring. Earnest thought that he had better remove his finger from her fanny.

140

A Few Problems

Archbishop of Canterbury, 'So how is it going, my dear general?'

General Sir Hampton-Smith, 'We are making good progress, but there has been some resistance.'

Archbishop, 'From who?'

General, 'There is the Gay Revolutionary Front in Brighton who are putting up a tough fight and the Guildford Satanists are also causing problems.'

Archbishop, 'Send in more troops.'

General, 'We are running a bit short with the witch trials and the crucifixions. They take a lot of manpower.'

Archbishop, 'What about the conscripts?'

General, 'There is no one to train them; there are not enough weapons available, and many of them have deserted.'

Archbishop, 'We need to hunt them down.'

General, 'We just don't have the resources. A lot of the deserters are officers. They don't all have our belief in the cause.'

Archbishop, 'What *good* news do you have?'

General, 'Two armoured divisions have annihilated the football team. The players, officials, owners and at least 90% of the supporters have been killed. It was hard work, but it was done in a logical, pragmatic fashion.

'The supporters were killed by armour-piercing shells and flame throwers. There was some resistance, but we had machine-gun nests at strategic points ready to slice the dissenting fans into small pieces. It was unfortunate that some of the away fans were caught in the crossfire, but that sort of thing often happens in a grudge match.

'We were a bit more subtle with the actual players. They all voluntarily placed their heads in a guillotine. The referee objected and was accidentally set on fire by a flame thrower as he was running off the pitch.'

Archbishop, 'I'm a bit confused as Sheffield Wednesday were not playing today.'

General, 'We definitely terminated a team in Sheffield.'

Archbishop, 'What have you done? You have eliminated the wrong team, *my* team! How could you?' The archbishop was in tears. 'What have you done?'

General, 'Archbishop, these things happen in the fog of war.'

Archbishop, 'Not to my team! You just don't know how angry I am. Someone will have to pay.'

If he had his way, it would be the general, but he needed him.

General, 'Do you want the armoured division to move to their next task: the total destruction of Rotherham?'

Archbishop, 'Yes, please, that will cheer me up. They can also take out Doncaster and Wakefield. Nobody will miss them.'

General, 'That will be done, your lordship. I'm preparing the air force. Do you have the coordinates for Hell?'

Archbishop, 'I will get them from Gabriel. Keep me up to date on any other problems.'

General, 'Well, you need to be careful near your cathedral. A gang of Humanist hitmen have been spotted in the area along with a group calling themselves the "Mormon Marauders".'

Archbishop, 'I never thought that the path of righteousness would be an easy one.'

General, 'I'm glad that you are being positive about things as you and your family have been threatened by several terrorist groups.'

Archbishop, 'Who would dare to do that?'

General, 'For a start there are the Vegan Vigilantes, the Buddhist Buccaneers, the Sex-Slaying Slaughterers, the Exeter Executioners, the Bolton Butchers, the Kensington Killers, the Ambleside Assassins, the Dagenham Destroyers, the Everton Exterminators and a rival group, the Everton Eradicators.

Archbishop, 'Stop, you are saying that they are all out to get me?'

General, 'Yes your holiness, I wouldn't want to be in your shoes. I would certainly avoid going to Yorkshire.'

Archbishop, 'I must say that I'm a bit surprised. I've just delivered what the public wanted.'

General, 'I think the crucifixions have put a lot of people off.'

Archbishop, 'Why is that?'

General, 'A recent survey identified the following issues:

- Smell: putrefying bodies can let off a very strong whiff
- Noise: the sound of late-night moaning, groaning, and screaming has disturbed local sleeping patterns
- Sexual deviance: some of the scantily clad victims have been abused by young lads which has led to jealousy
- Hygiene: a number of the victims seem to be ignoring the normal housekeeping rules by urinating and defecating in public
- Medical: body parts are falling off and are left to rot.'

Archbishop, 'We may need to rethink our policy.'

141

What are Nuns for?

Archbishop of Canterbury, 'I'm sure the nuns are not there for your sexual gratification.'

Gabriel, 'But I need two or three fresh women each day.'

Archbishop, 'Why is that?

Gabriel, 'I'm spreading the word of God.'

Archbishop, 'By fucking them and letting them fall to Earth?'

Gabriel, 'But they are guaranteed an entrance to Heaven.'

Archbishop, 'That may be the case, but there have been many complaints. People don't expect to find half-naked nuns landing in their back gardens. The nuns don't like it and nor do Londoners.'

Gabriel, 'Surely you can spare two or three nuns per day?'

Archbishop, 'That's not the point. What you are doing is wrong.'

Gabriel, 'I'm Gabriel, I know what's right or wrong. Taking a nun up in the sky, fucking her and letting her fall to Earth is not wrong.'

Archbishop, 'It must be.'

Gabriel, 'Surely it's no worse than crucifying innocents.'

Archbishop, 'They are not innocent, they are deviants.'

Gabriel, 'But aren't the nuns committing a crime by marrying Jesus? Isn't that bigamy?'

Archbishop, 'It would certainly "BE BIG OF ME"!' He could never resist that joke.

Gabriel, 'Let's agree on two per day.'

Archbishop, 'OK, that seems fair.'

Gabriel, 'Mind you, I only want the pretty ones.'

Archbishop, 'Could you be more careful with where you drop them?'

Gabriel, 'It's not easy. You have to take into account the wind, the weight of the girl, her aerodynamic characteristics, the level of struggling, etc.'

Archbishop, 'Fair enough. I have a question for you. Our general friend wants to know how we are going to attack Hell. We don't know where it is.'

Gabriel, 'You are joking. You are telling me that you head the Church of England and you don't know where Hell is?'

Archbishop, 'You've had your fun. Tell me where it is.'

Gabriel, 'Get me the fresh meat first and then I will tell you.'

Archbishop, 'Do they have to be nuns?'

Gabriel, 'I don't mind a bit of variety, but I enjoy shocking the nuns. They are just humans, and there are millions of them. I might as well enjoy a few of them. Who cares?'

The archbishop was getting more and more concerned about Gabriel's behaviour. And some of Gabriel's stories about God were also shocking. Perhaps he should indulge, himself. He *did* get excited watching the young girls being tortured for information about the atheists in hiding.

142

What can I say?

Narrator, 'NO, NO, NO. This novel is a stinking pile of shit. It has sunk to a level that would embarrass most pornographers.

'There is gratuitous sex on every other page. The language is abusive. There is probably not a single person on the planet who will not be offended by this book in some way.

'Clearly, this needs further investigation:

Page No	Foul Words Used
12	Twat
13	Arse
14	Shits, Arsehole
15	Shit
18	Shitstorm, Fucking
22	Fart, Bastard, Fuck
28	Pissed
31	Bugger
32	Fucking
33	Fuck, Fucked
34	Fuck, Fucking, Fucked, Cunt X2
35	Arse
36	Todger
37	Shit, Fucked
39	Fuck
42	Shit
47	Piss, Pissed, Fuck
48	Arse, Fuck
50	Fucked

55	Bugger
57	Shitting
59	Shit
60	Blow job
61	Blow job X2
62	Todger
63	Trouser Snake
65	Shit
66	Fucking X2, Whore X2
68	Bastard
69	Whore
71	Piss
75	Arse
77	Fuck, Shit
81	Fucked, Fucking
89	Shit
91	Fuck
92	Fuck, Fucked, Whores
97	Todger
104	Fucking
105	Bastard
107	Fucking
112	Fucking
116	Shagging
120	Crap
123	Todger
124	Shitter, Crap
135	Shit
136	Arse, Arses
145	Fucking X2
146	Arse, Shit, Buggers, Shitty
149	Crap
163	Bitch, Fuck X2, Fucking
168	Turd X3
169	Shit

170	Fucking
171	Shit
177	Shits, Piss, Pissing, Fucking
178	Fucking
185	Piss
186	Cunts
187	Arse, Farts, Turd, Shit, Shitstorm
206	Bugger
207	Buggers
216	Fuck
221	Pissed
224	Cretin
227	Fucking, Todger
228	Fucked, Fucking, Todger X2
231	Bugger
234	Fucking
239	Bitch, Twat
240	Fucking
253	Fuck X2, Fucked, Fucking
254	Whores
255	Fuck X2
261	Shit

'I was going to list all of the sexual acts page by page but what's the point? No decent publisher is going to put this book on the market.

'At one stage, I thought Alan was simply a tosser. Now I know that he is a perverted swear-mongering deviant.'

143

Everyone gets their Comeuppance

Narrator, 'I can't believe it. Why me? What have I done?

Author, 'What has happened?'

Narrator, 'My family has been wiped out.'

Author, 'Never!'

Narrator, 'In one day, I've lost my wife, two daughters, my two grandchildren and my son-in-law.'

Author, 'Was it a family get together?'

Narrator, 'No, they were killed in separate events.'

Author, 'So what actually happened?'

Narrator, 'It started with my daughter who offered herself to the ice-hockey team if they won the championship, knowing that the chances of that were zero. She didn't know what to do when the team won, but the team did.

She was stripped and laid on the ice, ready for their victory fuck. A pillow had been placed under her bottom to help the whole process. However, they hadn't fully realised that her naked skin had stuck to the ice. Nevertheless, the team took their winnings one by one. The fourth player had just finished the job when they spotted the ice-smoothing machine coming their way.

'This machine is automated. It crushes, cleans, and smooths out the ice. The lads shouted at my Jenny to get out of the way, but she was stuck. The ice-smoothing machine continued and crushed, cleaned, and smoothed Jenny's head. The final remaining player decided to take his victory prize while he could. Some people might find that shocking, but he really didn't want to miss out.

'The Manager had planned to join in the fun, but he decided not to. I think some men have enough moral fibre to say no to fucking headless girls in a public place. (Author, this wasn't the reason. The Manager had been fucking Dolores, the Narrator's wife, for fourteen years. There was a possibility that he was Jenny's father.)

Author, 'That is shocking. I'm so sorry for your loss and what a way to go!'

Narrator, 'Then it got worse: the Manager of the hockey team phoned my wife to tell her about the terrible event. I listened to the phone message. I was a bit surprised when he called her, "My fucky bum-bum". But lots of people use nicknames.

'Sadly, my wife hadn't realised in her distress that she was driving down the wrong side of the dual carriageway.

'From the car, she phoned my other daughter, who was bathing my granddaughter in the sink. Don't ask me why. When the phone went, my other three-year-old granddaughter rushed down the stairs, tripped, fell down the stairs and broke her neck. My daughter rushed to her aid, but it was too late. When she returned to the sink, she found that Tracy had sank under the water and drowned. You can imagine just how distraught she was.

'Despite uncontrolled sobbing, she managed to phone her husband, who immediately got in his car to rush home. The last thing he expected was a head-on collision with a car driving down the wrong side of the dual carriageway. Who would?'

Author, 'I really can't believe this. So much bad luck in one day.'

Narrator, 'That wasn't the end of it. When the police contacted my daughter to let her know that her husband and mother had been killed in an accident, she simply took a sharp knife and slashed her throat.'

Author, 'We have had our differences, but I'm so sorry.'

Narrator, 'Wait a minute… *you* wrote this, didn't you?'

Author, 'Certainly not. It's not in this book, is it?'

Narrator, 'I suppose not.'

144

Publish or be Damned

Publisher, 'That was a fairly mean trick to play on the Narrator.'

Author, 'There are still worse things to come: disease, bankruptcy, prison, a range of humiliations, a few accidents, etc.'

Publisher, 'I understand where you are coming from. He is a bit of a stick-in-the-mud, but he does have some fair points.'

Author, 'What are you saying?'

Publisher, 'For a start, the use of swear words is getting worse.'

Author, 'I don't swear much myself. I only use them for dramatic effect.'

Publisher, 'There are more subtle ways of doing that. You have used the word 'cunt'. Quite a few times. For a lot of people, that word is a real no-no.'

Author, 'It's just a word.'

Publisher, 'I agree, but it's still a word that offends a lot of people. I'm not a censor. I look to you to censor your own work.

'The other area is graphic sex. It is getting a bit too much.'

Author, 'What specifically is upsetting you?'

Publisher, 'Well there are quite a few examples:
- Sexual intercourse with a headless corpse
- Mid-air intercourse with nuns
- The fingering of Stella on a bramble bush

I could go on.'

Author, 'They are all vital parts of the story.'

Publisher, 'I want to see more balance. So far, it is too sexist. We need stronger female stories where women are in control.'

Author, 'OK, I can do that.'

145

Witches in Pershore

Witchfinder General, Pershore, 'Bring the suspect in.'

Witchfinder, 'Yes Ma'am.'

A boy in his late teens was dragged in. He had already lost some of his fingernails.

Witchfinder General, Pershore, 'I hear that you are not being co-operative.'

The lad shook his head.

Witchfinder General, Pershore, 'You say, "No Ma'am". Do you understand?'

A whack around the head usually helped.

Suspect, 'Yes Ma'am.'

That was proof that a whack helped.

Witchfinder General, Pershore, 'You have been accused of heinous crimes. What have you got to say?'

Suspect, 'It was my three-year-old sister who accused me.'

Witchfinder General, Pershore, 'And what is your point?'

Suspect, 'She caught me pleasuring myself.'

Witchfinder General, Pershore, 'So you admit that you were having sex with a succubus?'

Suspect, 'No, I'm not sure what that is. I was just using my hand.'

The Witchfinder General turned to her assistant and said, 'Strip him.' She ripped his clothes off and looked him in the eyes and said, 'You won't be needing these again.'

She used a knife to cut his pants away.

Witchfinder General, Pershore, 'Now show us what you were doing.'

Suspect, 'You want me to have a wank in front of you?'

Witchfinder General, Pershore, 'It's called masturbating.'

She wacked him again as it's the only way these idiots learn.

Suspect, 'Why do you want me to do it?'

Witchfinder General, Pershore, 'We want to see if your succubus returns.'

Suspect, 'I refuse.'

Witchfinder General, Pershore, 'Then it's off with the genitals. It won't be the first time you know.' She showed him a box of cut-off penises and testicles. The suspect quickly started pumping away.

Witchfinder General, Pershore, 'Harder, we want to see some real action.'

Witchfinder General, Pershore, 'Witchfinder If he doesn't come soon then chop that todger off.'

Witchfinder, 'Yes, Ma'am.'

And she sharpened her knife. It's amazing what a little bit of motivation can do. The lad came as ordered. He was embarrassed, but what could he do?

Witchfinder General, Pershore, 'Who is next?'

Witchfinder, 'It's the local bank manager.'

Witchfinder General, Pershore, 'I can't see him getting out with his genitals intact.' They both laughed.

146

Publish or be Damned Number 2

Publisher, 'When I said that I was keen on the book having stronger female parts, I didn't mean S&M.'

Author, 'Well, you need to make your mind up about what you want.'

Publisher, 'By the way, the Narrator has put in a formal complaint.'

Author, 'Who to?'

Publisher, 'The Publishing Guild. They do have the power to stop the book from being published.'

Author, 'On what grounds?'

Publisher, 'He is using some old, quite complex publishing laws from medieval times. It seems to focus on profanity, blasphemy, disturbing the peace, criminal neglect, copyright infringement and breaking some of the acts within the race relations legislation. It's not good.'

Author, 'What is the plan?'

Publisher, 'From our perspective, we don't want to be involved in an expensive court case.'

147

Mother Superior isn't Happy

Archbishop of Canterbury, 'I know. I know. It's not a good use of nuns.'

Mother Superior, 'My girls are not there for the sexual gratification of a deviant angel even if he is Gabriel.'

Archbishop of Canterbury, 'I know but he likes them young and innocent.'

Mother Superior, 'My girls used to volunteer, but there is now a distinct lack of enthusiasm.'

Archbishop of Canterbury, 'I can understand that, but they do get immediate entry into Heaven.'

Mother Superior, 'That's not what Gabriel has told them. Apparently, if you pleasure Gabriel, then you are breaking your vows to Jesus. That's instant damnation. The girls are not keen on that.'

Archbishop of Canterbury, 'I can understand that.'

Mother Superior, 'My girls have all seen the pictures of dead bodies of naked nuns all over London. They have landed in the strangest of places including The Tower of London, Buckingham Palace, and Wembley Stadium while a game of football was in progress. The photos are hardly complimentary with their bits on show. In fact, the locals seem to enjoy making sure that they are fully exposed.'

Archbishop of Canterbury, 'I know what you mean. Some people just lack respect.'

Mother Superior, 'It's worse than that. There is a morbid interest in naked nuns. One young man was charging to see one of the bodies. Another was offering photo opportunities: you could choose the position of the corpse. Two of my girls survived the fall but not the local attention.'

Archbishop of Canterbury, 'What do you mean?'

Mother Superior,' Well the locals were a bit annoyed that they were still alive, so they took things into their own hands.'

Archbishop of Canterbury, 'What happened?'

Mother Superior, 'As I said they took things into their own hands. And I mean hands, the hands were around the nuns' necks.'

Archbishop of Canterbury, 'That is absolutely shocking.'

Mother Superior, 'What's even more disturbing is that a dead nun is worth over a thousand pounds on the black market.'

Archbishop of Canterbury, 'What do people do with them?

Mother Superior, 'You don't want to know.'

The Mother Superior was wrong. The Archbishop of Canterbury was desperate to know.

Archbishop of Canterbury, 'So you are saying no to supplying your nuns?'

Mother Superior, 'In broad terms that's true, but there could be a deal.'

Archbishop of Canterbury, 'What sort of deal?'

Mother Superior,' Well I have a few novices that are not going to make the grade. They could be made available.'

Archbishop of Canterbury, 'What sort of deal are you thinking of?'

Mother Superior,' Well so far you have had eighty-four nuns that have been deposited all over London. I'm looking for some payment for them.'

Archbishop of Canterbury, 'That's a bit unfair, but I can see where you are coming from. How about £500 per girl? I will pay you £42,000.'

Mother Superior, 'I'm happy with that, but I want £1,000 for each new girl.'

Archbishop of Canterbury, 'That's a bit steep.'

Mother Superior, 'But I can get that price on the black market for a dead one. These are live frisky girls that will satisfy the demands of Gabriel.'

Archbishop of Canterbury, 'Fair enough, how many can you get?'

Mother Superior, 'If I hunt around, I can probably get 150.'

Archbishop of Canterbury, 'Then it's a deal.'

Mother Superior, 'Just checking, have you got my private bank account details?'

148

How do we get to Hell?

Archbishop of Canterbury, 'I've sorted out some fresh nuns for you.'

Gabriel, 'Thank you, Archbishop.'

Archbishop, 'Is there any chance that you could be a bit more discreet about where you drop them?

Gabriel, 'What can I do? I'm just the messenger of God.'

Archbishop of Canterbury, 'The nuns are revolting.'

Gabriel, 'I thought you were guaranteeing that they would be young and pretty.'

Archbishop, 'The old ones are the best.'

Gabriel, 'I thought that they were going to be young.'

Archbishop of Canterbury, 'Your humour knows no bounds.'

Gabriel, 'Now you will want to know the whereabouts of Hell.'

Archbishop, 'That's correct.'

Gabriel, 'Here you are. This device opens portals to Hell and Heaven.'

Archbishop of Canterbury, 'Can we use it to scout out the area before we attack?'

Gabriel, 'You need to be prepared. If you open it, demons will be waiting to stream through to Earth. Anyway, we need to coordinate our campaigns.'

Archbishop, 'Of course. Who do we liaise with in Heaven?'

Gabriel, 'Michael.'

Archbishop, 'Are there any plans yet?'

Gabriel, 'Not until you guys create one.'

Archbishop, 'So the onus is on us?'

Gabriel, 'Most definitely. We are pretty hopeless at this military stuff. We are more lovers.'

Archbishop, 'But you just drop them out of the sky. Eventually, we will run out of volunteers.'

Gabriel, 'Should we consider some form of conscription?'

Archbishop, 'Most conscripts face the possibility of death. Here it is almost guaranteed. When should we talk about our military plans?'

Gabriel, 'There's no real urgency. You still need to gather your resources.'

149

Hell could be a Problem

Archbishop of Canterbury, 'OK, I'm free now, please give me your update.'

General Sir Hampton-Smith, 'As before, we are still making good progress, but the resistance is growing. Rotherham and Wakefield have been utterly destroyed, but we had a slight mishap with Doncaster. The lads decided that Barnsley was a better bet. The transport options were a lot easier; Barnsley was just a short trip down the M1.'

Archbishop of Canterbury, 'But my parents live in Barnsley.'

General Sir Hampton-Smith, 'Not anymore.'

Archbishop, 'So far you have destroyed my team and killed my parents.'

General, 'That's not good, but we can only blame the troops on the ground. We need to get the real work underway. When do we attack Hell?'

Archbishop, 'I now have a device that will give us access to Hell. I was warned that when we use it, demons will swarm out. We need to plan for that. Michael, one of the top angels, is organising Heaven's resources. I'm trying to fix a meeting.'

General, 'We need to scout the area before an attack. Is that acceptable?'

Archbishop, 'Yes, but we will still have the demon problem. And we also need to get agreement in advance.'

General, 'Fair enough. What sort of timescale are you thinking of? We can move reasonably quickly, although we need to understand what we are going to find once we use the device. Do we arrive in space, in water, in the air or even on land?'

Archbishop, 'That hadn't crossed my mind.'

General, 'There are lots of other things that we need to investigate:

- How big is Hell?
- Is it the same size as Earth, or bigger?
- How is it structured? Are there lots of individual countries, regions, towns?
- Is there an underground structure?
- Are there roads?
- Is there a breathable atmosphere for humans?
- What is the temperature going to be?
- Do our troops need environmental protection?
- What type of military force do they operate in Hell?
- Are we just up against demons and angels?
- Is there a local population?
- What sort of weaponry do they have?
- How do you kill an angel?
- How do you kill a demon?
- Will our weapons work on them?
- Will we need fighter planes?
- Will we need bombers?
- Can we get a map of Hell?
- Are we going to target Beelzebub himself?
- How do we get back to Earth?
- How many combatants have they got?
- Do they have different types of combatant?
- Is there a water supply?
- Will our phones work?
- Will radar work?
- How big a force can we get through using the device?
- How do we integrate our force's with Heaven's?
- Do we have a joint command?
- Who is ultimately in charge?
- What about medical facilities?
- What happens to our troops who die in Hell?
- Do combustion engines work in Hell?
- How do we identify good and bad angels?
- Do they take prisoners?

- Do we take prisoners?

'I can think of a lot more questions.

'But before we even start, we need to define the mission objectives.'

Archbishop, 'What do you mean?'

General, 'Well we casually talk about destroying Hell, but what does that mean? Is the plan to totally remove it from existence? Are we just killing the inhabitants? All of them? Is the intent to kill the Devil?

'I need a clear, concise mission statement. Do you understand?'

Archbishop, 'Yes, General, I do. I will have a word with Gabriel.'

General, 'Excellent. Are there any other missions for my men?'

Archbishop, 'Could you take out the Welsh and Scottish Parliaments?'

General, 'Just the buildings?

Archbishop, 'No, take out all of the MPs as well.'

General, 'Certainly.'

150

International Response

The Archbishop of Canterbury and Gabriel addressed a combined meeting of the following Protestant Church organisations in the USA:

American Baptist Churches in the USA

The Episcopal Church

The Evangelical Lutheran Church in America

The Presbyterian Church (USA)

The United Church of Christ

The United Methodist Church

The meeting was going reasonably well but became a rousing success when Gabriel took to the stage. The evangelicals were incredibly enthusiastic. Gabriel particularly enjoyed the foot-stomping, hand-clapping and spontaneous singing. There was also some spontaneous fucking, but that was all hushed-up.

Luckily, the Archbishop had brought a few novice nuns with him to satisfy Gabriel's needs. Some of them loved flying on the transatlantic flight but were less enthused about free falling over New York.

There was similar enthusiasm from the USA Catholic Church.

In a few days, the archbishop had guarantees of considerable financial and military support from the USA Government. In fact, factions within the Administration and the Pentagon wanted a similar revolution to that in the UK.

The Pope had rallied support in Europe, Africa, and China. An extensive Muslim force was being put together.

The archbishop was coming under pressure to start the campaign.

151

Yorkshire Revolts

The Archbishop of Canterbury, 'I understand that there is a problem in Yorkshire.'

General, 'That appears to be the case. I think the destruction of Rotherham and Wakefield upset a lot of people. Strangely, no one seemed to be bothered about Barnsley.'

Archbishop, 'I can understand that. What about Sheffield United?'

General, 'The city is split. If you are a Wednesday fan, it was a good thing. Anyway, any protesters have been eliminated.'

Archbishop, 'Crucifixions?'

General, 'No because of the issues raised earlier. We tried the guillotine, but that was hugely resource-hungry, so we switched to motorway dumping. We throw the protesters off motorway bridges. It serves two purposes: elimination of protesters and traffic calming. Sadly, we had to stop that after a while because the Watford Gap pile-up stopped the motorway traffic for two days.'

Archbishop 'I thought we were going to ban the use of motorways.'

General, 'That was the plan, but there were too many logistics problems. We couldn't distribute food quickly enough. There were riots in Weston-Super-Mare, Bogner Regis, Littlehampton, and Swansea.'

Archbishop 'I hope that those towns were effectively dealt with.'

General, 'They certainly were. Every fifth woman under the age of twenty-five was given a Bible and was initiated as a nun for your stockpile.'

Archbishop 'Good thinking. We need to build the stocks up as it would appear that Michael has similar tastes to Gabriel...'

General, 'That's terrible news, but there is a very healthy demand for dead nuns. It's amazing what you can do with them.'

Archbishop, 'What do they use them for?

General, 'Assuming that you have had them properly treated by a good taxidermist they make exquisite household ornaments. You can use them as flowerpots, toothbrush holders, mannequins, pincushions, hat stands, etc. The uses are endless.

'One of my friends has house plants coming out of every orifice. Another uses one as a signpost in his restaurant with the words, *"Make a habit of Nun today"*. He's selling a make of wine.'

'I'm sure that that you don't want to know more about some of the more salacious uses.'

He was wrong. The archbishop really wanted to know. He wondered how the General got his rocks off.

Archbishop 'Are you married, General?'

General, 'No, your eminence, I've never had time for that home-building malarkey.'

Archbishop 'How do you satisfy your natural manly urges?'

General, 'Valet.'

Archbishop 'Are you a homosexual?'

General, 'Certainly not; I always make sure that my valet is an attractive young woman.'

Archbishop 'And you seduce them?'

General, 'Certainly not. I make it very clear during the interview what services are required.'

Archbishop 'And they don't mind?'

General, 'Certainly not; they are young women with healthy needs of their own. I always go for married ones as that usually stops them wanting a full-time relationship.'

Archbishop 'And how long have you been doing this?'

General, 'Many years, your eminence.'

152

A Nun is Saved

The Archbishop of Canterbury had started to wonder about his chastity. Everyone else seemed to be at it, including the angels. Why was he being so chaste? Who actually cared?

He decided to take decisive action and called for a novice nun. He didn't know her name, but she had beautiful blue eyes. He called her into his spartan room.

Archbishop 'What is your name?'

Novice Nun, 'Mary, your lordship.'

Archbishop 'And do you know what is in store for you?

Novice Nun, 'Yes, your lordship.'

Archbishop 'Tell me.'

Novice Nun, 'Well Gabriel is going to strip me, fuck me, fly me up to a great height and drop me.'

Archbishop 'And you don't mind?'

Novice Nun, 'Mother Superior told me that it's a great honour and that I will go straight to Heaven.'

Archbishop 'Are you not frightened?'

Novice Nun, 'I'm terrified, your lordship.'

Archbishop 'I might be able to offer you an alternative.'

Novice Nun, 'Anything, your lordship.'

Archbishop 'I might be a man of the cloth, but I'm still a man.'

Novice Nun, 'I understand.' She removed her apron, scapular and underskirts to stand naked in front of a man for the first time. She had heard from the other girls that you bend over and open your legs. So she got herself into position.

The archbishop removed his outer garments and underwear and said a little prayer. The nun handed him a cloth. Because he had a puzzled look on his face, she said, 'Remember, I'm a virgin.'

He lined up his erect member, broke through the hymen, and entered the holy of holies. They both lost their virginity together: an eighteen-year-old girl and a sixty-four-year-old man.

He was in love, and she was saved from falling from a great height. It wasn't long before she had him organised.

153

The Scots are Revolting

General Sir Hampton-Smith, 'Your Eminence, I have to inform you that the Scots are revolting.'

Archbishop, 'You can say that again.'

General, 'Destroying their Parliament and First Minister has not gone down too well.'

Archbishop, 'She shouldn't have stood in front of the tank.'

General, 'They did try to miss her, but they have a very tight turning circle.'

Archbishop, 'They reversed over her!'

General, 'That might be the case.'

Archbishop, 'Let's be honest, they reversed over her thirteen times.'

General, 'Let's move on.'

Archbishop, 'Do we have the revolt under control?'

General, 'Not really, we are still struggling with the Yorkshire insurrection and the fact that the Guildford Satanists have teamed up with the Godalming Gamblers to form a mobile attack unit which is causing us problems.

'I'm concerned that the invading Scottish army will unite with the Yorkshire Yeomanry. It's all getting a bit chaotic. That and the food shortages are making keeping the peace quite challenging.

'And before you say it, more crucifixions are not the answer.'

Archbishop, 'But we need to teach these heathens a lesson.'

General, 'It appears that sometimes the lesson is the problem.'

Archbishop, 'I hope that you are not turning soft before our great victory.'

General, 'Your Eminence, we are a long way off from a victory.'

Archbishop, 'You mentioned food shortages.'

General, 'Yes, your eminence, they are getting quite critical.'

Archbishop, 'Why is that happening?'

General, 'There are several reasons. Firstly, our force is rapidly approaching a million men and women. They need a lot of feeding.

'Secondly, some of our recruits would typically be part of the food business: farmers, food processors, distributors, shop staff, etc.

'Thirdly, we shut the motorway network down for a while. Food wasn't being distributed.'

Archbishop, 'I see. What's the solution?'

General, 'Get on with the mission.'

154

Hell Prepares

Lucifer called a Council of War. It was about time. Actually, it wasn't about time, it was about the defence of Hell.

The attendees were:
- Lucifer himself
- Asbeel
- Tamiel
- Aglibal
- Hanibal
- Harut
- Kabarel
- Malakbel

They had just been feasting on the bones of unbaptised babies. The skulls were not fully formed, which made them edible. When the meal was finished, Lucifer said, 'The threat is real, there is a huge, combined angel and human military force being formed against us.

'I happen to know that the humans have been given an IDAG (Inter-Dimensional Aperture Generator). They are coming.

'We need to review our defence plans. Each of you has a level of Hell to defend. I call upon Asbeel to go through the general defence plan.'

Asbeel, 'Let me take you through the plan:
- We have 50 demon legions with a million demons in each legion
- We have 10 angel legions with 100,000 angels in each legion
- There are over 50,000 Dragoni with 200,000 fighters

- There is the Imperial Guard of 100,000 devils
- On Earth, we have a combined army of ogres, orcs, and trolls of nearly half a million ready to take up arms
- Also on Earth, there are 40,000 werewolves and 60,000 vampires awaiting orders
- We have built up a considerable stock of munitions.'

Lucifer, 'Thank you. Tamiel can you take us through the plan?

Tamiel, 'Yes, my lord. Our biggest problem is that we don't know where the attack is going to happen. So we have positioned a single demon legion on each level.

'The Angel legions will act as a mobile force ready to assist the demon legion or legions that have been attacked. It is likely that Heaven's forces will strike at the same time as the humans, so there will be multiple attack points.

'The good news is that when the humans use IDAG, we get a warning. Just enough to get 100,000 demons to the aperture.

'The plan is that these demons will enter through the aperture and attack Earth. The danger is that they will lose their discipline and attack The Fay, but they should cause some short-term havoc. It will be a great distraction.

'The Dragoni will be a heavy-duty hit force used to back up any of the demon legions that are struggling.

'The Imperial Guard will defend our lord.'

Lucifer. 'Thank you, Tamiel. Harut, what is the situation regarding weapons?'

Harut, 'Since our last war with the angels, we have developed a range of horrible weapons. They will work a treat on the humans. They include flesh strippers, acid bombs, fast working biohazards, blister bombs, genetic killers, and of course, an extensive range of lava weapons. The enemy will get a hot old time.'

Lucifer, 'Excellent. Aglibal tell me about your plans for the Earth-based forces.'

Aglibal, 'A piece of land called Britpop seems to be the main focus for the human preparation. There is some sort of civil war going on, but a considerable force is being prepared.

'Once we have agreed on the likely attack date, we will do the following:

- Order the vampires to take out all political, military, and religious leaders
- Order the werewolves to destroy all communication hubs: motorway intersections, telephone exchanges, railway stations, airports, etc.
- Order the orcs, ogres, and trolls to attack the military forces.'

Lucifer, 'Excellent. That does bring us to the key question of when we expect the attack. Malakbel, what do we know?'

Malakbel, 'Our sources up there suggest that everything is ready. 'They are just waiting for two things:

- To have a planning meeting with the humans
- God to push the go button

'I would recommend that we attack Earth during their planning meeting.'

Lucifer, 'That sounds like a plan to me. Any disagreements?'

The attendees had learnt not to disagree. If they did, then they would become lunch.

155

What's Happened to the Weather?

This is the BBC News. I've asked our weather expert for his take on things.

Professor Dot Derringer, 'There cannot be any argument now about climate change. Governments have been warned for the last twenty-five years.'

BBC Interviewer, 'I think we accept that, but does climate change explain some of the strange phenomena we are experiencing?'

Professor Dot Derringer, 'Such as?'

BBC Interviewer, 'I'm pretty sure that you know what I'm talking about, but I will list them:

- The River Thames turning blood red
- Lake Windermere icing over during a heatwave
- Volcanic activity in Sussex
- Huge lightning bolts in Sussex, Plymouth, Stafford, Manchester, and Belfast
- Raining fish in Cirencester
- Giant holes appearing in Bromsgrove, Rochester, Darlington, Newcastle, and Poplar High Street
- Hailstones the size of bricks
- A thunderclap that smashed most of the windows in Birmingham
- Jelly rain falling in Hartlepool
- The River Mersey drying up
- Glaciers forming in the Chilterns
- Rivers of fire in Aberdeen
- Geysers in Guildford

The list goes on.'

Professor Dot Derringer, 'These are all natural phenomena that can be explained.'

BBC Interviewer, 'Well, go on.'

Both the reader and author know that these things are happening because The Fay has ceased to manage the Earth.

156

What's Happened to the Land?

The land was turning to shit. Ancient trees were dying. Crops were failing. Bees stopped fertilising. Wildlife stopped fornicating. Cows stopped producing milk.

The scientists had no explanation. It was as if Nature had lost the plot. Or just couldn't be bothered. Or wanted revenge on humankind.

Both the reader and author know that these things were happening because The Fay has ceased to manage the Earth.

Fayden, 'I've called this meeting because Mother Gaia is suffering. If we don't do something, we will not have a planet to live on.'

Rufus, 'It is pretty serious. I've never seen it so bad.'

Elderberry, 'But we are rushing towards the biggest conflict ever. It is probably only a few days away.'

Fayden, 'I agree. We are doomed if we do something and doomed if we don't.'

Rufus, 'True, do we die fighting or die hiding?'

Elderberry, 'I say fighting. I've had enough of the hiding, but is it fair on our people?'

Fayden, 'I agree. We are doomed if we do something and doomed if we don't. Sorry, I had already said that earlier.'

Rufus, 'In that case, do we go for five blasts?'

Fayden, 'I would say yes.'

The other two agreed. Fayden took a deep breath and went for five blasts of the horn. The world would be saved, or would it? Or would it be the biggest mistake the three of them had ever made?

157

What's Happened to the Narrator?

It appears that the Narrator has built up a bit of a fan base. The sudden and tragic loss of his family has affected many of our readers. (Editor: The book hasn't been published yet.) Letters, flowers, and even small presents have been sent to the office. The author would like to say that money is preferred at this stage. It would undoubtedly help the Narrator more during this tragic time.

And it *was* a tough time for the Narrator. He had begun to suspect that his wife was having an affair. There were a few clues: the videos of her practising naked yoga with a male friend, the love letters, and the pile of used condoms in her bottom bedside cupboard. Of course, it wasn't proof, but it made him wonder.

He later found out that both his wife and two daughters worked at the local strip club. They were famous for their mother-and-daughter acts. Of course, that was just a way of helping out the household finances. He was surprised just how much money his wife had in her off-shore accounts.

He was annoyed that he couldn't get his hands on the money as he had some substantial debts due to his medical conditions. Since he had become a narrator, he had suffered a range of disorders including Parkinson's, MS, asthma, scabies, heart disease, irritable bowel syndrome, palsy, glandular fever, scarlet fever, numerous bouts of influenza and dementia. He had recently been surprised to discover that he had contracted leprosy. The combination of the above had not helped his mental health.

He also had some STDs. He had only slept with his wife twice in the last year, but she told him that you could catch it from toilet seats. Since then, he had always defecated in the garden, which was why he was being prosecuted for indecent exposure. That was somewhat ironic considering his family's side line.

He never got the insurance money as his wife lied about her profession on the application form, and it turned out that his son-in-law was a drug dealer. His assets were confiscated as part of the proceeds of crime act, and the bank account he used for the transactions belonged to the Narrator. He was guilty by implication. Prison was looming.

Several bankruptcy claims had been made against him, and there was every possibility that he would lose his house. He wondered how he would cope as he needed access to fresh water to stop the gangrene smelling. Not that the water supply would continue if he didn't pay the bill soon.

What really pissed him off was that his first book was almost complete. He had never been good with technology. He cursed himself over and over again for not saving his work. It was a masterpiece. It was going to show that tosser Alan Frost how a book should be written. Who's laughing now? It certainly wasn't him. He couldn't laugh due to the twenty-odd boils on his tongue.

But then you have to look at the sunny side of life.

158

Young Mike Turns up

Trumpets sounded the angelic presence of Michael.

Gabriel, 'Since his victory in the last war he has always liked to make a big entrance. I wish I could stick his halo up his arse.'

Archbishop of Canterbury, 'How come you haven't got a halo?'

Gabriel, 'Because of his victory countless years ago he was awarded a sainthood. Anyway, he will be over soon saying, "It is I, Michael".'

Michael, 'It is I, Michael. You must be the archbishop.'

The archbishop knelt before him. Michael gave him his hand to kiss.

Archbishop of Canterbury, 'This is General Sir Hampton-Smith.'

General Sir Hampton-Smith put his hand forward to shake, and said, 'Morning your angelness.'

Michael, 'I never touch humans; one doesn't know where they have been, but good morning to you.'

General, 'So you won't be needing the young girls that we have collected for you?'

Michael, 'I am Michael. The young girls will be anointed.'

General, 'Does that mean you plan to drop them from a dizzy height?'

Michael, 'You are very impertinent for a human. Do you know that I am Michael?'

General, 'I've just about mastered the name.'

Michael, 'And just so you know, I don't plan to drop them. I hope that you have selected some chubby ones for me.'

General, 'Chubby?'

Michael, 'You have seen the cherubs. That's typically how we like our women. Thick arms, large thighs, buxom breasts, huge arses, and full bellies. I need meat, something you can get your teeth into.'

General, 'To be honest we haven't gone for the larger woman, but there are plenty of them around. I will get my team onto it.'

Michael, 'Anyway, we haven't got time for that we have a war to plan.'

General, 'I agree.'

Michael, 'So what do you want us to do?'

General, 'What do you mean?'

Michael, 'Obviously we have left the planning to you. You are the experts in mass killing and genocide. We don't pretend to be your equals in slaughtering.'

General, 'I understand. We need to know more about Hell and the campaign objectives.'

Michael, 'The campaign objective is to destroy Hell.'

General, 'I understand. We need to know more about Hell and the campaign objectives.'

Michael, 'The campaign objective is to destroy Hell.'

General, 'What does that mean?'

Michael, 'It means that we destroy Hell.'

General, 'Let me suggest some possible objectives, and we can discuss:

- Hell will cease to exist
- Hell will surrender to God
- We eliminate all of the inhabitants of Hell
- We kill Satan
- We do all of the above.'

Michael, 'Yes.'

General, 'Yes, what?'

Gabriel, 'God just said destroy Hell.'

General, 'What's your interpretation of that?'

Gabriel, 'Hell will cease to exist.'

General, 'So we are going for a complete destruction of Hell. When we have finished there will be nothing left.

'OK, how big is Hell?'

Michael, 'It's as big as it needs to be.'

General, 'How big is that?'

Gabriel, 'We don't have the finite concept of size that you have.'

General, 'If we want to destroy Hell, I need to have an understanding of its size.'

310

Michael, 'It's roughly 100,000 times larger than Earth.'

General, 'How could we destroy something that large?'

Michael, 'We were hoping you would know.'

General, 'I think we need to redefine our objectives.'

Michael, 'What do you suggest?'

General, 'How about eliminating the inhabitants?'

Michael, 'I think I could sell that to the boss.'

General, 'How many inhabitants are there?'

Michael, 'Unlike Heaven, no one is keeping any statistics, but I would estimate the following:

Being Type	Quantity
Angel	1,500,000
Demons	50,000.000
Dragoni	250,000
Imperial Guard	100,000
Inhabitants	100,000,000+

General, 'What forces would be arrayed against us?'

Michael, 'Everyone except the inhabitants.'

General, 'But that's 52 million.'

Michael, 'We are hoping that you can match that and more. The population of Earth is seven billion and growing, so we thought that you would provide 100 million troops.'

General, 'You are joking.'

Michael, 'I've never joked in my life. One demon army is composed of a million.'

General, 'OK, we can secure additional forces. I have other questions.'

Gabriel, 'Fire away.'

General, 'I understand that when we use the portal, demons are likely to attack us. How would they know we are coming?'

Michael, 'To keep things fair the portal has a warning signal for the other side.'

General, 'Why do that? It stops any chance of a surprise attack.'

Gabriel, 'A surprise attack would be unfair. We are not uncivilised, you know.'

General, 'That's a strange interpretation of being civilised. How many demons will be waiting for us?'

Michael, 'Fifty thousand at the aperture and 950,000 in support.'

General, 'That can't be true.'

Michael, 'It certainly is.'

General, 'When we use the aperture, where will we land?'

Michael, 'Where you want to.'

General, 'So we could land on land?'

Michael, 'Of course.'

General, 'Are there are roads?'

Michael, 'No.'

General, 'Will our tanks operate OK?'

Michael, 'Probably not; we have never tried them as no machinery works in Hell.'

General, 'What about our guns?'

Michael, 'They probably won't work.'

General, 'How do we kill a demon?'

Michael, 'How do you normally kill them?'

General, 'We don't. There aren't any for us to kill. What about the angels? How do we kill them?'

Michael, 'We can't tell you, it's a secret.'

General, 'This seems a lot more difficult than I had originally thought. Can we send over a small scouting party?'

Gabriel, 'Of course but they will be met by the demons.'

General, 'Is there any way we can sneak some scouts in and get them back for a debriefing?'

Michael, 'What do you mean "get them back"? Once in Hell, you stay in Hell. I thought that was obvious.'

General, 'So you are saying that our main army can't come back after using the portal?'

Gabriel, 'That's correct.'

General, 'How would we feed them in Hell?'

Michael, 'You can't. They would be in Hell.'

General, 'But we are destroying Hell.'

Gabriel, 'I can't see the problem. They are only humans. They don't live long. Let's get down to the detailed planning.'

General, 'I think we need a short break.'

159

Decision Time

Archbishop of Canterbury, 'That seems to be going quite well?'

General, 'Are you mad?'

Archbishop, 'Language!'

General, 'Can't you see how impossible it is? The objectives are too vague.

'There will be 50,000 demons waiting for us at the portal

Then there are 950,000 demons waiting to back them up, and then a further fifty-odd million

Then it's a one-way trip—we are sending a million of our troops to Hell. They won't tolerate it.

Most of our machinery will not work

Our weapons won't work

We don't know how to kill demons and angels, and they won't tell us

The angels see humans as cannon fodder. They really don't care about us.

I can't and won't lead this force.'

The archbishop shuffled around in his cassocks, found his revolver, and shot the General in the head.

Archbishop, 'Goodbye, General, that is the fate of all non-believers.'

160

Decision Time 2

Aglibal, 'Your Satanic Majesty, the angels and humans are having their planning meeting at this very moment.'

Satan, 'Excellent, remind me of our plan for Earth.'

Aglibal, 'Of course, your satanic majesty:

- The vampires are going to kill all of the political, military, and religious leaders
- The werewolves are going to destroy all of the communication hubs: motorway intersections, telephone exchanges, railway stations, airports, etc.
- The orcs, ogres, and trolls are going to attack the military forces.'

Satan, 'Instruct them to go ahead.'

Aglibal, 'Of course, Your satanic majesty. I also had another idea.'

Satan, 'What's that?'

Aglibal, 'Shall we use our IDAG to release some demons and Dragoni onto Earth?'

Satan, 'Technically it would mean that we are starting the war. What the hell, let's go for it.'

Aglibal, 'How many?'

Satan, '100,000 demons and 1,000 Dragoni.'

Aglibal, 'Of course, Your satanic majesty.'

161

A Crisis on Earth

General Buckmaster was trying to get through to General Sir Hampton-Smith. The archbishop took the call.

Archbishop of Canterbury, 'The General is indisposed; can I help?'

General Buckmaster, 'It's hard to believe, but we are under attack by werewolves and ugly giant brutes.'

Archbishop of Canterbury, 'Tell me what's happening.'

General Buckmaster, 'Our troop concentration centres are being attacked by ugly troll-like creatures. It would appear that our bullets just bounce off them, but they can't resist our tanks.

'I'm told that Watford Gap Service station is being attacked by werewolves. Just a minute... I'm picking up that Membury, Chieveley, Birmingham International Railway Station, the M5/M50 interaction and Gatwick Airport are also under attack.'

Archbishop of Canterbury, 'By werewolves?'

General Buckmaster, 'Yes, your eminence. Our Control Centre is also under attack, but it is a very secure environment so we should be OK.'

Archbishop of Canterbury, 'Keep me updated.'

General Buckmaster, 'Yes, your eminence. Before you go, there have been further updates coming in:

- We have lost the Watford Gap Services, and the M1 has been shut
- The Houses of Parliament are being attacked by a brood of vampires
- English Heritage is upset as we have lost Stonehenge to the trolls. They are taking the stones to build bridges
- Trolls are also attacking Edinburgh Castle

- Carlisle Railway Station has succumbed to the werewolves
- The BBC is fighting off both vampires and werewolves
- Ogres have taken over the MOD depot at Tewkesbury
- The Channel Tunnel is under werewolf control
- The Queen is in a secure room surrounded by bloodsucking vampires. There are rumours that Prince Harry has been consumed and is now one of them
- Hordes of orcs are roaming Salisbury Plain looking for members of Her Majesty's Armed Service to devour
- Plymouth is under siege by trolls

All I can say is that things are deteriorating rapidly.'

Archbishop of Canterbury, 'Just do your best, General.'

General Buckmaster, 'Yes, your eminence, but I have to tell you that most of the motorway hubs have been secured by the enemy; also, a few naval ships have been captured by the enemy and they are now bombarding Liverpool.'

Archbishop of Canterbury, 'I've got to go now.'

General Buckmaster, 'Just when I thought things couldn't get worse. A giant hole has appeared in the sky. Thousands of demons of different sizes are streaming through along with hundreds of full-size dragons.

'And the two outer layers of the defence perimeter have been breached. I'm not sure how long the Control Centre can withstand this attack.'

The archbishop put down the phone. He wasn't in the mood for bad news, and there was a lot of it.

162

Where Angels Fear to Tread

Archbishop of Canterbury, 'My friends we are under attack from large ugly beasts, vampires and werewolves and now some demons and dragons have entered the fray.'

Gabriel, 'I think that it's probably time that I made my departure.'

Archbishop of Canterbury, 'Aren't you going to stand side by side with us humans fighting the creatures of the dark?'

Michael, 'I would like to stay, but I have got pressing business in Heaven.'

Gabriel, 'I think I've got pressing business as well.'

Archbishop of Canterbury, 'But we need your expertise in fighting them.'

Michael, 'I would like to help, but it's probably best that I leave before the demons get here.'

Gabriel, 'Michael is right. They might be deliberately targeting us.'

Archbishop of Canterbury pulled out his revolver for the second time that day. He pointed it at Michael and said, 'You will stay. It is God's will.'

Both of the angels laughed, and slowly, very slowly, the archbishop lifted the gun to his head.

Gabriel, 'I would say that it's been nice knowing you, but I would be lying, and angels don't lie. You are a nauseating, aggravating little prick who has done irreparable damage to the human race. There is little chance that you will make it to Heaven, but if I do see you there, I'm going to give you a huge kick in the balls. Goodbye.'

Michael, 'I would like to think that Gabriel's words were a bit harsh, but he is right. You are a shit; you humans are just scum. I'm not sure why we are even bothering to talk to you. And once you get up from

Gabriel's kick in the balls, expect another one from me.'

Gabriel, 'Come on, brother, our job has almost been done.'

The revolver was cocked, and the archbishop pulled the trigger. The walls of the room would need redecorating.

163

Hello I'm back

Yes, it's Danny. Not the original of course but a reasonable facsimile. I've had to come back because our dearly loved and admired Narrator has moved onto pastures new. In fact, he is *under* some pasture. You don't borrow money from the Mafia and expect lenient repayment terms.

So where are we?

Basically, the Earth is in a shitload of trouble:

- The weather is shit
- The land is shit
- The angels' behaviour is shit
- The vampire attacks on key people are shit
- The military situation is shit
- The archbishop was shit
- The capture of the communications hubs by the werewolves is shit
- The ogre infestation is shit
- Stonehenge is now shit
- The troll damage throughout the UK is shit
- The demon invasion is shit
- The now leaderless Government is shit

Let's put it this way: things are not good.

Now that's far quicker narration than we normally get.

Now, do you want to know my predictions?

Of course, you do:

- We won't hear a thing from God or the angels. Was this their plan all along?
- The vampires and werewolves will do a *Twilight* and fight each other for eternity

- The demons will track down The Fay and gorge themselves on their life essences. Not a good time for the little people
- The demons will eventually die off because they can't stand continual exposure to light
- Over a period of time, The Fay will sort the weather and the land
- The trolls will build their houses under bridges
- The orcs and the ogres will get jobs in New Zealand working on *The Hobbit* 3, 4, 5 and 6.
- Satan will continue to watch box sets

So what becomes of the humans? Who knows and who cares?

That's the end of my narration.

164

I object

I can't say that I ever liked the Narrator. Let's be honest; he was a first-class twat. I accept that the story now needs a Narrator, but why Danny? For a start, a lot of the story is about him and let's not be shy; he is a mass murderer.

How do we know that it wasn't Danny who killed the Narrator? And how can he just suddenly come back? It destroys a lot of the book's narrative.

And lastly and most importantly, he has more or less given the end of the story away. That elf is a pillock.

165

I object as well

Danny here again. I'm a bit pissed off. That Alan Frost thinks he is God. Well from a writing point of view anyway. We characters are allowed to have thoughts and opinions of our own.

And I don't like the insinuation that I killed the Narrator. It's unfair and unjust. If he carries on like that, he won't have any characters left. They are getting a bit thin on the ground again.

Anyway, if Frosty doesn't like it, he will soon be pushing up the daisies too.

166

I object even More

Look, this is my book. I'm not having characters, even important ones bullying me. It's outrageous.

See below.

Danny tried his hand at narration but failed miserably. Anyway, he had to help his comrades fight the demon horde. The job of the Narrator subsequently became vacant. Stella Weller thought that she might apply.

167

Time for lunch

The Fay had an in-built demon detector in much the same way that demons could smell out the little people. The Fay knew that demons could only spend four or five days in the sunlight before it killed them. It was usually a case of spontaneous combustion.

The only thing the Fay could do was hide. The deeper underground, the better. It wasn't much protection because the demons had very sharp claws and even sharper teeth. And once they got into a feeding frenzy, there was little they could do as the demons would rip the ground apart.

It wasn't the Fay flesh that they were after but their essence, or spirit, if you like. Typically, the demons would rip the head off their Fay victim and literally suck them dry. Sometimes they ate the body, but that was unusual. During the 'Great Demonia' half of the Fay population was sucked to death. Piles of desiccated bodies and ripped heads were stacked up.

One of the Fay tactics was to avoid contact with other Fay. When the Fay were together, their smell increased significantly. Fayden and the two lords realised that they were in significant danger as there had been quite a Fay gathering. Fayden had often postulated that it was the magick that the demons could smell, which was somewhat ironic as Fay magick doesn't work on demons.

The three of them hid under a sturdy tree root, listening. They could hear the noise of their own bodies, especially their hearts. Then a dirty red broken nail scraped along the tree root, feeling and prodding. It almost touched Lord Elderberry. Then suddenly there was a demonic scream and a scaly foot crushed against the root and Elderberry went flying. Flying into the arms of a female demon.

She held Elderberry in her calloused hand. His head was poking out of the top, and the legs were dangling below. It was the classic King Kong grip. He tried to struggle, but her grip was immense. The look of anticipation in her eyes was intimidating. It was clear that Elderberry was doomed.

The demon went for a side bite as the fangs got in the way. Elderberry's head was sliced off and flicked away. Like a bag of sherbet, Elderberry's essence was poured into the demon's mouth. That was the end of a creature who had lived thousands of years. Fayden contemplated the waste of a great fairy, but her own survival was not guaranteed.

Lord Rufus Randytoad of the Roundheadians decided to run. It was partly to protect his Queen. The run didn't last for long as a gnarled demon foot captured him between its toes. The demon snapped his neck and drained him. Fayden just looked on in horror. It was her turn next. When you have the possibility of living forever, death is always a tragic waste. The humans know that their lives are going to be short, they understand.

Then members of the Royal Guard arrived. She wanted them to run as there was absolutely nothing that they could do against the demons. But then something miraculous happened. The five demons just exploded. Blood and guts flew everywhere. Danny had arrived with a weedkiller spray.

Fayden, 'How did you know that weedkiller would work?'

Danny, 'I didn't.'

Fayden, 'We need large stocks of this stuff.'

Danny, 'I'm on the case, I have an Amazon account and a credit card.'

Fayden, 'There is much more to you than I realised.'

Danny, 'In the short term we need a weedkiller hit squad.'

168

General Buckmaster to the Rescue

Ministry of Defence, 'General, I need to tell you that both the Archbishop and General Sir Hampton-Smith have been compromised. We have been through the chain of command to find that there have been many assassinations. The angels have also deserted us. You are now in command.'

General Buckmaster, 'Thank you. I'm honoured.'

General Buckmaster to Operations Control, 'Issue the following commands:

- Inform all military units that I've taken command
- Cancel the invasion of Hell
- Put all units on alert, orders to follow
- Show me our available assets.

Operations Control, 'The following assets are available:

- Ten multi-purpose divisions (Each division is a fully functional unit consisting of armoured infantry brigades, artillery, logistics, engineering, air defence and signals) totalling a million men
- 1 armoured division
- 1 paratrooper division
- 1 Specialist Infantry Group
- Twenty-five battle groups of a thousand men each

The Air-Force and Naval Command Centres are also awaiting your orders.

General Buckmaster to Operations Control, 'Issue the following commands:

- Assign a geographic area to each division based on their current location

- Order them to assess the position in their area and report back
- Inform them that they need to liaise with the battlegroups that are being allocated individual tasks
- Allocate a battlegroup to retake Watford Gap and open the M1
- Allocate a battlegroup to support the Police at Westminster
- Allocate a battlegroup to retake Edinburgh
- Allocate a battlegroup to retake Carlisle
- Allocate a battlegroup to retake Tewkesbury
- Allocate a battlegroup to retake the Channel Tunnel
- Allocate a battlegroup to retake Plymouth. Secure naval support
- Allocate a battlegroup to retake the Salisbury Plain
- Allocate a battlegroup with SAS support to rescue the Queen
- Order the Navy to eliminate the rogue naval units in Liverpool
- Order the Air Force to investigate the demon invasion
- Order Signals to distribute their resources around the country so that we obtain real-time feedback.'
- Allocate a battlegroup to retake Birmingham International Railway Station
- Order all remaining battle groups to retake motorways and comms centres.'

Operations Control, 'Sir we have had a mysterious call from Danny who says that the demons can be destroyed by weedkiller.'

General Buckmaster, 'Talk to DOE about the use of weedkiller. Find out what product they would recommend for spraying. We don't want to destroy the countryside in our attempt to kill the demons.'

169

Heaven has a Laugh

God, 'I can't believe that they fell for our little trick. We had to find an acceptable way of releasing the demons on Earth to teach The Fay that they can't casually go around killing angels.'

Gabriel, 'And the humans fell for it hook, line and sinker.'

Michael, 'They even agreed to supply nuns for our sexual gratification. I wonder what they have done with the chubbies I asked for.'

God, 'Lords Elderberry and Randytoad have been killed by the demons. Do you want their Queen killed?

Michael, 'Gabriel, what do you think?'

Gabriel, 'Tricky one. Clearly, she deserves to die, but we don't really want The Fay leaderless at this stage.'

Michael, 'In that case, let her live but kill as many of those pesky rodents as you can.'

God, 'It was good of Lucifer to go along with our little wheeze.'

Gabriel, 'And it's certainly stirred the humans up, but it looks like they are making a comeback.'

God, 'What are we going to do with the archbishop?'

Michael, 'What do you mean?'

God, 'Peter wants to know. He recognises his dauntless loyalty to me, but he killed to get his way.'

Gabriel, 'I thought he was a boring twat. We don't want him in Heaven.'

Michael, 'He is far too irritating to be with us. The problem will be that Satan won't want him.'

God, 'I will tell Peter to make him a walker.'

Gabriel, 'That means that he will remain a ghost forever.'

Michael, 'That's too good for him, but it is rather amusing.'

God, 'Anyway, Earth will be back to normal soon. We will have to think of another entertaining wheeze.'

170

The Humans Advance

General Buckmaster to Operations Control, 'Give me an update.'

Operations Control, 'Generally good progress all around. Specifically, I can update you as follows:

- Every Division is now committed. They are finding numerous outbreaks in the strangest of places. Starbucks seems to be one of the favourite targets for the enemy
- Watford Gap is still a hotspot, but the werewolves are in retreat. The local commander wants to know what she should do with the two-hundred-odd naked humans
- Westminster is under control. Again, the local commander is seeking advice. He wants to know how you can tell the difference between a vampire and a Member of Parliament
- Edinburgh Castle is now free of trolls, but the pubs are doing a very brisk trade.
- The werewolves in Carlisle have caught a train south. They are being tracked by the RAF
- The BBC has employed two of the vampires to work in the News Department
- The ogres at Tewkesbury have blended in with the local population. Attempts are being made to separate them by using intelligence tests
- The Channel Tunnel is back under French control. Many of the locals in Kent preferred the werewolves
- The International Railway Station at Birmingham has not been particularly cooperative. They are arguing that if orcs have a valid ticket to travel, then they have no right to stop them

- DOE has recommended a weedkiller that is relatively safe, and it is being sprayed in the demon zone. The demons are exploding on contact with the chemical.'

General Buckmaster, 'That's all very encouraging. Are there any hotspots I need to know about?'

Operations Control, 'There is a strong infestation in Hartlepool. The local commander has recommended a tactical nuclear strike. Will you approve it?'

General Buckmaster, 'How many locals would be affected?'

Operations Control, 'About 15,000, of which 50% are unemployed.'

General Buckmaster, 'Tell her to go ahead.'

Operations Control, 'The dragons are causing a problem with their fire and dung.'

General Buckmaster, 'Dung?'

Operations Control, 'Yes, every time they shoot a fireball about a ton of dung shoots out of their arse. So far, about two hundred people have been killed by dung deposits. And it's far too hot to be of any use as manure.'

General Buckmaster, 'I thought the RAF were tackling the dragons?'

Operations Control, 'They are, Sir, but modern jets are too fast, and they haven't got the manoeuvrability. Helicopters have been quite successful, but they are very vulnerable to the dragon's fire blasts.

'The Spitfires and Hurricanes in the memorial flights have been used to great effect. There is a problem with the dead dragons falling out of the sky. In one case a dead dragon devastated Dudley so badly that the zoo had to close. Thirty-two, day visitors were flattened. Locals were annoyed that the zoo refused to return their entrance fee.'

Things were slowly getting back to normal, whatever that meant.

171

Satan doesn't enjoy the Joke

Satan, 'So this was just one of God's jokes?'

Aglibal, 'That's what he is saying, but really it was an elaborate plan to get us to send demons to Earth. They knew that they would attack The Fay. It was all about avenging the loss of two of their angels.'

Satan, 'So how do we get revenge on God?'

Aglibal, 'The usual way. We will refuse to accept anyone from St Peter until they apologise.

'Anyway, God's plan didn't really work. The humans have destroyed the demons by spraying weedkiller on them.'

Satan, 'I'm a bit surprised that the humans knew that.'

Aglibal, 'One of the Fay told them.'

Satan, 'That makes it even more ironic.'

Aglibal, 'It certainly does.'

Satan, 'What resources have we still got engaged?'

Aglibal, 'It's hard to assess. The humans are quite enterprising and diligent in hunting our forces down.'

Satan, 'You might as well recall what's left.'

Aglibal, 'Yes, your satanic majesty.'

172

The Round-up

General Buckmaster to Operations Control, 'What's the latest situation?'

Operations Control, 'Sir, the enemy is retreating on all fronts. The dragons are literally disappearing. Most of the orcs and ogres are also disappearing, but the trolls are refusing to leave their new bridge homes.

General Buckmaster, 'Have we got a national damage report yet?'

Operations Control, 'We have a consolidated report covering the whole episode. Shall I give you an overview?'

General Buckmaster, 'Yes please.'

Operations Control, 'The key points are as follows:
- Rotherham, Wakefield, and Barnsley are devastated cities. The local populations have been effectively eliminated
- Hartlepool is a nuclear wasteland
- Sheffield United Football Club and their supporters have been annihilated
- The Welsh and Scottish Parliaments, with all of their MPs, have been eliminated
- Nearly 50% of the nuns in the UK have been lost
- Most of the UK's MPs have been lost
- There has been considerable collateral damage
- Stonehenge has been removed.'

General Buckmaster, 'What about human casualties?'

Operations Control, 'We don't have any accurate figures yet, but a broad survey suggests two million civilians and thirty thousand military.

There are some outstanding issues that need your input:
- We have a considerable number of prisoners. How should we treat them? Are they covered by the Geneva Convention?

- We have an office full of nuns. What shall we do with them?
- What do you want us to do about the troll problem?
- Who owns the dragon bodies?'

173

The Fay Escape

Fayden had mixed emotions. She was grieving for their lordships but she was ecstatic that the demons have been defeated. It was a shame that the sacrifices had been made. She was also relieved that The Fay wouldn't have to go back into hiding.

But what did all this mean?

It was hard to work out what had happened. It looked like the humans had allied with Heaven to attack Hell, but then Hell attacked the humans first and now it had all petered out. A whole horde of strange beings had been roaming the Earth, including the demons. Then the humans sprayed the demons with weedkiller. She reckoned that Danny somehow had a hand in this.

Then she heard that part of the land up north was dead beyond death. She wasn't sure what it meant, but there were thousands of dead humans, orcs, and ogres. She also discovered that there were still gangs of trolls wandering around. It wasn't going to be easy to revitalise the Earth.

174

An Insult too Far

As you know, I'm not shy in terms of being rude. We elves are famous for speaking our minds, and I'm probably the worst. But this author has been unnecessarily offensive to large swathes of the population.

In the tradition of our previous, now deceased, Narrator, I've analysed and charted the level of insult:

Page Number	Insult
3	The Queen
3	Edward Heath
5	Haywards Heath
6	Haywards Heath
7	Haywards Heath
11	Wife
17	Irishmen
18	Wife
19	Mother
42	Burgess Hill
Chapter 25	Pet killings
Chapter 31	The handling of rape
Chapter 33	Discussion on male genitalia
59	Burgess Hill
60	Wivelsfield Green and Burgess Hill
61-62	Those with Tourette's Syndrome
65	Insulting women
66	Threat of incest
71	Those with Tourette's Syndrome
118	Sexual exploitation. Slavery
Chapter 97	God is insulted

Chapter 114	God is insulted
	Sussex has been unfairly targeted
	General criticisms of the Police
	General criticisms of religion
	Constant sex and sexual innuendos
	Shocking depiction of angels
	Trivialisation serious human conditions
	Too much graphic violence
	Insulting Government ministers
	Numerous insults regarding Archbishop of Canterbury
	Treatment of nuns
Chapter 127-130	Disgusting use of sperm
Chapter 123	Insult to Humanists
250	General insults to many groups
256	Gays in Brighton
256	Satanists in Guildford
256	Sheffield United
257	Rotherham, Wakefield, and Doncaster
257	Mormons and Buddhists
257	Exeter, Bolton, Kensington, Everton
	Yorkshire seems to be getting unfair treatment
	Extreme sexual perversions
	S&M
271	Corruption In the church
274	Barnsley
278	Use of nuns
Chapter 149	The Scots
312	Hartlepool

The above is probably not comprehensive, and I haven't included the bad language as this has already been covered before. And to be honest the chapter and page numbers are often wrong, but who cares!

You are probably still wondering why I'm the Narrator. I got the Editor and General Buckmaster on my side.

175

So Where are We Now?

General Buckmaster was effectively the UK's dictator. There was no Prime Minister; the majority of the MPs had been devoured, and the Queen was in shock after the attempted vampire attack.

The Tories had been discredited after siding with the archbishop and the angels. As the details of God's 'joke' became known, there was a massive public reaction against him. His little jest had resulted in the death of millions of humans. It wasn't that funny.

Conversely, the Humanist and atheist movements had been effectively eliminated; not by the archbishop, but by the fact that supernatural entities are now known to exist. God had killed off the non-believers, but he had not acquired any additional followers.

In fact, there was a growing faction that demanded revenge against God. He was hardly the loving father that the Christian Church promoted.

The great tidy-up had started:

- Survey teams were wondering how they could treat the radioactivity in Hartlepool. Some of the local residents who didn't look that well were demanding rebates for their council tax and the loss of their allotments
- There was discussion about combining the two Sheffield football teams into a single city team that could dominate the Premier League, but after mass protests and a few deaths, it was decided to carry on in the lower leagues
- It was decided that there was no point in rebuilding Rotherham
- Wakefield was converted into a motorway service station
- Barnsley was completely forgotten about
- The Martlets Shopping Centre in Burgess Hull was rebuilt,

but it was on a considerable slope, and it didn't need any heating systems

- Wivelsfield was turned into a large fish pond, and Haywards Heath was voted the most boring town in England for the tenth year in a row
- New elections were called for all of the Parliaments. The favourites were the Green Party
- Stonehenge was put back together, but it was never quite right
- Dead Nuns had gone up in value as they were now much scarcer
- Dead orcs were also selling well and tasted particularly nice with BBQ sauce
- In Tewkesbury, the intelligence tests proved inconclusive as the ogres scored higher than the locals. Based on just appearance alone many of the locals were arrested
- The werewolves and vampires returned to their ancestral homes—local conservative offices, while the surviving orcs and trolls joined the Labour Movement.
- The chubby nuns formed a choir called The Chubby Nuns
- Scotland achieved independence and was given Hartlepool as a bonus
- The witchfinders returned to their regular jobs as chiropodists
- There was a vote, and most Londoners preferred a red Thames
- The archbishop's private nun became the first female Archbishop of Canterbury as no one else wanted the job
- The Guildford Satanists with help from the Woking Werewolves and the Vauxhall vampires formed a chain of self-help clubs and blood banks
- There was much building and reconstruction to be done which led to an economic golden age for the rich
- There was an ample supply of turnips for the poor
  General Buckmaster was enjoying his affair with the new Archbishop of Canterbury.

176

The General Election

The traditional parties still put candidates forward, but there had been an enormous shift in the general public's political outlook. They wanted revenge. Someone had to pay for the loss of loved ones and old friends. Someone had to pay for the loss of property, although no one cared about Barnsley.

The Tories was seen to be the friends of the angels, and Labour was seen as the home of the trolls. The Liberal party had decided to avoid power by changing their leader once again. The Greens were expected to do well, but the desire for revenge was not really their scene.

General Buckmaster decided to form a party to meet the population's desire. General Buckmaster met the general public's needs by generally offering revenge at the general election. It was a landslide victory.

General Buckmaster entered Number 10. His partner, the Archbishop of Canterbury, wasn't sure what to do, so she sold Canterbury Cathedral to the President of UAE, resigned, and became the Chancellor of the Exchequer. It's amazing what an ex-nun with a fine pair of legs can do.

The General realised that his power-grab was based on just one factor: revenge. And that was what he was going to deliver. He wasn't sure how but he would deliver!

177

Civil Committee on Alien Life Forms

General Buckmaster had ordered a committee to investigate 'alien' life forms that had not been encountered before.

The first challenge was to identify these new life forms and classify them. They could only be included in the study if there had been some empiric proof for their existence.

The following chart was prepared:

Name	Description	Exist?
Angel	Multiple visitations. Documented on film. Named individuals	Yes
God	Referenced by Angels	No Proof
Satan	Referenced by Angels	No Proof
Demons	Documented on film. Destroyed by weedkiller	Yes
Orcs	Held in captivity	Yes
Trolls	Held in captivity. Colonies still living under bridges	Yes
Vampires	Held in captivity. Working in the Conservative Party and the BBC	Yes
Werewolves	Held in captivity (naked humans)	Yes
Ogres	Held in captivity	Yes
Elves	Considerable reports but most evidence had been destroyed	No Proof
Dragons	Documented on film. Dead bodies in storage	Yes
Witches	No clear documentation	No Proof
The Fay	Their presence has been discussed	No Proof

After considerable discussion, it was felt that none of the above were natural allies of humanity.

One of the National Parks was allocated to the orcs, ogres, and trolls. It was assumed that they got on well together. This was not the case, and they had to be separated at a later date at a considerable cost in human life. It wasn't easy tempting the trolls out of the under-bridge homes. However, in the long term, humanity had secured some new allies.

A new system of registering vampires and werewolves was introduced. A detailed study of their physiology led to significant progress regarding the cure of cancer, heart disease and several blood diseases. It was also thought that some of the research would lead to the extension of human lifespans.

The dragon remains were allocated to universities and museums. It wasn't the case that their DNA structure didn't fit into the natural order of things that surprised the scientists. It was the fact that they had no DNA at all. This was also true of angels and demons. The view was that they were constructed beings. Possibly the work of God?

Surprisingly, orcs, ogres and trolls had similar DNA structures to humanity. Although it hadn't been tested, it looked like all three could successfully mate with humankind.

The Committee was tasked with the following:

- Identifying ways of detecting werewolves and vampires
- Carrying out a full DNA study of all the new life forms
- Obtaining proof of the existence of God and Satan
- Determining if witches existed
- Investigating the Fay
- Setting up a Department of Alien Life forms with a sophisticated library
- Identifying weapons that can be used against the alien life forms
- Investigating magic
- Investigating mind control
- Investigating teleporting
- Investigating previously unsolved mysteries

Do human souls exist? If they do, what happens to them on death?

There was so much for humanity to investigate. New words were needed for new sciences.

178

Military Committee on Alien Life Forms

General Buckmaster had also ordered a second Committee to be set up to determine how revenge could be enacted. This would be staffed by the military. In reality, their task was to identify the guilty party and choose the best way of obtaining revenge.

Name	Crime	Guilty?
Angel	Worked with God in carrying out the deception	Yes
God	Responsible for instigating false plan that led to the death of millions	Yes
Satan	Responsible for attacking Earth and killing millions	Yes
Demons	Ordered to attack Earth by Satan	N/A
Orcs	Ordered to attack Earth by Satan	N/A
Trolls	Ordered to attack Earth by Satan	N/A
Vampires	Attacked humans	Yes
Werewolves	Attacked humans	Yes
Ogres	Ordered to attack Earth by Satan	N/A
Elves	Not clear if they exist, but probably guilty of murder	Yes
Dragons	Documented on film. Dead bodies in storage	N/A
Witches	No clear documentation	N/A
The Fay	Their presence has been discussed. Possibly guilty of murder	Yes

It was decided that the orcs, ogres, and trolls were simply following orders and should not be punished. Vampires and werewolves were guilty because they were human variants attacking humans.

God, Satan, and the angels were declared guilty. The position regarding The Fay was still vague.

General Buckmaster had been effectively given the approval to punish the offending parties.

179

The MOD do their Job

General Buckmaster ordered the weapons to be prepared. Everything was done in absolute secrecy. They didn't want the Americans to find out as they would stop it.

It was going to take them a few months to develop the technology, but as money was no object, it should be ready on time. A new launch site was developed in the Shetlands on the basis that if there was a massive disaster, it wouldn't matter that much.

December 4th was chosen as the launch date. This would become the most important date in history. So what else happened on that date?

1154—Adrian IV elected Pope. The only Englishman to become pontiff.

1259—Treaty of Paris: English King Henry III and French King Louis IX end 100 years of conflict between the Capetian and Plantagenet dynasties

1489—Battle of Baza - Spanish army captures Baza from Moors

1534—Ottoman   Sultan Suleiman   the   Magnificent occupies Baghdad

1619—Thirty-eight colonists from Berkeley Parish, England disembark in Virginia and give thanks to God. Considered by many the first Thanksgiving in the Americas.

1674—Father Marquette builds first dwelling in what is now Chicago

1688—General John Churchill (later 1st Duke of Marlborough) changes allegiance from James II to William of Orange

1691—Emperor Leopold I takes control of Transylvania

1691—Spanish king Carlos II names Maximilian II Viceroy of Southern Netherlands

1745—Bonnie Prince Charles reaches Derby

1791—Britain's *Observer*, the oldest Sunday newspaper in the world, first published

1829—Britain outlaws "suttee" in India (widow burning herself to death on her husband's funeral pyre)

1833—American Anti-Slavery Society formed by Arthur Tappan in Philadelphia

1918—US President Woodrow Wilson sails for the Versailles Peace Conference in France

1930—Vatican approves rhythm method for birth control

1941—Nazi ordinance places Jews of Poland outside protection of courts

1942—US bombers strike Italian mainland for the first time in WWII

1942—Holocaust: In Warsaw

1943—Commissioner Landis announces that any baseball club may sign Negroes

1944—Germans destroy Rhine dikes

1945—Senate approves US participation in the United Nations

1952—Killer fogs begin in London, England; the term "smog" is coined

1954—The first Burger King is opened in Miami, Florida, USA

1961—Tanganyika becomes 104th member of UN

1964—The Beatles release their "Beatles For Sale" album

1968—Following a civil rights march in Dungannon, Northern Ireland, there is a violent clash between Loyalists and those who were taking part in the march

1971—McGurk's Bar bombing: the UVF exploded a bomb at a Catholic-owned pub in Belfast, killing fifteen Catholic civilians and wounding seventeen others.

1978—Pioneer Venus 1 goes into orbit around Venus

1985 "Les Misérables" opens at Palace Theatre, London

1988—USSR performs nuclear test at Novaya Zemlya, USSR

1991—Muslim Shi'ites release last US hostage Terry Anderson (held 6½ years)

1995—Atherton (185*) bats for 643 minutes to save Johannesburg Test

1996—NASA's 1st Mars rover launched from Cape Canaveral

2018—First successful birth resulting from uterus transplant from a deceased donor in São Paulo, Brazil

1993—Frank Zappa, American rocker, composer, activist, and filmmaker dies

2017—Christine Keeler, British model, and showgirl (Profumo affair), dies

180

Boom!

The IDAG was used, and two portals were opened. Two missiles left the Shetlands and flew into the apertures. They contained the largest and most sophisticated atomic weapons ever designed by humanity. They were designed to explode fairly quickly in case the powers that be could use their 'powers' to stop the explosions.

Two unimaginable massive explosions took place, and the portals were closed. The missile sent to Hell also contained huge quantities of the main chemical that weedkiller was made from.

Like the previous portal encounter to Hell, a few thousand demons escaped to Earth. This time, humanity was waiting for them. The atmospheric area around the portal had been saturated with weedkiller, and most of the demons exploded on contact. Some made it to Earth, but teams were waiting to capture them.

The Civil Committee on Alien Life Forms had specially prepared vehicles to hold the creatures. They were keen to experiment on them. One or two escaped and immediately started tracking down The Fay.

The portal to Heaven was guarded by a single angel who fell into Earth's atmosphere. He was chased by a fleet of helicopters with large nets. The angel was struggling to evade them and was eventually caught and taken to the CCALF citadel for experimentation. Just how magickal was an angel feather? They would find out.

181

Unhappiness in Heaven

God, 'What was that?

Michael, 'It appears to be an almighty explosion, your magnificence.'

God, 'Please don't use the word "almighty".'

Michael, 'It's a very, very large explosion, your magnificence.'

God, 'It felt a bit like the big bang.'

Gabriel rushes in.

Gabriel, 'Terrible news, your brilliance.'

God, 'What has happened, my son?'

Gabriel, 'The explosion has shattered three quarters of Heaven. Parts of it have collapsed into Hell. Most of the human souls are confused and rushing around aimlessly, screaming in pain.'

God, 'Are the angels going to their assistance?'

Gabriel, 'No, my fantasticness, they are burning. Their skin is blistering, and their wings are falling apart.'

God then noticed that Gabriel's wings were turning grey.

God, 'Who has done this?'

Gabriel, 'We obviously suspected Hell, but they have experienced a similar explosion. What are you going to do?'

God, 'I'm not sure what I can do?'

Gabriel, 'But you are almighty.'

God, 'That is true, but I've learnt not to react too quickly as it often makes things worse.'

Another angel rushed in.

Metatron, 'Your fabulousness, I have to tell you that the Pearly Gates have been destroyed and St Peter has suffered severe burns. Demons are also attacking from Hell.

God, 'Have we got our defences in place?'

Metatron, 'Not really, our angels are not in a fit state to fight.'

182

A Mixed Reaction in Hell

Satan, 'What a brilliant explosion. Someone has done a first-class job.'

Kokabiel, 'It was magnificent, your Most Evilness, but there are a few issues. Heaven has crashed into Hell, and over half of Hell has disappeared.'

Satan, 'Disappeared?'

Kokabiel, 'It's fallen into the Armageddon Chasm.'

Satan. 'Won't that kickstart the Armageddon process?'

Kokabiel, 'That's very likely, your horribleness.'

Satan, 'Surely that's a good thing?'

Kokabiel, 'A lot depends on your outlook. It would be the end of days. The end of everything.'

Satan, 'Well, I was getting a bit bored, but I've still got so many box sets to watch.'

Kokabiel, 'Yes, I'm rather enjoying *The Prisoner*. Do you think that it is a metaphor for Hell?'

Satan, 'I wondered that. If we could track Patrick McGoohan down, we could ask him.'

Kokabiel, 'The other problem is that the vast majority of our demons have been destroyed.'

Satan, 'We can always make some more.'

Kokabiel, 'But sadly it takes too long. The few we have left are attacking Heaven.'

Satan, 'What's the resistance like?'

Kokabiel, 'Their angels are not in a good state: severe burns and wing damage. I'm wondering if there is much point in attacking Heaven.'

Satan, 'It would just be fun to stick my fingers up God's nose. What other resources do we have?'

Kokabiel, 'Not many. The orcs, trolls and ogres have been housed in the Lake District. The werewolves and vampires are under firm human control and are either working in Parliament or the entertainment industry, and the dragons are refusing to fight.

Satan, 'Bit of a bugger then. Bring on Armageddon.'

183

Further Problems

Michael, 'Your tremendous holiness, we have another problem.'

God, 'Calm down my son, every problem can be solved.'

Michael, 'Its terrible news. Half of Hell has fallen into the Armageddon Chasm, your nobleness.'

God, 'Fucking hell! Has it started the Armageddon process?'

Michael, 'Yes, I'm afraid so.'

God, 'How long have we got?'

Michael, 'Twenty-one days. Can't you stop it?

God, 'No, I designed it that way.'

184

A Military Success

The UK military were well pleased with their missile strikes. The only problem was that they couldn't determine how successful they had been. However, the main objective had been achieved. Humanity had got revenge on heaven and hell.

They were also pleased that they had captured an angel and twenty-odd demons. They even managed to capture one of the little people. She was saved from having her head ripped off by a demon.

They were amazed that she was a perfect replica of a full-size human. She was actually quite pretty with stern, purposeful eyes. She was trying to communicate, but it wasn't any language that humanity had encountered before.

185

Or Was it a Failure?

General Buckmaster, 'Tell me again.'

Home Secretary, 'OK, Prime Minister, no one can die.'

General Buckmaster, 'What do you mean, no one can die?'

Home Secretary, 'Exactly that. Death has stopped. Nothing is killing people, accidents, disease, murder, etc.'

General Buckmaster, 'So if a steamroller squashed someone, they would carry on living?'

Home Secretary, 'Yes, flat Stanley would carry on living despite the catastrophic injuries. And the pain would be too much to bear.'

General Buckmaster, 'What has caused this?'

Home Secretary, 'It started when the atom bombs were exploded. Perhaps there is nowhere for the souls to go.'

General Buckmaster, 'What is the scientific view?'

Home Secretary, 'They are as shocked as we are.'

General Buckmaster, 'What are the consequences?'

Home Secretary, 'In the short term, it is mostly pain management. It's also putting a lot of funeral directors out of business.'

General Buckmaster, 'Perhaps it's a good thing?'

Home Secretary, 'Some of our Christian friends say that it is foretelling the end of days: Armageddon.'

186

More beer

God and Satan were having another beer. They weren't sure whether Hell had conquered Heaven or not.

God, 'So you think you have won?'

Satan, 'Not really; what's winning or losing?'

God, 'Well, you have conquered what's left of Heaven, but it won't do you any good.'

Satan, 'I guess you are referring to Armageddon. How many days are left?'

God, 'Four.'

Satan, 'What actually happens?'

God, 'Nothing really; everything ceases to exist.'

Satan, 'Including me?'

God, 'Yes, everyone and everything.'

Satan, 'Those humans have got a lot to answer for.'

God, 'I guess that we pushed them too hard. It's a dangerous thing, free will.'

Satan, 'What's going to happen to you?'

God, 'Nothing, but I will be all alone with nothing.'

Satan. 'Will you start it up again?'

God, 'I've done that two or three times. I'm not sure if I can be bothered again. I quite fancy a long rest.'

187

A-Day minus three

General Buckmaster, 'So you have managed to talk to the little person?'

Director-General Civil Committee on Alien Life Forms, 'The language they use is an ancient combination of Aramaic, Hebrew and early dynasty Egyptian. It turns out that she is the Fairy Queen.'

General Buckmaster, 'And I'm Humpty Dumpty.'

Director-General, 'After some long conversations I actually believe her. Her name is Fayden. She said that she could easily teleport herself out of here if she wanted to, but she had a message for us.'

General Buckmaster, 'And that was?'

Director-General, 'Armageddon is only two days away. Our attack on Heaven and Hell initiated the Armageddon process.'

General Buckmaster, 'So that's not tomorrow but the day after.'

Director-General, 'That's right.'

General Buckmaster, 'And do you believe her?'

Director-General, 'Not really, but she is very adamant about it.'

General Buckmaster, 'Did you ask her why people are not dying?'

Director-General, 'Yes, she said that it was because our bomb destroyed the Pearly Gates.'

188

A-Day minus two

Hello, this is going to be my final entry as the Narrator. I often wondered how I would feel on my last day. Actually, I don't feel much. Perhaps I haven't really accepted that tomorrow is Armageddon.

It is, however, a chance to review my life, but that can be dangerous. Some might say that my actions have inexorably led to Armageddon. If I hadn't met June when she was a young girl, then we wouldn't all be facing the void tomorrow. I'm not trying to avoid the consequences of my actions, but am I really guilty or am I just a player in a much larger game?

And if I knew what the ultimate effects of my actions would be, would I have changed them? Probably not. If I'm honest, I take some pride in the fact that I caused the end of days.

Goodbye. I hope your last day is a good one.

189

A-Day minus None

ARMAGEDDON